DARING DUCHESSES

They'll scandalise the Ton

Back in society after becoming widows, three duchesses dare to contemplate the wicked delights of taking a lover…

Except they haven't bargained on the gentlemen who rise to the challenge being *quite* so gloriously devilish!

SOME LIKE IT WICKED

SOME LIKE TO SHOCK3

Also read Sophia's story
SOME LIKE IT SCANDALOUS
Historical *Undone!*

AUTHOR NOTE

Welcome to the second story in my world of the *Daring Duchesses*. The introduction to these two books appeared in the Historical *Undone!* eBook, SOME LIKE IT SCANDALOUS, which told Dante and Sophia's story.

This book is about Pandora and Rupert.

The stories of these three duchesses, and the men with whom they fall in love, have been especially fun to write. The women are all so different, and their background stories equally so, yet their friendship, although newly formed, is one that they all know will endure. Just as they know the love each one finds with the gentleman of their dreams will last a lifetime.

Enjoy!

SOME LIKE IT WICKED

Carole Mortimer

First published in Great Britain 2012
by Mills & Boon, an imprint of Harlequin (UK) Limited.
Large Print edition 2013
Harlequin (UK) Limited, Eton House, 18-24 Paradise Road,
Richmond, Surrey TW9 1SR

© Carole Mortimer 2012

ISBN: 978 0 263 23259 2

Harlequin (UK) policy is to use papers that are natural, renewable and recyclable products and made from wood grown in sustainable forests. The logging and manufacturing process conform to the legal environmental regulations of the country of origin.

Printed and bound in Great Britain
by CPI Antony Rowe, Chippenham, Wiltshire

Carole Mortimer was born in England, the youngest of three children. She began writing in 1978, and has now written over one hundred and fifty books for Harlequin Mills & Boon®. Carole has six sons: Matthew, Joshua, Timothy, Michael, David and Peter. She says, 'I'm happily married to Peter senior; we're best friends as well as lovers, which is probably the best recipe for a successful relationship. We live in a lovely part of England.'

Previous novels by the same author:

In Mills & Boon® Historical Romance:

THE DUKE'S CINDERELLA BRIDE*
THE RAKE'S INDECENT PROPOSAL*
THE ROGUE'S DISGRACED LADY*
LADY ARABELLA'S SCANDALOUS MARRIAGE*
THE LADY GAMBLES**
THE LADY FORFEITS**
THE LADY CONFESSES **

The Notorious St Claires
**The Copeland Sisters*

You've read about *The Notorious St Claires* in Regency times. Now you can read about the new generation in Mills & Boon® Modern™ Romance:

The Scandalous St Claires:
Three arrogant aristocrats—ready to be tamed!
JORDAN ST CLAIRE: DARK AND DANGEROUS
THE RELUCTANT DUKE
TAMING THE LAST ST CLAIRE

Carole Mortimer has written a further 150 novels for Modern™ Romance, and in Mills & Boon® Historical *Undone!* eBooks:

AT THE DUKE'S SERVICE
CONVENIENT WIFE, PLEASURED LADY
SOME LIKE IT SCANDALOUS†

†*Daring Duchesses*

To Peter, With All My Love

Chapter One

May 1817—Highbury House, London

'Do smile, Pandora; I am sure that neither Devil nor Lucifer intends to gobble you up! At least… it is to be hoped, not in any way you might find unpleasant.'

Pandora, widowed Duchess of Wyndwood, did not join in her friend's huskily suggestive laughter as they approached the two gentlemen Genevieve referred to so playfully. Instead she felt her heart begin to pound even more rapidly in her chest, her breasts quickly rising and falling as she took rapid, shallow breaths in an effort to calm her feelings of alarm, and the palms of her hands dampened inside the lace of her gloves.

She did not know either gentleman personally, of course. Both men were in their early thirties whereas she was but four and twenty, and she had never been a part of the *risqué* crowd which surrounded them whenever they deigned to show themselves in society. Nevertheless, she had recognised them on sight as being Lord Rupert Stirling, previously Marquis of Devlin and now Duke of Stratton, and his good friend, Lord Benedict Lucas, two gentlemen who had, this past dozen years or so, become known more familiarly amongst the *ton* as Devil and Lucifer. So named for their outrageous exploits, both in and out of ladies' bedchambers.

The same two gentlemen Genevieve had moments ago suggested might be considered as likely candidates as lovers now that their year of mourning for their husbands was over…

'Pandora?'

She gave a shake of her head. 'I do not believe I can be a party to this, Genevieve.'

Her friend gave her arm a gently reassuring squeeze. 'We are only going to speak to them, darling. Play hostess for Sophia whilst she deals with the unexpected arrival of the Earl of Sherbourne.' Genevieve glanced across the ballroom to where the lady appeared to be in low but heated conversation with the rakish Dante Carfax, a close friend of Devil and Lucifer.

Just as the three widows were now close friends...

It was sheer coincidence that Sophia Rowlands, Duchess of Clayborne, Genevieve Forster, Duchess of Woollerton, and Pandora Maybury, Duchess of Wyndwood, had all been widowed within weeks of each other the previous spring. The three women, previously strangers, had swiftly formed an alliance of sorts when they had emerged from their year of mourning a month ago, drawn to each other by their young and widowed state.

But Genevieve's suggestion a few minutes ago, that the three of them each 'take one lover, if not several before the Season was ended', had thrown Pandora more into a state of turmoil than anticipation.

'Nevertheless—'

'Our dance, I believe, your Grace?'

Pandora had not thought she would ever be

pleased to see Lord Richard Sugdon, finding that young gentleman to be unpleasant in both his studied good looks and over-familiar manner whenever they chanced to meet. But, having found it impossible to think of a suitable reason to refuse earlier when he had pressed her to accept him for the first waltz of the evening, Pandora believed she now found even his foppish company preferable to that of the more overpowering and dangerous Rupert Stirling or Benedict Lucas.

'I had not forgotten, my lord.' She gave Genevieve a brief, apologetic smile as she placed her hand lightly upon Lord Sugdon's arm before allowing herself to be swept out on to the ballroom floor.

'Good Lord, Dante, what has put you in such a state of disarray?' Rupert Stirling, the Duke of Stratton, enquired upon entering the library at Clayborne House later that same evening, and instantly noticing the dishevelled state of one of his two closest friends as he stood across the room. 'Or perhaps I should not ask...' he drawled speculatively as he detected a lady's perfume in the air.

'Perhaps you should not,' Dante Carfax, Earl of Sherbourne, bit out. 'Nor do I need bother in asking what—or should I say, whom—is succeeding in keeping Benedict amused?'

'Probably best if *you* did not,' Rupert chuckled softly.

'Would you care to join me in a brandy?' The other man held up the decanter from which he was refilling his own glass.

'Why not?' Rupert accepted as he closed the library door behind him. 'I have long suspected that my stepmother would eventually succeed in driving me either to drink or to committing murder!'

Pandora—having found herself trapped in a corner of the ballroom with Lord Sugdon once their dance came to an end, and only managing to escape his company a few minutes ago when another acquaintance had engaged him in conversation—could not help now but overhear the two gentlemen's conversation as she stood on the terrace directly outside the library.

'Then let it be drink this evening,' Dante Carfax answered his friend. 'Especially as the Duchess has been thoughtful enough to conveniently leave a decanter of particularly fine brandy and some excellent cigars here in the library for her male guests to enjoy.' There was the sound of glass chinking and liquid being poured.

'Ah, much better.' Devil Stirling sighed in satisfaction seconds later after he had obviously taken a much-needed swallow of the fiery alcohol.

'What are the three of us even doing here this evening, Stratton?' his companion drawled lazily as he threw wide the French doors out on to the terrace with the obvious intention of allowing the escape of the smoke from their cigars.

'In view of your dishevelled state, your own reasons are obvious, I should have thought,' the other gentleman remarked. 'And Benedict kindly agreed to accompany me, once I told him of my need to spend an evening away from the cloying company of my dear stepmama.'

Dante Carfax gave a hard laugh. 'I'll wager the

fair Patricia does not enjoy being referred to as such by you.'

'Hates it,' the other man confirmed with grim satisfaction. 'Which is the very reason I choose to do it. Constantly!'

Devil by name and devil by nature...

The thought came unbidden to Pandora as she remained unmoving in the shadows of the terrace, having no wish to draw the attention of the gentlemen to her presence outside by making even the slightest of noises.

The aroma of their cigars now wafting out of the open French doors was a nostalgic reminder to Pandora of happier times in her own life. A time when she had been younger and so very innocent, with seemingly not a care in the world as she attended such balls as this one with her parents.

Occasions when she would not have felt the need, as she had this evening, to flee out on to the terrace in order to prevent any of Sophia's *ton*nish guests from seeing that Pandora had finally been reduced to humiliated tears by Lord Sugdon's blatant and crude suggestions...

Not that most of the *ton* would care if she did find herself insulted, many of society not even acknowledging her existence, or troubling themselves to speak to her, let alone caring if she constantly found herself being propositioned by those gentlemen brave enough to risk her scandalous company.

Indeed, if it were not for the insistence of Sophia and Genevieve in having her also received at whatever social functions they chose to attend, then Pandora believed she would have found herself completely ostracised since she had ventured to return to society a month ago.

'A futile exercise, as it happens,' Rupert Stirling continued wearily, 'now that my father's widow is also recently arrived at the Duchess's ball.'

'Oh, I am sure that Sophia did not—'

'Don't get in a froth, Dante, I am not blaming your Sophia—'

'She is not *my* Sophia.'

'No? Then I was mistaken just now in the perfume I recognised as I entered the room?'

There was the briefest of pauses before the other gentleman replied reluctantly, 'No, you were not mistaken. But Sophia continues to assure me I am wasting my time pursuing her.'

Pandora's mind was agog with the implication of this last conversation. Sophia? And Dante Carfax? Surely not, when Sophia lost no occasion in which to criticise the rakishly handsome Earl of Sherbourne…

'Would not the taking of a wife solve at least part of your own problem, Rupert, in that the Dowager Duchess would then have no choice but to leave off living openly with you in your homes, at least?' Dante now asked.

'Do not think I have not considered doing just that,' the other man rasped.

'And?'

'And it would no doubt solve one problem, but surely bring about another.'

'How so?'

'In that I would then be saddled for the rest of my life with a wife I neither want nor care for!'

'Then find one you do want, physically, at least. There are dozens of new beauties coming out each Season.'

'At two and thirty, my taste in women does not

include chits barely out of the schoolroom.' The to-ing and fro-ing of Rupert Stirling's voice indicated that he was pacing the library in his agitation. 'I cannot see myself tied for life to a young woman who not only giggles and prattles, but knows nothing of what takes place in the bedchamber,' he added disdainfully.

'Perhaps you should not dismiss the existence of that innocence so lightly, Rupert.'

'How so?'

'Well, for one thing, no one could ever accuse *you* of a lack of finesse in the bedchamber, which would surely allow you to tutor your young and innocent wife as to your personal preferences. And secondly, innocence does have the added benefit of ensuring—hopefully—that the future heir to the Dukedom would at least be of your own loins!'

'Which may not have been the case if Patricia had succeeded in giving my father his "spare"— an occurrence which would have succeeded in rendering me fearful for my very life whilst I slept,' the Duke of Stratton stated venomously.

Pandora was aware she no longer remained silent outside on the shadowed terrace merely to avoid detection, but was in fact now listening unashamedly to the two gentlemen's conversation. Two gentlemen, having seen them from a distance but a short time ago, it was all too easy for Pandora to now envisage.

Dante Carfax was tall and dark with wicked green eyes, his impeccable evening attire fitting to perfection his wide and muscled shoulders, flat abdomen and long powerful legs.

Rupert Stirling was equally as tall, if not slightly taller than his friend, his golden locks fashionably styled to curl about his ears and fall rakishly across his intelligent brow, his black evening clothes and snowy white linen tailored to emphasise the powerful width of his shoulders, narrow waist and long and muscled legs. His eyes would no doubt be that cool and enigmatic grey set in his haughtily handsome fallen-angel face, with a narrow aristocratic nose, high cheekbones and a wickedly sensual mouth that could smile with sardonic humour or thin with the coldness of his displeasure.

A displeasure that at present appeared to be directed at the woman his late father had married four years ago.

Pandora had been only twenty at the time, and not long married herself, but she remembered that the whole of society had then been agog with the fact that the long-widowed seventh Duke of Stratton, a man already in his sixtieth year, had decided to take as his second wife the young woman it was strongly rumoured had been romantically involved with that gentleman's son before he returned to his regiment to fight in Wellington's army against Napoleon...

Pandora, along with all of society, was also aware that the new Duke and his stepmother had occupied the same house ever since the death of his father the previous year—or rather houses, because whether in town or the country, Rupert Stirling and his father's widow invariably now occupied the same residence.

'As I recall, you always did have reason to fear for your life when in the bedchamber with that particular lady,' Dante drawled drily in reply to the other man's previous comment.

Pandora felt the colour warm her cheeks at

overhearing such intimate details of Rupert Stirling's relationship with the woman who was now his widowed stepmother. Perhaps, after all, she had listened long enough to the gentlemen's conversation, and should now return to the ballroom and make her excuses to Sophia before leaving? Yes, that would probably be for the best—

'Half the gentlemen present this evening are currently following my stepmama about the ballroom with their tongues hanging out,' the Duke said scathingly.

'And the other half?'

'Appear to be panting after a petite golden-haired woman in a purple gown—'

'I believe you will find that her gown is violet in colour.'

'I beg your pardon?'

'Pandora Maybury's gown is violet, not purple,' Dante Carfax murmured.

Having already turned towards the house, with the intention of leaving the men to the privacy of their brandy, cigars *and* conversation, Pandora found herself stilling, a chill of apprehension now running down the length of her spine at suddenly hearing her own name mentioned.

'Barnaby Maybury's widow?' the Duke asked.

'Just so.'

'Ah.'

What little colour had returned to Pandora's cheeks during the minutes she had spent outside in the fresh air now drained away as she heard the unmistakable contempt underlying the Duke of Stratton's knowing utterance.

Dante gave a throaty chuckle. 'I know your preference is for women who are dark of hair, tall in stature and voluptuous in figure, Stratton.'

'And Pandora Maybury, being petite and fair haired and slender of figure, is so obviously none of those things—'

'I defy even you to notice anything else about her once you have gazed into the exquisite beauty of her eyes!'

'Should you, in the circumstances, be noticing the beauty of another woman's eyes, or any other part of her anatomy, Dante?'

The other man chuckled at the sarcasm evident in his friend's tone. 'I dare any gentleman, whatever the circumstances, to ignore the beauty of Pandora Maybury's eyes.'

'Pray tell what is so special about them?'

'They are exactly the same shade of colour as the gown she is wearing this evening. Violets in the springtime,' Dante added with obvious appreciation.

'Can it be that your prolonged state of unrequited desire for our beautiful hostess has finally succeeded in completely addling your brain?' Rupert drawled with obvious derision.

'You are the second person this evening to suggest that might be the case,' the other man snapped. 'But, I assure you, where Pandora Maybury's eyes are concerned, I merely state the truth.'

'Violets…?' The Duke was still the sceptic.

'The deep, dark colour of violets in springtime,' Dante maintained firmly. 'And surrounded by the longest, silkiest lashes I have seen on any woman.'

'And these are the same violet-coloured eyes and long silky lashes, no doubt, which succeeded in luring not one man to his death, but two?' The Duke's tone was scathing.

Pandora drew her breath in sharply even as she dropped down weakly on to the wrought-iron bench seat that stood against the wall of Clayborne House, having long been aware of how society thought of her, but never actually having heard anyone openly make the accusation in her presence before.

Except, of course, she was not in the presence of her accusers, merely an eavesdropper who, as the saying went, wasn't hearing anything good about herself.

'I believe I might take my leave as you are so out of sorts,' Dante now told Rupert.

'I will stay here and finish my brandy and cigar before making my own excuses,' the Duke answered.

Pandora was still too lost in her own misery to take any further heed of what they were saying. Too overwhelmed by the unhappiness of the memories their previous conversation had conjured up to do anything other than allow that misery to claim her, as it had so often this past year since her husband and Sir Thomas Stanley had both died so needlessly, and in doing so created a scandal which would be talked about for months, if not years. She—

'Ah, here you are,' a familiar voice oozed at her out of the surrounding darkness. 'And all alone, too,' Lord Sugdon added with satisfaction as he stepped into the dim candlelight escaping through the lace curtains at the library windows.

Pandora eyed him warily as she rose slowly to her silk-slippered feet. 'I was just about to go back inside—'

'Oh, surely not?' The young Lord Sugdon stepped closer still. 'It would be a pity to waste the moonlight. And the privacy this terrace affords us…' he added with a suggestive leer in the direction of the swell of her breasts visible above the low neckline of her gown.

'Nevertheless, I feel I really should return— Lord Sugdon!' she gasped in protest as he reached out and pulled her roughly into his arms. 'Release me at once!' She pushed against his chest in her efforts to escape the confining steel of his arms about her waist, struggles he completely ignored as he now lowered his head with the obvious intention of claiming her lips with his own. Just the thought of his moist, full lips upon her own was enough to make Pandora's stomach churn in sickening protest.

'You don't mean that—'

'I most certainly do!' Pandora insisted emotionally, sure that if she did not escape his steely grip very soon that she might actually swoon. Which she did not believe for one moment, from the expression of carnal intent now darkening Lord Sugdon's face, would succeed in securing her release either; indeed, the man looked as if he were more than capable of taking advantage of her while she lay unconscious and unknowing in his arms. 'You must stop this immediately, my lord!'

'Like it a little rough, do you, my beauty?' Sugdon grinned in satisfaction. 'You will hear no complaints from me on that score!' One of his hands released her waist long enough to grasp the neckline of her gown before pulling on the delicate fabric until it ripped and allowed her chemise-covered breasts to spill into view. 'Now there's a pretty sight to behold, to be sure.' His gaze was heated on her semi-naked breasts as he licked the fullness of his lips in anticipation.

Pandora gave a choked sob, knowing that her life—a life that had been overshadowed by so much unhappiness these past four years—had just lowered to a depth of depravity she could never have imagined before this evening. 'Please, you must not do not do this!' she pleaded desperately as she continued to push ineffectively against the strength of Lord Sugdon's hold upon her.

'You know that you want me to.' His hand now cupped one of her breasts, his fingers digging painfully into her tender flesh. 'That you have been begging for just this all evening.'

'You are wrong if you think that, sir!' Pandora gasped. 'Now please—'

'It is you who shall please me in a few moments, my lovely— Why, you—!' He snarled angrily as Pandora's hand landed painfully against his cheek. 'You shall pay for that, you little—'

'I believe you will find, Sugdon, that when a lady says no as vehemently as this one is so obviously doing, that it is better to err on the side of caution and accept that she really might be turning down your advances.'

Pandora staggered back into the bench as she found herself suddenly released from Lord Sugdon's hot and repulsive embrace, uncaring of the bruising of the metal into the back of her legs as she clutched her ripped gown tightly over her breasts, her face deathly pale as she stared across the terrace at her unexpected—and totally improbable—saviour.

Lord Rupert Stirling, eighth Duke of Stratton. Otherwise known to the *ton* as simply Devil...

Chapter Two

Rupert had been enjoying the last of his cigar and brandy when his solitude had been rudely interrupted by the sound of voices outside on the terrace. Believing at first that it was merely a man and woman involved in a lovers' tiff, he had chosen to ignore them and continue his contemplation of the unhappy predicament in his own life. Namely, how best to deal with the problem of Patricia Stirling, his late father's Duchess.

Having to think of the woman at all was enough to incite Rupert's ire, at the same time as he accepted that he could not contemplate continuing with their present living arrangements any longer. Something had to be done, and soon. He—

The volume of the conversation outside on the terrace had then become such that Rupert found it difficult to think at all. So much so that he stood up to cross the library to where the French doors stood open, his intention to tell the couple to take their damned argument elsewhere. Instead of which it instantly became apparent to him that it was not a lovers' tiff at all, but a gentleman whom he easily recognised as being that young pup Lord Richard Sugdon forcing his attentions upon a lady whom Rupert could not see clearly, held tightly in Sugdon's arms as she was, but who was nevertheless obviously protesting those attentions, both verbally and physically.

A petite and fair-haired lady wearing a purple—correction—*violet*-coloured silk gown. None other than Pandora Maybury, Duchess of Wyndwood, if Rupert was not mistaken. And he rarely was...

'Now see here, Devlin,' Sugdon began to bluster in protest.

'That would now be your Grace, the Duke of Stratton,' Rupert corrected icily as he turned his glittering gaze to the younger man. 'And I believe I have already seen and heard enough to know that you are bothering this lady.'

'There's nothing of the lady about *her*—' Sugdon's insult came to an abrupt halt as Rupert grasped him by his neckcloth before pushing him up against the brick wall of the house.

Rupert lowered his face to within a few inches of the younger man's flushed one, more than pleased to have a direction in which to vent his own inner frustrations. 'Firstly, the *Duchess*,' he bit out softly and succinctly, 'is a member of the *ton* and so most certainly she is a lady. Secondly, she has clearly refused your attentions. Am I correct so far?' The chill warning in his tone was enough to make the other man's cheeks pale.

Sugdon's Adam's apple moved nervously up and down in his throat. 'Yes.'

Rupert's fingers tightened in the neckcloth. 'Thirdly, if I ever see you within ten feet of her Grace again, I will ensure that you live to regret it. In fact, I believe it would be beneficial to your health if you were to take the next few days in which to deal with your affairs here before retiring to your home in the country for the rest of the Season.'

'I—'

'Finally,' Rupert continued in that same dangerously soft tone, 'before taking your leave you may apologise to the Duchess for your wholly unacceptable behaviour towards her just now.'

The younger man's face twisted into a sneer. 'I have no intention of apologising to one such as her.'

'*Now*, Sugdon. Before I forget there is a lady present at all and decide to beat you to within an inch of your life.' Indeed his mood was such this evening that Rupert would welcome—even positively enjoy—the opportunity of physically venting some of his seething emotions on the other man.

'The woman has been flaunting her attractions for weeks now—'

'I most certainly have not!' Pandora gasped in scandalised protest, having listened to the exchange in ever-increasing dismay, and knowing, from the resentful glare Lord Sugdon now sent in her direction, that he held her totally responsible for his present humiliation. Quite how he came to that conclusion, when Pandora had done absolutely nothing to encourage his shocking behaviour, nor personally called upon the Duke of Stratton for help, was completely beyond her comprehension, but believe it Lord Sugdon most certainly did.

She repressed a shiver of apprehension as she turned away from the promised retribution in his glare to instead look at the Duke of Stratton. 'I would far rather you just released him, your Grace, so that he might then leave my presence as quickly as is possible,' she pleaded huskily.

Rupert Stirling did not so much as glance in her direction. 'Not before he has made his apologies to you.'

Pandora shot another nervous glance in Lord Sugdon's direction, accepting that, whilst he might fear the Duke's immediate retribution, he harboured no such feelings of awe where she was concerned.

Indeed, she feared she would even now be prostrate on the terrace if looks could actually kill!

Lord Sugdon drew himself up stiffly as he spoke resentfully, 'I apologise, your Grace.'

She moistened the dryness of her lips before attempting a reply. 'Your apology—'

'Is not accepted.' Once again it was the Duke of Stratton who answered the younger man. 'For what reason are you apologising, Sugdon?' he prompted. 'In acknowledgement of your unacceptable behaviour just now towards her Grace? Or is it only that you regret being caught in the act of attempting to physically assault her?' he added knowingly.

The younger man shook his head vehemently. 'I fail to see why you are making such a fuss when everyone knows the woman is nothing more than an opportunist, on the look-out for the next man to share her bed now that her year of mourning her husband is over. Unless, of course, that next man is you, Stratton, in which case I apologise for having stepped upon your toes—or any other part of your anatomy—' He got no further with the insult as the Duke suddenly released his neckcloth in order to swing back his arm and land a punch firmly upon the other man's jaw, resulting in Lord Sugdon toppling unconscious to the ground.

'Your Grace!' Pandora stood up to stare down in alarm at the prostrate and unconscious man.

Rupert at last spared a narrow-eyed glance at the obviously dismayed Pandora Maybury, his gaze becoming positively appreciative as he took in the fact that the ripped front of her gown revealed surprisingly plump breasts beneath the thin material of her chemise, the nipples that adorned their firm, pouting tips showing a deep and alluring rose.

Her cheeks flushed a similar colour as she became aware of his intent gaze, her hand once again moving up to clasp the ragged edges of her gown together in order to hide that delectable plumpness from his view.

Rupert looked at her between hooded lids, taking in the gold of her hair arranged in fashionable curls at her crown, with several loose tendrils at her temples and nape, her face a pale oval in the moonlight, lashes lowered as she stared down at the prostrate man, making it impossible as yet for Rupert to see the full splendour of those 'exquisitely beautiful' violet-coloured eyes his friend had earlier described with such eloquence.

She moistened plump lips with the tip of her

tiny pink tongue before speaking huskily. 'What shall we do with him?'

Rupert arched dark, arrogant brows. 'I have no intention of doing anything with him, madam. In fact, it is my intention to leave him exactly where he fell.'

'But—'

'No doubt he will have a slight jaw-ache when he awakens,' he added with satisfaction. 'But that, and the injury to his pride, will no doubt be all that he suffers. Unless, of course, Sugdon was right all along and you were actually encouraging the roughness of his attentions and now regret my interference?' Rupert eyed her speculatively.

She gasped, that blush in her cheeks deepening in colour. 'How can you even suggest such a thing?'

He shrugged broad shoulders. 'Some women prefer a little…enthusiasm, in their lovemaking.'

'I assure you I am not one of those women!' she snapped indignantly. 'Now if you will excuse me—'

'You cannot possibly go back into the house with your gown in that condition.' Rupert made no effort to contain his impatience as he began to shrug out of his black evening coat. 'Here, put this about your shoulders.' He held the jacket out to her. 'And I will go and arrange for the carriage to take you to your home.'

Pandora was careful not to allow her fingers to come into contact with the Duke's as she took the tailored jacket from him, struggling slightly as she attempted to hold the front of her gown together at the same time as putting the jacket about her shoulders.

'Oh, for goodness' sake, woman, let me!' The Duke sighed his irritation with her struggles as he strode across the terrace to take the jacket from her and place it about her shoulders himself, Pandora at once enveloped in the warmth it had absorbed from his own body, along with the smell of his cologne and the cigar he had recently enjoyed. 'I will go inside and see to the carriage and at the same time ensure that our hostess is made aware of your departure due to a headache.' He glanced down in disgust as the other younger man gave a pained groan as he began to stir. 'A very large headache!'

Pandora's lashes lowered as she avoided meeting Devil Stirling's piercing grey gaze. 'I—I do not believe I have thanked you as yet for your timely intervention, your Grace. I am much appreciative of your rescue just now.'

'How appreciative, I wonder?'

Her lashes rose sharply at the speculation she heard in his tone. 'Your Grace?'

'Never mind,' he dismissed tersely as he straightened. 'Perhaps you should come through to the library, and then you may close and lock the doors after I have left and so ensure that you are not disturbed before I return.' He gave the rapidly recovering man at his feet another cold glance.

Pandora gave an apprehensive shiver despite being huddled in the warmth of the Duke's jacket, a warmth accompanied by a wholly masculine smell—the sandalwood and pine cologne, expensive cigar and another pleasant odour that was possibly uniquely Rupert Stirling—which was as reassuringly comforting as it was disturbing to the senses. 'I will do so, gladly,' she agreed as she preceded the Duke into the candlelit library, some of her trepidation leaving her as soon as she heard him locking the doors behind them before pulling the curtains across to secure her privacy.

With the lessening of those feelings of immediate danger came the full realisation of what had just happened to her. The knowledge of what more might have happened to her if Rupert Stirling had not come to her rescue. Lord Sugdon, for all of his foppishness, was a large man and so much stronger than her, and if the Duke of Stratton had not come to her aid then she feared the other gentleman would have continued with his ravishment to the bitter end.

'I believe it would be best if you don't dwell on thoughts of what might have occurred,' Rupert advised as he easily guessed the reason for the colour draining from Pandora's cheeks.

'Not dwell on it?' she choked emotionally. 'How can I not dwell on it when but for your own intervention he—he might have—'

'Oh, good lord, now you are crying!' Rupert gave a small groan as he saw the evidence of those tears as they spilled over her long silky lashes before proceeding to fall down the delicacy of her pale cheeks and knowing himself to be as impotent as the next man when faced with a woman's tears. 'Recall that I did intervene, madam, and let that be an end to it,' he begged hastily.

Those long silky lashes now rose, at last allowing Rupert his first glimpse of Pandora's 'exquisitely beautiful' eyes. Eyes, he instantly discovered, that were indeed the colour of the deepest, darkest violets in springtime. Eyes a man—and at least two other men, to his certain knowledge—might gaze into and find himself lost to all reason as he drowned in those seductive violet depths...

'I apologise for troubling you with my tears, your Grace.' Pandora was visibly battling to stop any more of those tears from falling as she delicately patted the evidence from her cheeks with a lace-edged handkerchief she had recovered from the beaded reticule at her slender wrist.

Rupert had indeed been troubled—was still troubled, if the truth be told, but by the mesmerising effect on him of those violet-coloured eyes, rather than the tears this woman had shed. 'If you have any sense at all you will not attempt to move from the library until I have returned from arranging for the carriage to take you home.'

Pandora could not help but flinch at the unmistakable steel she could hear underlying the Duke's dictatorial tone, along with the expression of deep irritation on his aristocratically handsome face as he glared down the length of his arrogant nose at her, as if he now regretted having come to her aid at all. Or perhaps, having done so, he was merely eager to rid himself of the responsibility of her as quickly as was possible?

'I assure you that I am perfectly sensible to my predicament, your Grace,' she confirmed softly. 'And should you appear out in the hallway without your jacket?' Her eyes were wide with consternation as she saw that was his intention.

'It would seem I have little choice when you are obviously more in need of it at present than I.' With one last brief glance in her direction the Duke turned abruptly on his heel and stepped out into the hallway before closing the door firmly behind him. 'Lock it,' he directed audibly from the other side.

Pandora quickly complied before pulling Rupert Stirling's jacket more tightly about her as she leant weakly back against the door. She felt slightly safer now, but knew she would not feel completely secure until she was well away from Clayborne House and most of the people in it.

Including her reluctant rescuer?

Yes, that did indeed include the Duke, Pandora acknowledged as she now seemed unable to stop her trembling. There had been something in Rupert Stirling's eyes when he had looked upon her in the candlelight just now, an expression of purely male assessment on his austere and aristocratic features, as he had seemed to take in everything about her in a single glacial glance. Followed by his swift exit from the library just now, as indication, no doubt, that having looked his fill, he was now in a hurry to be rid of her.

No doubt the Duke would have already made his planned excuses to leave if this obviously unwanted sense of responsibility towards Pandora had not delayed him.

Her legs began to shake in earnest as the full horror of what had almost transpired earlier once again washed over her. Indeed, if Rupert Stirling had not interceded, then she was certain that Lord Sugdon would have succeeded in his obvious intention of ravishing her. With or without her permission. And, in the case of Lord Sugdon, it would most certainly have been without!

Oh, she was well aware of what society thought and said about her, of the belief that she had cuckolded her husband with Sir Thomas Stanley, which had resulted in a pistols-at-dawn duel, which minutes later had left both gentlemen lying dead upon the ground.

All, and every part of it, a lie.

But it was a lie which the *ton* had wanted to believe a year ago, when Pandora had attempted to claim her innocence of any wrongdoing in her marriage. Unfortunately, tonight's events proved they did not believe in her lack of guilt now, either.

From the conversation she had overheard earlier between Rupert and Dante, it was obvious that they had also heard, and believed, the rumours that had been rife a year ago.

Before her marriage to Barnaby four years ago,

Pandora had been the naïve and trusting Miss Pandora Simpson, the only child of the impoverished landowner and Greek scholar from Worcestershire, Sir Walter Simpson, and his wife, Lady Sarah.

With Pandora's first successful Season behind her, during which she had received several offers of marriage from gentlemen she liked but whom her father considered unsuitable, she had later come to realise that none of those gentlemen had been wealthy enough for her father to tap for the funds necessary to alleviate the family's impoverished state due to Sir Walter's complete incompetence as a landowner; her father had always preferred his books to the running of his estate.

Then had come the offer during her second Season, from the young, handsome and extremely wealthy Barnaby Maybury, Duke of Wyndwood, an offer which Sir Walter had grasped greedily with both hands.

Perhaps Pandora was being a little unfair in laying the blame for her marriage upon her father, when he was no longer alive to defend himself, Sir Walter having succumbed to the influenza three winters ago, her mother following him only weeks later. After all, Pandora had been equally as flattered by the attentions of such a handsome and wealthy gentleman as Barnaby Maybury and excited at the prospect of becoming his Duchess.

Neither had there been any indication, during those heady days of her short betrothal to the Duke of Wyndwood, when he had been both charming and attentive towards her, of the nightmare her life would become once the two of them became husband and wife.

A nightmare which had refused to end following the scandal which had dogged her every footstep since her husband's death in a duel supposedly over her honour and culminating in the final and humiliating indignity of Lord Sugdon's attack on her earlier this evening.

Final—because this evening had shown Pandora that it would be better for everyone—but most especially herself—if she were to seriously consider withdrawing completely from society.

The majority of Barnaby's wealth had been left to a distant cousin, his male heir, upon his death, but her marriage contract had ensured that Pandora was left with some funds of her own, along with a property in London which was not entailed in the Duke's estate. Not in a particularly fashionable part of London, admittedly, but certainly a house she had been able to occupy in quiet seclusion during her year of mourning. But with the money she already had, added to what she might expect to receive from the sale of that house in London, she would surely be able to buy a suitable property and retire to the country, where hopefully she might be allowed to live out the rest of her days in peace and solitude?

She knew that Sophia and Genevieve would both decry such a course of action on her part. Both women had been kindness itself since declaring, when they'd first befriended Pandora, the one with kindness, the other with vehemence, that what wife had not, on occasion, wished to cuckold her husband and possibly even dispatch him?

Close as Sophia and Genevieve now were to her, Pandora could not reveal even to them that she was not guilty of doing either of those things. There were reasons, and others even more innocent than she who could be seriously wounded by the truth.

But after the unpleasant events of this evening, much as Pandora valued the other ladies' friendship, she now felt sure that the only future left to her if she stayed in London was to become prey to opportunists such as Lord Sugdon. A fate that was wholly unacceptable to her.

'You may safely unlock the door now, Pandora.' A brisk knock accompanied the Duke of Stratton's terse instruction.

Rupert knew at a glance, as he stepped into the room and closed the door behind him, that Pandora was a little more composed now than she had been earlier. She was very pale still, of course, that pallor giving a haunted depth to the deep violet of her eyes, but the expression on the delicate beauty of her face was one of resigned dignity rather than the emotional upset she had been verging on before he left the library just minutes ago.

Hers was a beauty of such delicacy—ivory skin, high and intelligent forehead, those incredible violet-coloured eyes, a short straight nose above the perfect bow of her full and sensuous lips, with a slightly stubborn tilt to her small and pointed chin—that Rupert found he was not in the least surprised that two gentlemen, her husband and her lover, had challenged each other to a duel in order to claim sole rights to that beauty.

His mouth thinned. 'Our hostess has been informed of your departure and the carriage is now waiting outside to take you to your home. I have brought this for you to wear.' He held up the black cloak he had requested from the Duchess of Clayborne's butler. 'It has the advantage of returning my jacket to its rightful place, as well as covering your own…damaged gown.'

'Thank you.' Her voice was husky and she kept her lashes lowered over those violet-coloured eyes as they exchanged Rupert's jacket for one of the Duchess of Clayborne's own evening cloaks.

Rupert pulled on his own jacket and straightened the cuffs before looking down at her with disapproving eyes. 'What on earth possessed you to walk outside with a man like Sugdon in the first place?'

Thick lashes surrounded those violet-coloured

eyes as they widened indignantly at the accusation in his tone. 'I did not go outside with Lord Sugdon! I had been standing outside on the terrace alone for some time when he found me—' She broke off her protest abruptly, the colour deepening in her cheeks, as she obviously realised she had just revealed her presence on the terrace directly outside the library whilst Rupert and Dante conversed privately.

How much of their conversation had she overheard? Rupert wondered ruefully. Certainly the latter comments concerning herself, if the deepening of that blush in her cheeks was any indication!

'Indeed?' His nostrils flared. 'And did you overhear anything of interest whilst standing there?'

She drew herself up to her full height of a little over five feet. 'Not in the least, your Grace.'

He quirked a mocking brow. 'No?'

'No.' Pandora had no intention of admitting to overhearing this man's conversation regarding his stepmother. The remarks about herself, on Dante Carfax's part at least, had not been too insulting, and the Duke's less-than-flattering opinion of her had, as with so many of the *ton*, been formed on hearsay rather than personal knowledge of her.

Or, at least that had been the case *before* Rupert Stirling had been forced to rescue her from the unwanted attentions of Lord Sugdon!

She sighed heavily. 'I think it best if I leave now, your Grace.'

'I think so, too,' he agreed. 'The Duchess's butler has arranged for the carriage to be brought to the back of the house rather than the front so that we might leave through the servants' hallways and kitchen rather than run the risk of running into any of the Duchess's other guests, and so cause them to question your current…appearance,' he added drily as Pandora gave him a startled glance.

'"We", your Grace?' she repeated slowly.

Ah, her surprise was not, as Rupert had believed, caused by their means of leaving the house, but more by the fact that he so obviously intended departing with her. 'We,' he confirmed authoritatively as he took a light grasp of her elbow before opening the door and indicating she should precede him out of the room.

Something Pandora made no effort to do as she instead looked up at him with obvious uncertainty. 'I have long been acquainted with what society has to say of me, your Grace, but I feel I should warn you—'

'And I am only too well aware of what that same society has to say about me, madam.' He scowled down the length of his arrogant nose at her. 'But you may rest assured that I am in no mood this evening to confirm any of the... less-than-complimentary remarks you may have heard in regard to my conduct towards the ladies.'

Pandora was pleased to hear it, having briefly wondered if she might not have succeeded in being rescued from one unacceptable situation only to now find herself in an even worse one!

Although she seriously doubted that most women would find the interest of a man as aristocratically handsome and challenging as the eighth Duke of Stratton in the least unacceptable!

Indeed, once upon a time, before her unhappy marriage, she would have been delighted—nay—

ecstatic, to have attracted the attentions of such a handsome and eligible gentleman as he. No longer. Pandora's only wish now was to draw as little attention to herself as possible.

'Then let us both depart, your Grace,' she accepted reluctantly as she reached up to pull up the hood of the cloak so that it covered part of her face and all of her hair.

A disguise that proved absolutely useless in helping her to pass unnoticed through the servants' hallways and kitchen!

How could it be any other way, when a gentleman as recognisable as Rupert Stirling strode arrogantly along at her side? Sophia Rowlands's household staff were obviously all agog at seeing a handsome Duke marching through their midst, their gazes speculative as they moved to the cloaked woman at his side.

'Not quite the unobserved departure we might both have wished for,' he acknowledged ruefully as they emerged outside into the dark lane at the back of the crowded and candlelit mansion house.

'No.' Pandora frowned as she saw there was only one carriage awaiting them there. A fashionable black carriage, which bore the Stratton coat of arms upon the door the groom now hurried forwards to open. 'My own carriage does not appear to have arrived as yet, your Grace—'

'Nor will it,' the Duke assured her briskly, maintaining that firm hold upon her elbow as he strode towards his own carriage. 'Whatever society may say about me, your Grace, my nanny and tutors ensured that I grew up knowing my manners perfectly, even if I do not always choose to put them into practice.' He raised an expectant brow as he waited for her to precede him into the interior of the ducal carriage. 'One of those precepts being that a gentleman does not abandon a lady in distress,' he added softly.

The only distress Pandora suffered at this moment was the thought of being seen driving through the streets in the Duke of Stratton's carriage and then arriving back at her home in that so-called gentleman's carriage rather than her own!

Chapter Three

She drew in a shaky breath. 'I believe I would rather this was an occasion upon which you chose to ignore the teachings of your nanny and tutors, your Grace.'

There was a stilled and expectant silence for several seconds and then the Duke gave a loud bark of spontaneous laughter. 'My friend Carfax omitted to mention that you are an Original, Pandora Maybury,' he finally murmured appreciatively.

'Possibly because I am not.' She became flustered as she recognised the speculation in the cool and assessing grey gaze now levelled at her.

'I beg to differ,' the Duke drawled.

'That is your prerogative, of course.' She nodded coolly. 'But I really would prefer to return to my home as I arrived, alone and in my own carriage.'

'Why?'

Her agitation increased. 'I— Well, because—'

'Can it possibly be that you are nervous at thoughts of travelling alone in the ducal carriage with me?'

'Of course I'm not!' Pandora glared up at him in the darkness.

'Good.' His mouth firmed with satisfaction as he all but lifted her inside the lantern-lit carriage and placed her on one of the plushly upholstered seats. He swiftly followed her inside to sit directly opposite her and nodded tersely to the groom to close the door, the movement of the carriage only seconds later evidence that they were now on their way.

On the way to where, Pandora was unsure, when the Duke had made no enquiry as to where in London her house was situated.

Rupert studied her between narrowed lids, able to take in her full appearance in the warm glow given off by the lantern inside the carriage. Her hair and lashes were of pure and deep gold, a perfect foil for those deep violet-coloured eyes, her skin the colour of ivory, her lips—full and pouting lips that hinted at the sensuous nature which had perhaps caused two gentlemen to fight a duel over her—the colour of ripe raspberries. The same colour as the nipples he had glimpsed through her chemise earlier, tipping those surprisingly plump breasts…

If released from their pins, would her golden curls be long enough to fall over those beautiful, pert breasts, thereby allowing those ripe berries to peak through invitingly? More interestingly, once fully unclothed, would the curls between her thighs be that same enticing gold—

Dear Lord, was his life not complicated enough, without sitting here contemplating what the notorious Pandora Maybury looked like naked!

'It really was unnecessary for you to manhandle me that way, your Grace,' she now spoke primly into the silence. 'I assure you I am both young and agile enough to climb into a carriage without your assistance.'

'And yet you made no effort to do so,' Rupert pointed out coolly, not at all pleased at the direction in which his thoughts had so recently been straying.

'Because, as I had already stated, I had every intention of seeking out my own carriage.'

'And I have already explained why that arrangement did not suit *me*.' Rupert's patience with this situation—what little he possessed—was wearing thin as he glared coldly across the width of the carriage at his reluctant companion.

Her lashes lowered as a blush coloured the ivory of her cheeks. 'I have told you how grateful I am for your help earlier this evening—'

'One would never believe so from your manner towards me now!'

Pandora gave a pained frown as she looked across the carriage at him. Perhaps his criticism was merited; she had behaved less than graciously towards him this past few minutes, because, despite wishing it were otherwise, she was utterly disconcerted at finding herself alone with Rupert Stirling in his carriage.

Every wary—and utterly weary—bone in her body had stiffened just now as she saw the speculative way in which his gaze had roamed so fa-

miliarly over her face and body. And against the
warning of the rational part of her brain, she was
equally as aware of his disturbing presence as he
sat opposite her.

The gold of his hair now fell rakishly across
his brow and curled about his ears and nape, the
glow from the lantern lending an austereness
to his high cheekbones and firmly squared jaw,
his lazy sprawl on the upholstered seat totally at
odds with the sharpness of that intelligent grey
gaze as he continued to look at her from between
narrowed lids. He was, without doubt, one of
the handsomest gentlemen Pandora had ever beheld—even more so than Barnaby, who had possessed boyish good looks as well as dark hair
and blue eyes.

Unfortunately, the Duke of Stratton's reputation
also rendered him the most potentially dangerous gentleman Pandora ever beheld, too, which
was the very reason she felt so totally out of her
depth in his company. 'It was precisely because
I did not wish to inconvenience you any further
this evening that I asked to return home in my
own carriage.'

The nostrils flared on that aristocratically straight nose. 'Do you suppose we could possibly talk of something else, Pandora?'

She blinked. 'Of course, if you wish it.'

'Indeed—' he nodded tersely '—I find myself exceedingly bored with the repetition of our present conversation.'

As no doubt he now regretted driving her home at all, Pandora accepted heavily as the Duke turned away dismissively to look out of the carriage window at the other carriages travelling London's moonlit streets.

Pandora had been much in society during the years of her marriage; indeed, Barnaby had considered it part of her wifely duties to accompany him to all the balls and parties given by the *ton* and so she had long ago learnt to engage in the polite and meaningless small talk that made up so much of the conversation at those entertainments, and to keep any of her original thoughts and ideas to herself.

Indeed, until Pandora had met and become friends with Sophia and Genevieve shortly after the start of the current Season, she had long as-

sumed that there were no intelligent ladies or
gentlemen left in society, let alone those who
found that inanity as tedious as she did herself.

It appeared that Rupert—*Devil*—Stirling was
yet another who did not enjoy meaningless conversation...

She sat forwards slightly, her interest piqued.
'Perhaps you would care to discuss literature?
Or politics?'

His brows rose. 'Really?'

Pandora nodded as she looked across at him
earnestly. 'My father was a Greek scholar, and
ensured that I am quite conversant on either subject.'

Rupert gave a reluctant quirk of his lips as he
once again found himself falling victim to those
mesmerising and beautiful violet-coloured eyes.
'I assume that is also the reason you have the unlikely name of Pandora?' The original Pandora,
if Rupert recalled his Greek studies correctly,
was reputed to have been a woman given a gift
by each of the gods, in order that she might bring
about the ruination of mortal men.

There was no doubting that this Pandora possessed the reputed beauty attributed to the original, but did she also have the power to bring about man's ruination?

If the gossip a year ago concerning that ill-fated duel was to be believed, then the answer to that question was a definitive *yes*!

Pandora eyed Devil Stirling warily. 'I believe that by naming me such my father believed I might be gifted with both grace and beauty.'

'Then he was not disappointed.' The Duke gave an acknowledging inclination of his head. 'But did he somehow forget that the opening of Pandora's box was also reputed to have released all number of evils upon man and beast?'

Pandora felt no warmth at his agreeing to her having been gifted with grace and beauty. How could she, when it was so quickly followed by this softly delivered insult? 'If my father were still alive, I am sure that he would have enjoyed debating with you as to whether or not that destruction was Pandora's doing or that of man himself.'

Gold brows rose over derisive grey eyes. 'Your father was of the opinion that every man—and woman—is instrumental in bringing about their own destruction?'

She arched fine brows. 'You disagree?'

Rupert could never before remember having a conversation with a woman on the subject of Greek mythology, let alone debating its philosophy. Obviously her father had been a learned man and it appeared to be an education he had felt no qualms in imparting to his only daughter.

Rupert's physical appreciation of her had already caused him to regret her presence in his carriage. He certainly did not wish to know that there was so much more to her than the flirtatious beauty malicious gossip had led him to believe.

'—telling me precisely where we are going, your Grace?'

'I beg your pardon?' Rupert frowned at this interruption to his musings.

'I asked if you would mind very much telling me where we are going?' The huskiness of her naturally sensuous voice had sharpened in her obvious anxiety.

He gave a lazy smile. 'I was unsure, once we were safely ensconced in my carriage, as to whether or not I would find myself with the dubious pleasure of dealing with a hysterical lady and advised my coachman to drive about London until you had calmed down enough for me to ascertain exactly where it is that you reside.'

'My home is in Jermyn Street, your Grace.' Pandora's smile was rueful as she waited quietly whilst he advised his coachman of their destination before continuing. 'I admit that I was upset by Lord Sugdon's familiar behaviour earlier, your Grace, but I don't believe I could ever be accused of being the sort of woman who swoons easily.' The Duke did not need to know that Pandora had been very close to doing exactly that when the erstwhile nobleman had ripped her gown and then crushed her in his arms so effortlessly.

'Then what sort of lady would you say that you are?'

She eyed him suspiciously, but could read nothing from his enigmatic expression as he relaxed back against the seat opposite her. 'The *ton* would have you believe—'

'And I am sure I have already made clear my own opinion of what the *ton* may or may not choose to believe or say, in regard to yourself or anyone else.' He gave a dismissive gesture with one long and elegant hand.

Pandora moistened her lips with the tip of her tongue. 'I am afraid I don't understand the question when my own opinion of myself must obviously differ greatly from that of others.'

'Why obviously?' He frowned. 'The *ton* believes me to be arrogant and proud, and something of a rake with the ladies, and I can find no argument with that opinion.'

She smiled at this blunt self-appraisal. 'But you are so much more than that, are you not?'

His brows rose. 'Am I?'

Pandora nodded. 'This evening you have been both chivalrous and kind.'

'I would advise you not to attribute me with virtues I do not, nor would ever wish, to possess,' he warned.

She shook her head in gentle rebuke. 'I have every reason to know you to be both those things after the manner in which you…dispensed so effortlessly with Lord Sugdon's unwanted attentions towards me earlier tonight.'

The Duke's mouth thinned. 'And if I were to tell you that my actions had very little to do with you? That my mood this evening was already such that I merely welcomed the opportunity to hit someone? Anyone? For whatever reason!'

Recalling the content of this man's earlier conversation with the Earl of Sherbourne, Pandora had some idea as to the reason for the Duke's bad humour. 'I would then say that the reason you acted in the way that you did was irrelevant, when it resulted in my rescue.'

Rupert looked quizzically across at her. 'And, if I may be allowed to say so, Pandora Maybury, I find you are not at all as the *ton* describes you.'

She laughed musically. 'Oh, you may certainly say it, your Grace—'

'Rupert.'

Her humour instantly ceased, her expression now one of uncertainty. 'I beg your pardon?'

He regarded her beneath hooded lids. 'I believe I should like to hear you call me Rupert.'

She sat as far back on the bench seat as possible. 'I could not possibly address you in so familiar a manner, sir.'

'Why not? You are a Duchess, I am a Duke, therefore we are social equals. Or are you already so awash with friends that you have no need of another?' Rupert added with cutting humour.

That slender throat moved convulsively as she swallowed before answering huskily, 'You must know that I am not.'

Yes, Rupert had already observed this evening that the only members of the *ton* who now bothered with her company were gentlemen who obviously had so much more than friendship in mind. Men like Sugdon. 'Our hostess, and her friend the Duchess of Woollerton, appear to value your friendship.'

Pandora's expression softened. 'They have both been kind enough to bestow that friendship upon me these past few weeks, yes.'

'So it has been commented upon.'

She looked across at him sharply. 'I trust not to their detriment?'

'Would it bother you if it were?' he asked curiously.

'Of course.' She gave every appearance of being agitated, her face flushed, her lace-gloved fingers now tightly gripping the cloak about her. 'I should not like to be the cause of either of those dear ladies being cut by certain members of society.'

'As you are yourself?' he pressed.

'Yes,' she acknowledged quietly.

He shrugged. 'I am sure both those ladies are of an age and confidence to choose their own friends. As am I,' Rupert added huskily.

Pandora eyed him warily. 'But we are not friends, your Grace, merely new acquaintances.'

'That is no reason to suppose that, with time, we might not become more than that.' Rupert studied her shrewdly. 'Tell me something of your marriage to Maybury.'

She looked startled at his abrupt change of subject. 'For what purpose?'

'It is a natural curiosity, surely, considering the method of his demise?' Rupert said.

'I see nothing natural about it, your Grace.' Her chin was raised proudly.

He gave an elegant shrug. 'That is possibly because you are too close to the subject.'

Her eyes flashed darkly. 'How should I be any other, when Barnaby was my husband?'

'And was it a love match? On Maybury's part, at least, one might presume it was.' He looked thoughtful.

Pandora frowned. 'As is the case with many in the *ton*, ours was an arranged marriage.'

'But happy? At least, initially?' he asked.

Not even initially!

It had become apparent to Pandora, almost immediately their marriage took place, that Barnaby had only married her because he required a young, and therefore malleable, wife for him to escort during the Season and to act as mistress in his many homes, both here in London and in the country. A wife who would not attempt to interfere in the way in which he chose to conduct his own life; having expressed no deep and passionate love for Pandora before their marriage, Barnaby had made it clear he considered it unreasonable of her to expect him to feel that way about her once they were husband and wife.

After much internal soul-searching, Pandora had realised she had no choice other than to accept this loveless marriage as being her lot in life. And if that acceptance had meant putting aside all of her girlish hopes and dreams of love and a grand passion in her marriage, then that was surely her own disappointment to bear, and no one else's.

She certainly did not intend to now share any of the details of that disappointment with the haughty and mocking nobleman in front of her, despite his insistence on asking her probing questions!

'We appear to have arrived at my home, your Grace,' Pandora realised thankfully. She sat forwards eagerly with the intention of alighting from the now-stationary carriage as the groom hurried to open the door for her. 'Once again, I am grateful to you for coming to my aid this evening.'

'I will call upon you tomorrow.'

'For what purpose?' Pandora, having just stepped down from the carriage, now turned sharply.

The Duke's teeth flashed a white smile in the moonlight as he stepped down beside her. 'Why, for the purpose of assuring myself as to your having fully recovered from this evening's ordeal, of course.'

There was no 'of course' or anything else about it, where this arrogant and disdainful gentleman was concerned. Nor did she wish for Rupert to call on her tomorrow or any other time.

She suspected, despite their efforts for it to be otherwise, that the news of the cloaked lady leaving Sophia's ball this evening in the Duke of Stratton's carriage, would be all over London by the morning, without adding to that gossip by him being seen calling at her house the following day!

'I assure you I am already fully recovered, thank you, your Grace.'

'Nevertheless, having rescued you, I now feel honour-bound to call upon you tomorrow to assure myself of your well-being,' he insisted.

Pandora looked up at him with frustration, very aware that he had only moments ago denied the existence of any such finer feelings in regard to his character, but at the same time aware of the restraint put upon her answer by the presence of the quietly attentive groom. Just because the man gave every appearance of being totally deaf to their conversation did not mean that he was not listening and remembering every word they spoke, in order that he might relay that gossip to the Duke's other servants once released from his duties later tonight.

It was pure arrogance on the part of the nobility to believe that their servants were not fully conversant with all their actions. And their foibles...

Pandora drew herself up to her full height before speaking coolly. 'You must do as you see fit, your Grace.'

'I usually do,' Rupert replied mockingly even as he lifted her hand to his lips, his intent gaze deliberately holding her startled one as he placed those lips upon her gloved knuckles. 'Until tomorrow, Pandora.'

She snatched her hand from his grasp as if burnt. 'Goodbye, your Grace.'

'Merely adieu, I assure you, my dear Pandora,' he murmured throatily, watching closely as she hurried up the steps to the front door of the mansion house, that door opening as she reached the top of those steps to slip silently inside without so much as a backward glance.

A scowl creased Rupert's brow as he now considered returning to his own London home.

And to the woman who would no doubt have made sure she would be awaiting him there...

Chapter Four

'How kind of you to call, your Grace!' Pandora's smile was one of vacuous politeness late the following morning as she rose to her feet in order to curtsy to Rupert as he strode with his usual arrogance into the blue-and-cream salon of her London town house. Endeavouring, as she nodded dismissal of Bentley, her butler, not to reveal by so much as a twitch of an eyebrow how disturbed she was that he had carried out his promise to call upon her this morning.

Which was not at all easy for her to do when the Duke looked so vitally handsome this morning. The gold of his hair was in tousled disarray upon his brow and about his ears and nape, those grey eyes piercing in that wicked, yet angelically handsome face. He was wearing a dark grey superfine over a silver waistcoat and snowy-white linen emphasised the width and power of his shoulders, black pantaloons hugging the long muscled length of his legs above highly polished black Hessians.

'Your Grace, allow me to introduce you to the family lawyer, Mr Anthony Jessop.' Pandora turned to the relatively young, dark-haired gentleman standing in the room with her. 'Mr Jessop, his Grace, the Duke of Stratton.'

Mr Anthony Jessop—the two gentlemen having acknowledged each other, the lawyer with a gracious bow, the Duke with a terse nod—now looked less than comfortable at finding himself the focus of Rupert's intense grey eyes as he gathered up his papers from the table. 'You will let me know as soon as things are settled, Pandora?' He turned to smile at her.

Having contacted Anthony Jessop at his offices first thing this morning and, that gentleman having duly called upon her a mere hour later, Pandora could not help but wish now that they had not concluded their business quite as efficiently as they had. She would have much preferred a valid excuse to encourage the Duke to leave her home!

'I will.' She rang for the butler, smiling warmly at the man who had been Barnaby's lawyer for some years before he died, and latterly her own. Pandora had found his help invaluable this past year, as she attempted to not only run her own London household but also manage her private finances.

The lawyer turned to nod at the slightly younger man. 'Your Grace.'

'Jessop.' There was no answering smile on Rupert's face as he waited until the lawyer had withdrawn in the company of the butler before speaking again. 'Springcleaning, Pandora?'

She gave him a startled look. 'I beg your pardon?'

'There appear to be several trunks in your front hallway. Possibly awaiting collection before the contents are distributed to the poor?'

Pandora drew in a sharp breath at the directness of the Duke's conversation; obviously they were to continue this morning in the same forthright manner as the previous evening—that is, with none of the social niceties!

Nevertheless, she would attempt to bring things back on track. 'May I offer you refreshment, your Grace?' Pandora looked across at him enquiringly.

He scowled darkly at her formal manner. 'No.'

'In that case, perhaps you would care to sit down, your Grace?' she invited smoothly as she indicated the armchair furthest away from where she had now resumed her own seat on the edge of the cream sofa beside the window.

An invitation he blatantly ignored as he instead strode forcefully across the room to lower his impressive height down on to that sofa beside her. Pandora immediately found his proximity overpowering as she tried—and failed—to ignore his barely leashed vitality. 'Perhaps you would care to explain what is going on, Pandora?' he pressed.

'Going on, your Grace?'

A humourless smile twisted his firm but sensual lips. 'The presence of both the trunks in your hallway, and the overfamiliar lawyer in your salon.'

'Is it not a lovely sunny morning, your Grace?' Pandora turned to look out into the carefully tended and sunlit garden at the back of the house. 'Did you choose to ride over this morning or come in your carriage?'

'Does it matter?' he dismissed impatiently.

'I was merely—'

'I know what you were "merely", Pandora—and I have no intention of sitting here exchanging polite inanities with you.' He eyed her grimly. 'I will ask again—why was your lawyer here at this early hour and what are those trunks doing outside in your hallway?'

She frowned her irritation at his single-mindedness. 'Could you not try to…to at least *pretend* to possess the art of polite conversation?'

'No.'

Pandora rose restlessly to her feet. 'As I assured you would be the case, I am perfectly recovered from last night's—unpleasantness. Thank you for enquiring.' She raised pointed brows.

Rupert ignored her obvious rebuke, could clearly see that—outwardly, at least—Pandora was indeed completely recovered from Sugdon's less-than-subtle attentions, the gold of her hair once again swept up and arranged in those becoming curls, with several loose tendrils at her temples and nape, the pale lilac of her fashionable gown a perfect backdrop for the deep-violet colour of her eyes, a gentle blush in those ivory cheeks.

Yes, outwardly, Pandora Maybury gave every indication of being the polite and gracious hostess she was obviously trying so hard to appear.

And no doubt she would normally have succeeded, if one failed to notice the slight shadows beneath those beautiful violet-coloured eyes—eyes which, despite Rupert's effort to convince himself otherwise, were now every bit as beautiful as they had appeared yesterday evening.

Or had no idea that the blush to her cheeks had been carefully applied rather than being natural. Or missed those lines of strain beside her politely smiling mouth. And the rapidly beating pulse in the long, graceful column of her throat and the shallow rise and fall of the fullness of her breasts above the low neckline of that lilac gown.

Or the presence of her lawyer—a man who, in

Rupert's estimation, had been far too familiar in addressing her as Pandora—and those damned packing boxes in the hallway!

Yes, if one failed to notice all of those things, then certainly she could be said to be completely recovered from the previous evening's ordeal!

'You will no doubt be pleased to know that I made enquiries earlier this morning and was informed that Lord Sugdon has refused all further social engagements and is at this very moment making arrangements to return to the family estate in Yorkshire by the end of the week.'

'I am gratified to hear it.' She nodded with obvious relief.

Rupert rose impatiently to his feet before barking, 'Enough that you will answer my earlier questions?'

'I would prefer that you did not raise your voice to me, sir!'

Better, Rupert acknowledged with inner satisfaction, as he now saw a spark of rebellion appear in those fine violet-coloured eyes. Much, much better. 'Very well, Pandora,' he drawled drily before deliberately making his tone more reasonable. 'Explain, if you please, why certain of your belongings are packed into trunks, and you have been visited by your lawyer this morning. At least, I am assuming he arrived this morning?'

She shot him an irritated frown. 'There are trunks in the hallway and I have been visited by my lawyer—*this morning*,' she added primly, 'because I am to leave London.'

Rupert scowled his displeasure at having his suspicions confirmed. 'Is it wise for you to leave London at the same time as Sugdon?'

An angry flush darkened her cheeks. 'A mere coincidence.'

'I am aware of that, but the rest of the *ton* is not.'

'I thought we had agreed that the *ton* will say what they wish, whatever I choose to do?'

Rupert frowned darkly. 'I don't enjoy having my own words used against me.'

Pandora shrugged slender shoulders. 'Even when they are the truth?'

'When are you leaving? To go where? And for how long?'

She gave a dismissive wave of her lace-gloved

hand. 'As soon as everything is packed and ready to be moved. As to where or for how long… I shall decide that in the next few days.'

Rupert gazed upon her with narrow-eyed criticism. Had he been mistaken in regard to this woman's courage the previous evening? The manner in which she had refused to break down completely after Sugdon's physical and verbal attack? The steadfast way in which she had met Rupert's every insult on the carriage ride to her home? 'In other words, you are allowing society to win and have decided to run away.'

'That is unfair!' The colour in the cheeks was now entirely genuine.

He shrugged. 'Life is unfair, Pandora, not I.'

Her chin rose. 'I am not running anywhere, your Grace. I have merely decided that society is not yet ready to…to forgive, or forget, the events of a year ago.'

Rupert's mouth twisted derisively. 'And it never will be if you tuck your tail between your legs and simply run away and hide.' To say that he was disappointed in her would be placing too much importance upon their brief acquaintance.

An importance his years of cynicism did not, and would not, allow for.

Devil take it, he only had to think of the unpleasantness that had taken place after his return to Stratton House the previous evening to be reminded of the fickleness that was women. An unpleasantness which now made it impossible for him to allow this situation with Patricia Stirling to continue another day—no, not even another hour.

'That is easy for you to say.' Unshed tears now moistened the deep-violet beauty of her eyes. 'I had hoped—' She gave a shake of her head as she determinedly blinked away those tears. 'I have realised, after the events of yesterday evening, that there is nothing here for me in London at present.'

'There are your two friends, the Duchesses of Clayborne and Woollerton.'

She sighed. 'Yes. And I am more grateful than I can say for their friendship. But even there I believe it would be better for both my friends if I were to leave London, at least for a while.'

Rupert snorted his disgust. 'As I said, you are running away.'

'Will you stop saying that as if I am guilty of committing some heinous crime!' Pandora glared her frustration, thoroughly annoyed with both Rupert and herself for having so quickly allowed him to turn this conversation to matters so personal—in spite of all her previous determination to the contrary.

She had decided last night, as she lay sleepless in her bed, that if the Duke should indeed come to call on her this morning—once he had found time to reflect on the social disadvantages of continuing an acquaintance with her, there was every chance, hope, that he might decide not to do so—that she would do everything in her power to ensure they met, and parted, as the polite strangers they were. However, Rupert's current, and continued, insistence on dismissing all idea of social politeness between them rendered that distance impossible!

Pandora shook her head wearily, gold curls bouncing. 'You were in the army, I believe?' she asked.

His scowl deepened at mention of the years he had spent in the army fighting against Napoleon. 'What does that have to do with anything?'

She smiled slightly. 'Did those years of conflict not teach you that it is brave to fight the battles that can be won, but sensible, even prudent, to withdraw from the ones that cannot?'

'No,' he stated with that now familiar arrogance, those grey eyes hard and uncompromising. 'I do not consider any battle as being lost before it has even been fought. And you should also have learnt by now that the *ton* are a fickle bunch, given to fads and fancies. And the one thing they *never* forgive or forget is cowardice. I, and consequently they, will no doubt consider your choosing to leave London because of a single incident to be exceedingly cowardly on your part.'

'It is not a single incident,' she gasped indignantly, 'but the last of many.'

'You are being a coward, Pandora.'

If Pandora were a woman who tended towards acts of violence then she knew that at this moment she would very much have enjoyed striking Rupert Stirling upon one of his haughty lean cheeks! As it was, apart from Richard Sugdon, she had never struck another person in the whole of her four-and-twenty years. She believed her years of being unhappily married to Barnaby to have slowly and inexorably dulled any spontaneity she might once have possessed, resulting in her now behaving in a cool and controlled manner in most, if not all, situations.

It would be most unwise of her to allow the annoyingly implacable Rupert Stirling to rile her into uncharacteristically volatile behaviour now. 'If that is your true opinion of my actions, then I'm afraid you will have to continue to believe that, your Grace.'

'If you "your Grace" me one more time then *I am afraid* I shall be forced to take an action I guarantee you will not in the least enjoy!' he warned through gritted, perfectly straight, white teeth.

'Why are you even bothering with me at all, yo—er—sir?' Pandora gazed across at him crossly even as those glacial eyes narrowed dangerously. 'Do you perhaps see my possible restoration into society as a project of pity with which you might amuse yourself for a day or until you became either bored or some other distraction piques your attention?'

That was a question which Rupert was as yet unwilling to answer. At this moment it was sufficient to admit that *he* needed Pandora Maybury as much as he believed *she* needed the protection of the Duke of Stratton.

He shrugged. 'My reason for coming here today—apart from assuring myself as to your well-being after the events of yesterday evening, of course,' he drawled just as pointedly as Pandora had minutes ago.

'Of course,' she echoed drily.

'—was to present you with an invitation,' Rupert continued firmly. 'From the Countess of Heyborough. She wishes for you to join her and the Earl in their box at the opera this evening.'

Pandora drew in a sharp breath at this unexpected—and totally bewildering—invitation. 'As far as I'm aware, I'm not even acquainted with the Earl and Countess of Heyborough.'

'But I am.'

Pandora tensed warily at Rupert's tone of satisfaction. 'I don't understand.'

'The Countess is my maternal aunt.'

'And she wishes to invite me to join her at the opera this evening?'

The Duke raised arrogant brows. 'I have said so, yes.'

She frowned. 'Would I be correct in supposing that you have also been invited to share that same box this evening?'

He gave a haughty inclination of his head. 'It is intended that I will make up one of the party, yes.'

'And this party will consist of...?'

'The Earl and Countess of Heyborough. You. And myself.'

'Why?'

His brows rose even further into his golden locks. 'What do you mean?'

'Why do you wish to act as my escort to the opera?'

Those sculptured lips thinned. 'I have my reasons.'

As Pandora had suspected... 'And are you about to share those with me?'

'No.'

Again Pandora was beset with the thought 'devil by name and devil by nature'... 'Are you so determined to once again witness my public humiliation that you are even willing to enrol the assistance of one of your relatives in order to achieve it?'

The Duke's jaw tightened ominously. 'Would you care to explain in what way my escorting you to the opera could in any way be considered a humiliation?'

She sighed her impatience. 'When other members of the *ton* present this evening not only ignore me, but choose to deliberately cut me. Snubs that perhaps might include even yourself and your aunt and uncle.'

Rupert now looked at her down the length of his impressive nose. 'I assure you, madam, that no member of the *ton* would dare to ignore you, let alone deliberately cut you, when you are in the company of the Duke of Stratton.'

He may be right in that conclusion, Pandora acknowledged ruefully; he was certainly a man to be reckoned with, both socially and politically, and as such he was unlikely to receive an insult from anyone. 'And what of your relatives—is their social standing also to be threatened because of what can only be considered an amusement, a whim, on your part?'

He was every inch the aristocratic Duke of Stratton as he gave Pandora a pityingly look. 'My aunt and uncle have no more interest in society's approval than I.'

'Even so—'

'Cease this interminable arguing, Pandora!' Rupert lost all patience with the conversation. 'We are both going to the opera this evening, in the company of the Earl and Countess of Heyborough, and let that be an end to it.'

Tears once again glistened in those beautiful violet-coloured eyes. 'What possible reason can you have for putting me through such an ordeal? Did I, or my husband, cause you some unintended slight in the past of which I am unaware? A slight that now requires my deliberate humiliation as atonement?'

'Don't be ridiculous, Pandora.'

'I'm not the one who is being ridiculous, Rupert—' She broke off, an expression of confusion on her delicately beautiful face at the realisation that in her distress she had lapsed into the familiar way of addressing him, after all. 'I'm sorry, but the very idea of accompanying you to the opera this evening is completely out of the question,' she continued evenly. 'I only attended Sophia's ball yesterday evening out of a desire to please her and because she has been so supportive and kind to me this past month. But, I assure you, I feel under no such obligation where you are concerned.'

Rupert felt a return of his previous admiration for this young woman's dignity and calm. It might be a complete fabrication on her part, but nevertheless it was still impressive to behold. Also, he found her concern for others, namely her two female friends, and now Rupert and his aunt and uncle, not quite in keeping with the reputation she had amongst the *ton* as having been consistently unfaithful in her marriage, an infidelity which had eventually resulted in her husband's death…

'Did I not come to your rescue against Sugdon yesterday evening?'

She eyed him uncertainly. 'Yes…'

He nodded tersely. 'Resulting in his having taken my advice, in that he is, as we speak, preparing to depart for cooler and windier climes?'

She smiled slightly at the use of his word 'advice'. 'Yes.'

'Then surely that means you are now obligated to me.'

'But—'

'I will call for you here in my carriage at seven-thirty this evening,' Rupert spoke firmly over her continued arguments.

Pandora gave a slightly dazed shake of her head. 'You have to be the most stubborn gentleman I have ever met.'

He gave her a confident and wholly unapologetic smile. 'I believe it has been mentioned before as being one of my character traits.'

Pandora eyed him quizzically. Rupert Stirling was arrogant, dictatorial, sarcastic, even ruthless—as well as being exceedingly stubborn, as she had just accused him. But he also possessed a sense of honour where even a disgraced lady's reputation was concerned, a mocking sense of humour that often included laughing at himself and a physical presence she was finding it increasingly difficult to ignore.

Rupert's looks and character were so completely different to those of her husband with his imposing presence, that arrestingly handsome face, impressive height and muscular build. Barnaby had been three or four years older than Rupert, but had looked younger with his boyish good looks and slight build. For all that Rupert was so determined to have his own way, he also filled Pandora with a sense of feeling protected and that no harm should befall her whilst she was in his presence, in a way which Barnaby never had despite his having been her husband for three years.

Except harm from Rupert himself, of course...

Pandora was not foolish enough to ever believe that he was offering her his public support out of the goodness of his heart! 'I would still like to know what it is *you* hope to gain from such a—a public acquaintance with me?'

Rupert raised his brows. 'Why should you assume I have anything to gain by it?'

Her eyes flashed deeply violet. 'I may be several years younger than you, your Grace, and be considered something of a pariah by society, but I advise you not to assume for one moment that my lack of years or social standing in any way renders me a fool.'

'I was not aware I had treated you as such.'

She shook her head. 'We had never even met properly before yesterday evening, and when we did it was certainly not under pleasant or flattering circumstances. Therefore, there must now be another reason for your seeming act of generosity in having persuaded your relatives to invite me to the opera. Perhaps it is that I am expected to act as a diversion of sorts, from attention being drawn to…to another relationship, which currently exists in your life?'

Rupert had already known this woman to be beautiful and equally as stubborn as he, and in possession of an impressive intelligence of mind.

He now knew she was astute in a way that would no doubt have reduced a lesser man than he to squirming discomfort! If, that is, that gentleman had been ignorant of the fact that Pandora had been privy to a certain private conversation between himself and one of his two closest friends… Although Rupert somehow doubted that the conversation Pandora had overheard had revealed all of the complexities of the relationship which currently existed between himself and the woman who was now his father's widow.

He gave a hard and humourless smile. 'You, my dear Pandora, are expected to be here, ready and waiting, and suitably attired for attending the opera, when I call for you at seven-thirty this evening.'

A reply which did nothing to answer Pandora's question, as was no doubt deliberate; Rupert appeared to feel no qualms whatsoever in intruding and commenting on the privacy of other people's lives, whilst at the same time refusing to reveal anything about his own.

Still, she couldn't help but privately believe his unexpected invitation to the opera was somehow connected to his stepmother, that in being seen in public with the notorious Duchess of Wyndwood, it would somehow distract attention from his other scandalous relationship.

Whilst Pandora's every instinct was to continue to refuse his invitation, her sense of fairness dictated otherwise; no matter how much she might wish it were not the case, his actions in rescuing her so dramatically yesterday evening meant that she was indeed obligated to Rupert.

She sighed and forced herself to straighten her shoulders. 'Very well, your Grace, I will accept the Countess of Heyborough's kind invitation to attend the opera this evening.'

'Why could you not have just said that five minutes ago?' Rupert glared.

'But only on the understanding,' Pandora continued firmly, 'that I won't be expected to accept a second such invitation from you.' She met his narrowed gaze unblinkingly.

As technically the invitation had not come directly from him, but from the generous heart of his Aunt Cecelia, after he had called upon her earlier this morning and explained what had happened last night, he now felt no hesitation in agreeing to Pandora's condition.

Besides which, having to spend one evening in a decade attending the opera would no doubt prove to be more than enough for his own jaded sensibilities!

Chapter Five

'I sincerely hope you are pretending an interest in this drivel rather than actually finding any enjoyment in it?'

Pandora did not show, by so much as a twitch of her bared shoulders, that she had overheard Rupert's hissed comment next to her earlobe, as she continued to stare down upon the stage where the hero of the opera was currently—and rather loudly—lamenting his lost love.

As promised, Rupert's ducal carriage had duly arrived at her home at seven-thirty that evening, that gentleman looking suitably and—Pandora admitted inwardly—breathtakingly handsome in his black evening clothes and white linen, a cloak draped about those broad and muscled shoulders, his rich gold curls revealed as being fashionably dishevelled once he had removed his tall black hat.

Pandora had coolly accepted his polite compliments on her own appearance: a deep-blue and feathered confection adorned her own fair curls, her silk gown of matching blue, its short-sleeved style leaving her shoulders bare, the high waist emphasising the full swell of her breasts, with pale-blue lace gloves covering her hands and arms to just above her elbows.

She had maintained that cool detachment as the two of them travelled to the opera, only thawing slightly under the Countess of Heyborough's genuinely warm greeting and her husband's twinkling blue eyes as he bent solicitously over her gloved fingers. A melting that had faded the moment Rupert took a proprietary hold of Pandora's elbow in order to escort her into the theatre. He had nodded and bowed imperiously in acknowledgement of the greetings he had received—several of them markedly startled once they realised the identity of the woman at the Duke's side. But, as he had promised, not a single one of those ladies or gentlemen had dared to offer her the cut direct in his presence.

Even so, Pandora's legs had been trembling so much by the time they reached the Heyboroughs' private box that she had been relieved to sink down on to the seat Rupert pulled out for her, before stepping back to fold his own lean length on to the seat directly behind her. A proximity he had just taken advantage of, the warm brush of his breath having felt almost like a caress against the bareness of Pandora's skin as he spoke so closely to her ear.

'Unless it has escaped your notice, your Grace, the heroine has just died and her lover is heart-broken,' she whispered discreetly, aware as she was that there had been much gossiping behind fans and sidelong glances made in their direction during the course of the evening, as many people watched the two of them rather than the performance taking place upon the stage.

'Then more fool him,' Rupert drawled uninter-estedly. 'Personally I would consider myself well rid of such a weak and mewling creature! Why is it that you never wear jewellery, Pandora?'

Those smooth and bare shoulders appeared to stiffen momentarily at this sudden change of subject before she brought her reaction under control and answered Rupert with that same infuriating coolness with which she had been treating him all evening. 'I have, on occasion, been known to wear my mother's pearls.'

'But not yesterday evening or tonight?'

Her mouth firmed. 'No.'

'Why not?'

'Could this conversation not wait until the opera has come to an end, your Grace?' She shot a meaningful glance in the direction of his aunt and uncle sitting in the box with them, the Earl and Countess giving every appearance of listening intently to the caterwauling rising up from the stage below.

Rupert affected a yawn. 'I might have expired from boredom before that happens.'

Pandora bit her top lip in order to hold back the chuckle she almost gave in response to his irreverent comment. In truth, this truly was one of the most depressingly morbid operas she had ever attended—and she had attended many of them during the years of her marriage to Barnaby. 'I believe your suffering is almost at an end,' she assured him.

'Thank God for that,' he muttered with obvious relief. 'I cannot believe that people actually attend such things with any idea of actually being entertained.'

'Perhaps their idea of entertainment is not as exacting as your own?'

'I believe I might find more to entertain me at a wake!'

This time Pandora could not hold back her smile of amusement. 'Then it is to be hoped you do not attend many of them.'

'More than I have the opera, thank God!'

Pandora frowned slightly. 'Why did you bother coming here at all this evening if you hate the opera so?'

There was silence behind her for several long seconds before Rupert answered quietly, 'Perhaps to see and be seen?'

She stiffened. 'Might one ask whom you wished to see, and be seen by, your Grace?'

'One might ask it, yes,' he said blandly.

Pandora allowed her gaze to drift away from the stage, where it was to be hoped the hero was in the latter stages of his lament, in order to surreptitiously observe the other members of the *ton* who had attended the opera, believing—no, expecting—that she would espy the Dowager Duchess of Stratton amongst their number.

Pandora was not a particular friend of Patricia Stirling's, the other woman being several years older and her friends much racier than any of Pandora's acquaintances, but she had met the other woman on several occasions in the past, and so knew her appearance to be exactly as Dante Carfax had yesterday evening described Rupert's preferred taste in women: tall and statuesque, with dark hair, eyes of pale blue and set in a classically beautiful face.

But despite a thorough, albeit discreet, search, Pandora failed to see her amongst the other theatregoers...

'Did you find what—or should I say, whom—you were looking for earlier?' Rupert raised mocking brows as he personally attended to Pandora's entrance into his carriage outside the theatre a short time later. His aunt and uncle had already departed, the Countess anxious to return home to check on the welfare of the youngest of her four children, who had been running a temperature earlier in the day; he made a mental note to send his little cousin Althea some tempting bonbons in the morning.

Pandora's gaze remained cool as Rupert removed his hat before entering the coach and making himself comfortable on the seat opposite. 'I wasn't aware I was looking for anyone in particular, your Grace.'

His mouth thinned at her continued formality even though there was no one else present to witness it. 'No?'

'No, your Grace—'

'I believe I have several times expressed my displeasure about being addressed in that priggish manner by you!' An evening of attending the opera, even in the company of a woman as beautiful as Pandora Maybury and his favourite aunt and uncle, had done nothing to soothe the inner feelings of oppressive disquiet he had suffered since the events of yesterday evening.

If anything, he now felt even more restless…

Restless?

Or aroused…?

There was no denying the arousal he had experienced earlier this evening, when he had called to collect Pandora and looked upon her eyes of velvety-drowning violet in the pale beauty of her face, the deep blue of her gown lending a pearly luminescence to the bareness of her shoulders and the full swell of her breasts visible above its low neckline. The interminable hours of sitting immediately behind her in the theatre box, allowing him to admire those pearly shoulders and the vulnerability of her slender, unadorned neck, as well as having his senses invaded by the lightness of her perfume, had only increased that physical awareness.

A physical awareness which now caused Rupert to shift slightly upon his upholstered seat, in the hopes of relieving some of the discomfort he was experiencing from the full and firm swell of his arousal.

Pandora seemed completely unaware of Rupert's physical discomfort as she continued to speak levelly. 'And is the voicing of your so-called *displeasure* usually reason enough for others to cease doing whatever it is they are doing to annoy you?'

'Invariably,' he clipped with satisfaction.

She raised haughty brows. 'Despite all appearances to the contrary, we have never so much as been formally introduced, your Grace.'

'Rupert Algernon Beaumont Stirling, the Duke of Stratton, Marquis of Devlin, Earl of Charwood, etc., etc.,' he drawled with all formality. 'Your servant, ma'am.'

'I very much doubt that.'

He raised his brows at her obvious scorn. 'I am sure I could produce several ladies who might vouch for my having…served them very well, in the past.'

'Besides which,' there was a warm blush in Pandora's cheeks as she continued firmly, 'I don't appreciate being used as a—a means of muddying the waters in regard to another…even less socially acceptable friendship in your life!' The fullness of her top lip curled upwards in her displeasure.

So the little cat had claws, Rupert noted appreciatively as he looked across at her, his eyes gleaming silver slits under his lids. Claws, which he could all too easily envisage scratching at and digging into his muscled back as he pounded himself remorselessly into—

What the devil!

His interest in Pandora was as a means to an end—Patricia Stirling's end, he hoped—and nothing to do with how much Rupert would or would not enjoy making love to her. Admittedly it would be an added bonus to his plans if, as Dante had advised, he could entice the beautiful Pandora into his bed, but it was not, by any means, a necessity.

'You made a similar remark to me this morning.' He eyed her with amusement. 'If you are referring to my father's widow, then I wish you would do so directly and cease these less-than-subtle hints.'

Those violet-coloured eyes glared her irritation. 'Why should I bother to explain myself when you so obviously know precisely to whom I am referring?'

How could Rupert not know, when all of London seemed to be aware that he and his stepmother had been sharing the same residence since the death of his father nine months ago! If not the reason for it...

Only Rupert's lawyer, Patricia Stirling herself, and Rupert's two closest friends, Dante and Benedict, knew the reason for his having to suffer the Dowager Duchess's continued presence in the ducal homes.

And his deceased father, of course, the besotted Charles Stirling, the seventh Duke of Stratton, and the gentleman wholly responsible for Rupert's present dilemma.

A dilemma which Rupert, with Pandora's assistance, now had every hope he might soon bring to a satisfactory end. 'Things are not always as they appear, Pandora,' he said evasively.

Pandora knew that, better than most! Although she failed to see how Rupert Stirling could possibly explain—even should he care to do so— his present living arrangements in such a way as to give them the appearance of being anything other than what they were: he and his widowed stepmother, a woman he was known to have been intimately involved with prior to his father's marrying her, had been openly living together since that gentleman's death.

Her gaze flicked over the Duke in dismissal. 'I believe this evening has taken care of any obligation I may have felt towards you, and as I neither expect, nor desire, to see you again after this evening, the subject of your present unorthodox living arrangements is of little interest to me.'

'Ah.'

Pandora's gaze sharpened warily on the aristocratically handsome face opposite, not at all reassured by the humour she saw glinting in those pale grey eyes and the cynical twist to that sensual mouth. 'What do you mean by "ah"?'

'Yet another subject I feel it would be best we wait until we are alone to discuss,' the Duke said with an expressive glance up to where his groom was perched upon the back of the coach.

Pandora couldn't help but approve of the way Rupert had taken account of the presence of his groom. So many of the aristocracy paid little heed to the presence of their servants when in conversation, seeming to regard them as they might a piece of furniture: of use, but without emotions or opinions of their own. A mistaken belief that all too often led to the servants knowing more of the personal business of their employers than was either prudent or safe. As Pandora knew to her cost...

She shook her head. 'I see no other opportunity in which we might ever converse alone.'

'The opportunity will occur, Pandora, when you invite me into your home for a nightcap, as a way of saying thank you for taking you to the opera this evening,' Rupert drawled.

'An outing I had no wish to attend in the first place!'

'Well...no,' he conceded drily. 'But it's still polite to say thank you.'

Had Pandora ever met such an infuriating gentleman in her life before as this one? If she had then she did not recall it. And she would most certainly have remembered if she had ever met anyone who annoyed and irritated her as much as this particular gentleman did!

And what annoyed and irritated her most was that she knew quite well it wasn't just those two emotions he made her feel…

Beneath the exasperation, there was a feeling of…of excitement, of awareness, that Pandora had never experienced before. A *frisson*, something, that made her aware of Rupert Stirling's every move and mood, even when she couldn't see him, as she hadn't been able to in the theatre earlier. She had certainly *felt* his presence behind her, been aware of his warmth, the insidious smell of him, of sandalwood and lemons and that something else that was unique to Rupert, that warmth and smell stirring her senses until she was aware of every breath he took as well as every shift in posture he made.

Pandora had no previous experience of those sensations to know how best to describe them, she only knew that she had felt them, deep inside her. That, in the close confines of the ducal coach, she felt them still, stirring her, arousing her, so that the tips of her breasts seemed to tingle inside her gown and between her thighs felt uncomfortably warm.

So much so that she now feared the very idea of being alone with him in the privacy of her home...

She straightened her spine against the upholstered bench seat. 'Then I will thank you now and save us both the trouble of any further attempt at politeness between us.'

'Oh, no, Pandora, that will not do at all.' Rupert chuckled huskily. 'The offer of a decent glass of brandy is the very least you owe me for having suffered through the opera this evening.'

'Our choice of entertainment was your own suggestion!'

'Only because I thought it would please you.'

Her eyes widened. 'You thought no such thing!'

'Do you presume, Pandora, after being acquainted with me for a scant twenty-four hours, to now know my character so well that you also know my thoughts?' Rupert raised sceptical brows.

'Well. No. Of course I don't know you well.' A blush once again warmed her cheeks. 'At all, really,' she amended with a frown. 'If I may say so, you're a decidedly enigmatic man at the best of times—'

'And these are certainly not the best of times,' Rupert cut in drily.

'They most certainly are not!' Those violet eyes glittered her displeasure.

He chuckled wryly. 'Do not fear, Pandora, all will be revealed once we are safely ensconced in the privacy of your home.'

A statement she did not find in the least reassuring!

'—talk to your household staff regarding the amount of candles they have left burning in your absence.'

Pandora, having fallen into a stony silence for the rest of the carriage ride to her home, a silence the Duke had happily emulated, as he, too, seemed lost in his own thoughts, now looked enquiringly across the carriage at him.

'Your home is lit up like Carlton House,' he explained in answer to her silent enquiry.

Pandora could see that for herself when she sat

forwards to glance out of the carriage. As the groom opened the door, every room at the front of the house seemed to be alight with burning candles. 'I don't understand…' she murmured faintly as she stepped down from the carriage.

'Perhaps your household staff have taken advantage of your absence to indulge in a leaving-London party?' Rupert suggested sarcastically as he stepped down beside her and placed his hat upon his head.

'Don't be ridiculous.' Pandora shot him an irritated glance when he took a proprietary hold of her elbow as they walked up the steps to the front door of the house.

He frowned darkly. 'That's the second time you have called me such today.'

'You deserved it,' Pandora snapped.

No doubt, Rupert acknowledged ruefully, and yet, apart from Dante and Benedict, he knew no one else of his acquaintance who would have dared to speak to the Duke of Stratton in such familiar and dismissive terms.

It seemed that his respect and admiration for Pandora Maybury grew exponentially. 'You are—' Rupert broke off his comment as the front door of the house was opened by the butler, and in doing so allowing the sounds to be heard from within the house—primarily a wailing Rupert found almost as painful to his ears as he had the singing at the opera earlier! 'What on earth...?'

All was pandemonium as Rupert put Pandora aside in safety before stepping into the small entrance hall of her home, the servants—dozens of them, it seemed, although Rupert doubted that Pandora actually needed to employ dozens of servants in this small mansion—milling about in what appeared to be unproductive disarray. The loud wailing was coming from a thin woman of middle years as she sat upon the bottom step of the staircase.

Rupert glared his disapproval. 'Cease that infernal racket, woman!' He nodded with grim satisfaction as the wailing, all noise, instantly ceased as everyone in the crowded hallway turned to look at him wide-eyed.

Rupert could now see that there were actually only six other people in the hallway besides himself: the elderly gentleman he knew to be the butler, two flighty-looking girls who were no doubts the upstairs and downstairs maids, a lady of middle years whom he presumed was the cook by her plumpness and the pinafore she wore over her beige gown and a bedraggled child of twelve or thirteen years, who might or might not be her kitchen maid. A motley crew, to be sure, none of whom Rupert would have seen employed in any of his own homes.

The woman seated upon the stairs started up her wailing again the moment Pandora stepped inside the house behind him. 'I'm so sorry, your Grace!' Tears now streamed down the woman's thin cheeks as she stood up to rush over to look at her mistress with appealing, if reddened, eyes. 'We none of us knew—we were all downstairs enjoying a late supper—I only discovered it when I went up to lay out your night things—all the beautiful things in your bedchamber...!' She began to wail once again.

Rupert gave a pained wince as the return of that screeching seemed to go straight through him and succeeded in giving him a headache. 'I will physically remove you from my presence if you don't stop that noise instantly,' he warned the woman coldly.

'Stop it, Rupert.' Pandora turned to give him a reproving frown. 'Can you not see how upset she is?' she admonished. 'Try and calm yourself, Henley.' Her voice softened into kindness as she crossed to the distraught woman. 'Enough to tell me what has happened, at least.' She took the older lady's hands in hers and gave them a reassuring squeeze.

Rupert, having absolutely no patience for the woman's sobbing and wailing, let alone her garbled explanation, turned instead to the butler who still hovered at his side. 'Explain, if you please?' he prompted quietly.

'It's just as Henley said, your Grace.' The elderly man frowned. 'Whilst we were all downstairs, partaking of a late supper, someone must have entered the house and gone up to her Grace's bedchamber.'

'And?'

The older man winced. 'And the room is in great disarray, your Grace.'

Rupert's arrogant brows rose. 'Have the authorities been called?'

The butler looked uncomfortable now. 'Not as yet, your Grace.'

Rupert scowled darkly. 'Why on earth not?'

'Well, I—' The man glanced briefly, uncomfortably, to where Pandora was still in quiet conversation with her maid. 'We only discovered what had occurred a few minutes ago, your Grace, and anyway, I was not absolutely sure that—'

'I think there has been quite enough chatter for one night,' Pandora stated. Having now learnt from Henley exactly what had occurred—in lurid detail!—in her absence, she had no wish to discuss it further in front of Rupert Stirling; he already knew far too much about her personal business for her comfort.

She certainly didn't need Bentley to tell the overly curious and shrewdly intelligent nobleman that the reason he had not called the authorities as yet was because he had been unsure of whether or not she would *want* him to bring this to their attention.

Pandora turned to the butler. 'Bentley, take everyone back down to the kitchen and see that they are all given a little brandy to calm their nerves—'

'But first bring a decanter of the same and two glasses to her Grace's blue salon,' Rupert instructed the elderly man imperiously even as he took a firm hold upon Pandora's elbow.

'You are white as a sheet, madam,' he added sternly as Pandora would have protested the need for strong alcohol.

Well…yes, she probably was. But she had thought—hoped— What did it matter what she had thought or hoped, when tonight's events had so obviously proved her wrong?

'Do as his Grace suggests, Bentley,' she instructed wearily, knowing that there would now be no persuading Rupert to leave her or her home until she had offered him some sort of reasonable explanation for what had happened here this evening.

Although quite how much of an explanation Pandora wanted, or indeed, intended to give him, she was as yet uncertain…

Chapter Six

'I am still waiting, Pandora,' Rupert prompted.

'What exactly are you waiting for?' A frown creased her ivory brow as she looked up from where she was seated upon the sofa on the other side of the unlit fireplace from where Rupert was standing, the glass of brandy he had poured for her minutes ago remaining untouched in her gloved hand. They had both dispensed with their evening cloaks and hats upon entering the salon, Bentley having quietly removed them after delivering the silver tray containing the decanter of brandy and two glasses.

Rupert moved to refill his own empty glass before answering Pandora in measured tones. 'I'm waiting for an explanation, of course.'

She raised fair brows. 'I'm not sure I understand—'

'A word of caution, Pandora,' he cut in grimly, instantly causing her expression to turn wary. 'I have never appreciated being lied to.'

'Very few people do,' she returned lightly as she took a tentative sip from the brandy in her glass before instantly making an expression of distaste.

'I especially don't appreciate being lied to by a woman,' he added.

'Does that include all women, or do you have a specific preference in that, too?' She placed the half-full brandy glass well away from her on a side table.

Rupert's mouth compressed at her levity. 'I believe you will find my mood much more…accommodating if you don't attempt to fob me off with sarcastic humour, either.'

'Perhaps I wouldn't feel the need to do so if I knew what it was you wished for me to tell you?' she murmured.

'I wish for the truth, madam!'

Pandora shrugged her shoulders dismissively.

'It has been my experience that one person's truth is not always the same as another's— Rupert!' she gasped in protest as he reached down to take a grasp of both her arms even as he thrust his face very close to her own.

He frowned darkly. 'Pandora, you expressed neither surprise nor distress upon hearing that someone had entered your home illegally whilst you were out at the opera this evening. Nor have you since gone up to your bedchamber in order to see what, if anything, may have been taken. Why is that?' His voice was now silky soft and all the more dangerous for it.

Her throat moved convulsively as she swallowed. 'I have had other, more immediate concerns—'

'More immediate than establishing whether or not any of your valuables have been taken?' he pressed determinedly.

The idea that she might have any valuables left in her possession which *could* be taken almost caused Pandora to laugh bitterly. Almost. For the expression on Rupert's face was of such fierceness, and so very close to her own, that she found it impossible to do anything other than continue to look into the angry glitter of those compelling silver eyes. 'There will be plenty of opportunity for me to go upstairs when you have gone.'

'Which could be some time when I have absolutely no intention of going anywhere until you have fully explained this situation to me,' the Duke assured her implacably.

'There is no situation,' she denied. 'An unknown person, or persons, seems to have entered my home this evening, deeply distressing my personal maid and leaving the rest of the household in uproar. That is the end to what I know of this business at the present time.'

Rupert continued to look at her searchingly for several long seconds, but could read absolutely nothing from the blandness of her expression or the calm look in those violet-coloured eyes as they gazed up into his.

Such fine and beautiful eyes. So deep a violet as to give the appearance of a deep, dark well. And as full of mystery...

Damn it, now was not the time for him to be

appreciative of the fineness of Pandora's eyes, or indeed any other part of her anatomy!

Rupert released her to straighten abruptly, but continued to look down at her along the length of his nose. 'I will come up the stairs with you now—'

'That will not be necessary—'

'Nevertheless, I have every intention of accompanying you to your bedchamber.' Rupert's lids narrowed as he saw a return of the alarm in her expression. 'What is it you are afraid of, Pandora?'

'I'm not afraid of anything!' She rose suddenly to her feet, two bright wings of colour now in the ivory of her cheeks, from temper, he believed. 'Very well, if you insist, you shall come up the stairs with me.' Those magnificent eyes flashed deeply purple. 'Although quite what you expect to find there, I have no idea! A lover, perhaps?' she added scornfully. 'Some man I keep hidden away in my bedchamber in order that he might share my bed at night?'

Rupert had far from forgotten the accusations

of infidelity made against this woman during her marriage. Accusations which he had not cared to hear then at second hand, and had even less interest in doing so now that he had actually met and spoken to her. No, if and when he were to ever hear the truth surrounding those accusations, then he had every intention of it being Pandora herself who revealed it to him.

There was a detachment about Pandora Maybury. A coolness which she had deliberately adopted in order to keep those hurtful comments at bay, perhaps? The same coolness, which Rupert knew he had been endeavouring to breach, by whatever means possible, since the moment he first met her.

He gave a brief smile now. 'I somehow doubt that.'

'You do?' She looked at him in challenge.

Rupert smiled again, confidently. 'Yes.'

Pandora eyed him coldly. 'Then you are singular in that belief.'

He gave a mocking shake of his head. 'I have told you, I make it a rule never to blindly follow where others in society lead.'

Her smile was completely lacking in humour. 'How nice to realise that your acquaintance with me is nothing more than a snubbing of your arrogant nose at society!'

Rupert had every hope that it was going to be so much more than that... 'If you're hoping to annoy me further, Pandora, then don't bother; I assure you that I, and my arrogant nose, are completely impervious to insults.'

'How fortunate for you!'

He crossed the room to open the door. 'After you...?' He stood back pointedly to allow her to precede him from the salon.

Which she did with a brisk sweep of the skirts of her gown as she moved past him, her chin raised haughtily high, those violet-coloured eyes glittering angrily, her cheeks once again aflame with temper.

Rupert followed more slowly, unsure himself as to what he expected to achieve by insisting on visiting Pandora's bedchamber with her—certainly not the obvious! But his instincts had served him well during his years in the army, and as such he knew there was something...not quite right in the calmness of Pandora's response to someone having entered her home uninvited this evening.

'Oh!' Pandora had believed she was prepared for what she would find when she entered her bedchamber. Henley's description earlier, of mayhem and destruction, had been given to her so vividly that Pandora had known of the shredded bed linen, the feathers scattered about the room from the ripped pillows and mattress, of overturned or broken perfume bottles on her dressing table, and drawers left open and now empty, with the clothes that had been inside thrown about on the floor.

Yes, she had known to expect all of those things upon entering her bedchamber, but still it had in no way prepared her for how shocked she would feel at seeing all of her personal belongings either ripped or broken. As if, not finding what they had come here for, the perpetrator had then become intent upon destroying everything she might hold dear.

'Sit, Pandora.' Rupert had lifted and righted the

overturned bedroom chair and now indicated she should sit down upon it—before, in his opinion, she fell down.

Her eyes were deep pools of pained violet in the now deathly pallor of her face as she sank down gratefully on to the brocade-covered chair, the fingers shaking on the hand she now raised to cover her trembling lips.

Rupert moved down on to his haunches in front of her to take her other hand into both of his. 'Who did this, Pandora?' he prompted gruffly.

She blinked, the sweep of her long silky lashes brushing against the tears that had welled up in her eyes and causing them to fall down her cheeks as she looked at him blankly.

'Pandora?' Rupert's hands tightened about hers. 'Tell me who is responsible and I will see that they are punished accordingly,' he assured grimly.

'I— Why should you imagine I might have any idea who was responsible?' She shook her head even as she pulled her hand free of his to stand up and move across the room to begin picking up the things scattered or broken on top of her dressing table.

Rupert frowned as he slowly straightened. 'Possibly because it has happened before?'

Pandora spun about sharply, her eyes wide. 'Why do you say that?'

Rupert had not known that for certain. Until now. Pandora's reaction to his question had just confirmed his earlier suspicions. 'I've told you, you were not surprised or distressed enough earlier. And Bentley looked to you when I questioned why he had not called in the authorities. Is it—could it be that someone has done this out of a malicious need to hurt you?'

Some of the tension eased from her shoulders. 'A jealous wife, perhaps?' she challenged scornfully.

Rupert drew in a sharp and steadying breath. 'It is not so out of the question, is it? Stanley had a wife, I believe?'

Pandora closed her eyes. Oh, yes, Sir Thomas Stanley, the man who had died whilst engaged in that same duel which had killed Barnaby, had most certainly had a wife. And two young children. Which was the very reason that Pandora had not, and never would, publicly reveal the complete truth about the events of a year ago.

She raised her lids, her gaze steady. 'Yes, he did,' she acknowledged wearily.

The Duke nodded tersely. 'That being the case, it's not such a leap to suspect she may be the one responsible for—'

'She is not,' Pandora cut in firmly. 'Clara Stanley moved to live in Cornwall with her two children not long after—after attending her husband's funeral.'

'Which doesn't mean she hasn't paid some-one—'

'For heaven's sake! She has not and did not, Rupert.' Pandora was losing all patience with this conversation.

Rupert looked at her closely, noting the strain in those violet-coloured eyes, the slight trembling to Pandora's bottom lip, the shaking of her hands as she bent to pick something up from the floor and set it back upon her dressing table.

She raised that same weary hand to her brow. 'It's very late, Rupert, and surely you must realise how improper it is for you to linger in this way in my bedchamber.'

'You are quite right—in that it is far too late for either of us to be concerned about our reputations. And with that in mind, I believe it best if you don't remain in this house alone tonight.'

'But I'm not alone—'

'I beg to differ,' Rupert cut in crisply.

'There are the servants—'

'An elderly man, two flighty young maids, a plump cook and her slightly addled-looking and very young assistant, and an hysterical lady's maid—'

'Bentley is not so elderly,' she defended in offended tones. 'Those two young maids are his granddaughters for whom he has been responsible since the death of their parents three years ago. Mrs Chivers is cheerfully rotund, and that very young assistant is her daughter, Maisie, who, although slightly…slow, is certainly not addled. As for Henley—I would far rather have her overabundance of emotion, than be forced to suffer the company of my previous maid.' Pandora's chin was raised stubbornly as she met his gaze in challenge.

'And why were you forced to suffer her company?' Rupert eyed her frowningly.

Her cheeks became slightly flushed. 'My husband previously engaged all the household staff.'

And left to her own devices this past year, Rupert realised that Pandora had chosen to employ an elderly butler because he was responsible for his two young granddaughters, a cook and her no doubt illegitimate—and 'slightly slow'—daughter, and a lady's maid who went into hysterics at the slightest provocation.

All of them servants who had no doubt previously found it difficult to attain employment. And yet Pandora had engaged all of them. Yet another contradiction to that reputation she had as being flighty and self-centred, as well as unfaithful...

Rupert sighed heavily. 'Pandora, can't you see that whoever came into this house earlier this evening may decide to come back again?'

'They never have in the past—' Pandora broke off, an expression of consternation on her face as she looked across at him accusingly. 'You said that deliberately in order to trick me!'

Yes, he had, and he would do it again, if it succeeded in leading him to the truth. Or, as much of the truth as Pandora was willing to share with him at this moment... 'I was right then, this has happened before?'

'Yes.'

'How many times?'

'Three in the last year—and, no, that does *not* mean that Clara Stanley must be the one responsible.' She glared her annoyance. 'Will you not leave that poor woman alone? Has she not suffered enough?'

Again, strange sentiments from the woman who was supposedly responsible for causing most, if not all, of Clara Stanley's suffering...

There was so much here which did not add up. So many questions that Rupert instinctively knew Pandora would not answer as yet. Truthfully, at least. Not that he had any reason to believe she had ever answered him untruthfully, she just had a way of avoiding the truth when it suited her to do so.

Rupert had heard the gentlemen in his clubs discussing the beauty of Pandora Maybury during the past four years, of her infidelity during her marriage, and it had been impossible not to learn of the gossip of the scandal surrounding the death of both her husband and the man accused of being her lover. But there had been little gossip of note about her since that scandal. No mention of her having taken a new lover. Or lovers. No gentlemen at his clubs having boasted of bedding the beautiful but deadly Duchess.

Of course it could just be that she was *too* scandalous, too notorious, for any of those gentlemen to wish to become involved with her, even privately, but somehow Rupert didn't think so; Sugdon, for one, had certainly not seemed to suffer from any such reluctance to bed her!

Rupert's mouth tightened, nostrils flaring, just at the memory of the scene he had interrupted the previous evening, of Pandora's gown ripped, her breasts all but visible through the thin material of her chemise. 'Is there anything missing that you can tell?'

She gave a shake of her head. 'Obviously I

won't be able to say exactly until after things have been put back to rights, but I don't think so, no.'

Rupert's eyes narrowed. 'Was anything taken those other three times?'

'Not that I'm aware, no.'

'Not that you are aware? How can you not know for sure?'

Pandora sighed at his obvious incredulity. 'My marriage contract stated that if Barnaby should die before me and our marriage was childless, I should be left a house of my own in which to live and funds to support myself. This house was never a part of the Wyndwood estate; in fact, I had no knowledge of its existence until Barnaby bequeathed it to me in his will. It came to me already furnished and I've changed very little since I moved here a year ago. But I believe all the furnishings are the same, and that the original paintings still hang upon the walls.'

In Rupert's experience there was usually only one reason for a gentleman to own a property in London of which his wife had no knowledge. Was it possible that, before his untimely death,

Barnaby Maybury had kept a mistress here, in the very same house he had bequeathed to his wife in his will? If that was indeed the case, then Rupert could imagine no greater insult to that wife. However, the clearness of Pandora's gaze and expression would seem to imply she remained totally in ignorance of the insult....

Yet another indication—if Rupert had needed one—that she wasn't at all the sophisticated and experienced woman the gossips expected her to be. Indeed, her soft-heartedness, even with regard to the employment of her household servants, gave every impression she was anything but those two things!

Could it be that Maybury's mistress had since returned to this house three—no, *four* times, in order to try to retrieve something of hers she had inadvertently left behind when she no doubt hastily removed her things from the premises? It was certainly one explanation, and one that Rupert intended to privately pursue.

If Pandora was in ignorance as to her husband's use for this house, then it was perhaps best, for the moment, if she remained that way.

Only the vulnerability of her nape and the back of her shoulders was now visible to him as she once again busied herself tidying the things upon her dressing table. A vulnerability which stirred Rupert's protective feelings in spite of himself.

He carefully stepped over the silk undergarments scattered upon the floor as he silently crossed the bedchamber to stand behind her. 'Pandora—what have you done?' he prompted sharply as she gave a gasp at the same time as she swiftly drew back her gloved hand from arranging the things on the dressing table.

'A sliver of glass just pierced my finger.' Pandora kept her face averted as she now held her injured hand against her breasts, fully aware that it was the realisation of Rupert's close proximity which had startled her, as much as the sudden pain of the glass entering her finger.

The more so, because until that moment, having been preoccupied in her own thoughts concerning all the events of this evening, she had been totally unaware of his disturbing presence standing so close behind her...

'Let me see.'

Pandora's back stiffened instinctively as he took a firm hold of her bare shoulders before turning her to face him, that golden head now bent as he took a gentle hold of her injured hand with the obvious intention of inspecting the damage.

'As there is blood oozing all over your glove you'll need to remove it,' he advised gruffly.

Pandora, having been staring, mesmerized, at that bent golden head, now gave a startled glance down at her hand, surprised to see there was indeed blood seeping through the lace. 'Oh, dear!' She freed her hand to peel the glove down her arm before carefully removing it. 'It doesn't look so bad...' There appeared to be only the smallest of puncture wounds in the soft pad of her index finger.

'Let me see.' The Duke once again took a firm grasp of her hand, frowning darkly as he looked down intently at the blood still oozing from the wound. 'Is the glass still inside?'

'I don't think so, no.' Pandora was no longer bothered quite so much by the shock of the accident as she was by having Rupert cradling her hand in his much larger one. Her breath hitched in her throat, her senses alert to every nuance of the touch of those long, slender fingers that so gently cupped her own.

'Perhaps it would be as well if I...' He did not finish his sentence as he raised her hand to his parted lips to take her injured finger into the moist heat of his mouth.

'What are you doing?' Pandora gasped at the intimacy of such an action, the cut to her finger completely forgotten as she felt the moist lap of his tongue against her flesh before he began to suck upon it gently. 'Rupert!' she exclaimed, her breathing becoming shallow.

Long golden lashes rose until that glittering silver gaze met and held hers even as he continued his tender ministrations.

Pandora ceased to breathe at all, totally ensnared, both by those mesmerising eyes gazing so deeply into her own, and the shocking intimacy of feeling what he was doing to her finger. It felt so...sensuous, forbidden and of such intimacy that she was helplessly aware of her breasts swelling beneath her gown, the tips hardening, and causing an aching warmth between her thighs. She felt herself totally unable to find the strength to look away from the perfectly chiselled lips around her finger.

It was, at one and the same time, the most caring, and yet erotically charged, moment of her life, that gentle suckling of her flesh causing the tips of her breasts to tingle, as if the softness of Rupert's lips were touching her *there* rather than her finger. The heat increased inside her core, dampening the delicacy of her folds and making her press her trembling thighs together in a vain attempt to suppress it.

'Oh, my goodness!' There was a shocked gasp from across the bedchamber as Henley entered the room without warning. 'I had no idea! I would not have— I believed his Grace to have already left...' She trailed off awkwardly.

Rupert ignored the flustered lady's maid as he moved so that his body shielded Pandora from the other woman's curiosity. His fingers tightened as she would have instantly snatched her hand away, his silver gaze brooding as he continued to look down into her now-stricken one as he slowly sucked upon her injured finger once more, twice, before releasing that digit from his mouth with a soft popping noise, the whole length of that tiny finger now moist from his ministrations. 'I don't think there's any glass still embedded in your finger,' he rasped.

Her cheeks were flushed, her breasts softly rising and falling in her agitation. 'Release me,' she hissed softly when her attempts to pull her hand from within the strength of his proved fruitless.

Rupert's lips curved into a mocking smile even as he placed those same lips one last time upon her injured finger before releasing her. 'My nanny was a great believer in kissing a hurt better as a healing method.'

Kissing a hurt better?

Pandora now ached in parts of her body she had not known *could* ache! But not in an unpleasant way. No, what she now felt, in her breasts and between her thighs, was all too pleasurable...

Chapter Seven

Pandora swallowed to ease the dryness in her throat before answering him waspishly. 'In that case, I believe I must be completely cured, your Grace!' She shot him a censorious glare before turning to look across the bedchamber at her maid. 'What is it, Henley?'

That poor lady looked completely undone by this added stress upon her already frayed nerves. 'I came to help—that is, I thought to— Perhaps I should come back later…?' Henley shot Rupert a nervous glance.

'I—'

'Do that,' the Duke cut in haughtily.

Pandora scowled at him before answering her maid. 'That won't be necessary, Henley. His Grace was just leaving,' she added pointedly.

Rupert raised lazily arrogant brows. 'I don't believe our present…conversation is over just yet, Pandora.'

A blush heated her cheeks, whether with embarrassment or anger she was unsure. 'Oh, I think we've said all that needs to be said on the subject for one evening, your Grace.'

'Indeed?' he drawled.

'Indeed.' Her mouth firmed. 'Henley, perhaps you would care to show his Grace out?'

'I—'

'I shall see myself out, thank you, Pandora.' The ice now literally dripped from his voice.

Then do so—now! Pandora wished to say. She knew it was ungrateful of her to feel that way. Rupert had been kindness itself to her since they had entered the house and found the whole of her household in uproar. Well…perhaps he had not been merely *kind* to her for all of that time—as the tingling of her breasts and thighs still testified!

'When—and if,' the Duke continued inexorably, 'I deem it necessary.'

When and if *he* deemed it necessary that he leave? He was unbelievably arrogant!

As far as she was concerned it would have been better by far if he had left some time ago! 'Leave us, would you, Henley?' She made the request gently, even as her flashing gaze was fixed immovably upon the arrogant idiot in front of her.

'Yes, your Grace.' Henley bobbed a curtsy. 'Of course, your Grace. Would you like me to—'

'For heaven's sake, just go, will you?' Rupert instructed. 'How on earth do you stand that woman's presence about you every day?' he demanded the moment Henley had closed the door of the bedchamber behind her. 'I'm sure I should be driven to madness by her nervous twitchings and hesitations!'

'Then it's as well you don't have to suffer them any further,' Pandora returned tersely. 'And how dare you give her the impression that you and I... *Imply* that you and I— I believe you should leave now!' She eyed him in utter frustration.

'So I ascertained some minutes ago.' He nodded unconcernedly.

'Well?' Pandora prompted some tense seconds later as he still gave no indication of leaving.

He raised those arrogant brows as he looked down at her with cool grey eyes. 'There was something of import I had intended to discuss with you this evening.'

Pandora stiffened warily. 'Oh?'

Rupert smiled ruefully as he saw that wariness. 'Obviously, the situation we found upon our return here has deemed that now is not the right time for us to have that discussion.'

'Obviously.'

His smile widened at the dryness of her tone. 'In which case I will return here tomorrow and we shall have our conversation then.'

Pandora tapped a foot in exasperation. 'You know, Rupert, you might find my mood to be far more accommodating if you were to ask rather than use such arrogant phrases as "I had intended" and "I will"!'

'Touché.' Rupert smiled as she turned his earlier comment back upon him. Proving her sharp intelligence once again, but also that she was not in the least the ordinary type of woman of his

acquaintance, who gushed and fawned over the Duke of Stratton.

Just as the physical evidence of Pandora's response to him a few minutes ago—a flush to her cheeks, the swelling of her breasts, the unevenness of her breathing—proved that neither was she immune to the physical intimacy fast developing between the two of them…

But would Pandora's physical awareness of him make what Rupert wished to say to her more, or less, acceptable?

Their conversation tomorrow would, he hoped, provide him with an answer to that question.

'Do sit down, Pandora, and tell me all that has happened to you since we last met,' Genevieve Forster encouraged avidly the moment the two of them were left alone in that lady's private parlour the following afternoon. 'And don't attempt to claim that nothing has happened, because several of my visitors this morning could talk of nothing else but your visit to the theatre yesterday evening in the company of Devil Stirling!' The reproving frown she gave Pandora was obviously on account of her not having informed Genevieve of it herself.

Devil Stirling...

Pandora had come to realise how well that name suited Rupert! He might have the golden looks of a fallen angel, but he was indeed a devil and one who enjoyed nothing more than tormenting her.

Or tempting her...?

Pandora was suffused with heat every time she so much as thought about those few moments of intimacy between them in her bedchamber the evening before. Although why she should feel so hot and bothered, just having Rupert Stirling kiss her finger, was beyond her comprehension. Which was one of the reasons she had called upon her friend today, in the hope that Genevieve, hopefully more understanding of such things, would be able to explain this strangeness of feelings to her.

She sat forwards in the chair to take the cup of tea Genevieve had just poured for her. 'The Earl and Countess of Heyborough were also there. In fact, I was their guest for the evening, not Rupert Stirling's.'

Genevieve raised russet brows. 'But at Stratton's urging, no doubt?'

Pandora felt the blush in her cheeks. 'I believe he did prompt his aunt into making the invitation, yes...'

'Well, of course he did! And?'

'And the opera was particularly tedious—'

'I have no interest in hearing about the opera, Pandora!' her friend admonished ruefully. 'But I do want to know everything else,' she added eagerly. 'Such as how you came to be so well acquainted with Devil Stirling in the first place that he prompted his aunt into inviting you to the opera. And, more to the point, what happened after he drove you home at the end of the evening!' Genevieve's blue eyes twinkled merrily.

The warmth increased in Pandora's cheeks, her pulse leaping, just thinking about the rasp of Rupert's tongue stroking against her injured finger, of his sucking that finger into the heated moisture of his mouth, of the way his devilish silver eyes had held her gaze captive as he did so... It was an act so stirringly intimate that for some minutes Pandora had completely forgotten the surrounding disarray of her bedchamber.

She moistened her lips before speaking. 'We met on the terrace the evening of Sophia's ball. Quite by chance,' Pandora added hastily; she had preferred not to confide in Genevieve and Sophia that an unknown person, or persons, had broken into her home several times this past year and she did not now intend to recount to Genevieve the details of Lord Sugdon's unpleasant attentions towards her the evening of Sophia's ball, either. Pandora deeply appreciated the friendship Genevieve and Sophia had given her this past month and she wasn't going to bother either of those ladies with the less acceptable details of her life. 'Talking of which…have you seen or spoken to Sophia since that evening?'

Genevieve's curls gleamed deeply red as she shook her head. 'Both of you have left me quite bereft of your company this past two days. Why?' Her interest quickened. 'Has something happened to her, too, which I should know about?'

It would perhaps be indiscreet of Pandora to

mention the comments she had overheard the evening of the ball indicating Dante Carfax's long-term interest in Sophia. 'I merely wondered if she had been pleased with the success of her ball,' she said lightly.

'And I believe you are merely trying to distract my attention from telling me of this new friendship of yours with Devil Stirling.' Genevieve pouted prettily.

'Not at all,' Pandora assured with a soft laugh. 'Indeed, I am as surprised by that gentleman's... attentions towards me, as you appear to be.'

'I don't see why. You are beautiful, and charming—'

'And surrounded by such scandal that most gentlemen tend to give me a wide berth in company and attempt to bed me in private!'

Genevieve gave an indelicate snort. 'That particular gentleman is no stranger to scandal himself!'

'Well...no.' Pandora frowned slightly at mention of Rupert's less-than-pristine reputation even before he began living so openly with his stepmother. A relationship he had seemed to completely disregard in Pandora's bedchamber the evening before! 'But it is not the same for a gentleman as it is for a lady.'

'Nothing in life ever is.' Genevieve grimaced.

Pandora eyed her curiously. 'You've not told me of your own progress in taking a lover.'

'Because there is nothing to tell as yet.' Genevieve looked deeply aggrieved by the fact. 'Now for heaven's sake, cease your delaying, Pandora, and tell me all!'

Pandora didn't tell her friend quite all of her acquaintance with Rupert, preferring to omit the reason for their initial conversation, as well as those moments of intimacy in her bedchamber. But she did relate everything else to the eagerly listening Genevieve.

That lady's blue eyes were wide with excitement by the time Pandora had finished her tale. 'And have the two of you had chance to speak again today?'

'Not as yet, no.' But Pandora knew that Rupert had called this morning, whilst she was out at the shops, leaving his card and promising to return this afternoon. Which was the very reason Pandora had chosen to pay a visit to Genevieve. Although she seriously doubted she would be able to avoid him for ever. 'What do you think it can be that he wishes to discuss with me?'

'Can you not guess?' Genevieve's eyes glowed with mischief.

During the hours since Pandora had last seen Rupert Stirling she had taken several guesses as to what the subject of that conversation might be—each of them more fantastic than the first!—which was why she had sought counsel of one of her friends.

'He is going to ask you to be his mistress, of course!' Genevieve announced excitedly.

Exactly the conclusion Pandora had come to.

'Would not such a request make his bed a little overcrowded, when there is already another lady occupying it?' she reminded Genevieve sharply.

'That is just too, too wicked, Pandora!' Genevieve laughed gaily at what she obviously took to be Pandora's dry humour. 'Obviously he has finally tired of Patricia Stirling and now seeks to replace her with you.'

'How flattering!' Pandora's scathing tone showed that she meant exactly the opposite.

'But is this not exactly what we discussed previously, Pandora?' her friend cajoled. 'For each of us to take an exciting lover, or lovers, before this tedious Season comes to an end?'

Yes, that was certainly what Genevieve had proposed, Pandora recalled all too clearly. A daring and scandalous suggestion, which Pandora had preferred not to answer directly at the time. She had since realised that Sophia had not seemed particularly enthused about it, either.

She stood up restlessly. 'That doesn't mean I would ever choose Rupert Stirling to be that lover.'

'Why on earth not?' Genevieve looked up at her incredulously. 'He has the looks of a Greek god. A fallen angel. A veritable—'

'Devil in disguise—and it is a thin disguise at that!' Pandora put in firmly.

'Did I hear someone mention my name?'

Pandora spun around so quickly at the sound of Rupert's amused voice that she felt quite dizzy. Even more so as she looked upon his handsome 'fallen angel' face as he stood slightly behind Genevieve's obviously disconcerted butler. Her heart seemed to cease beating as she took in his impeccable appearance in a superfine of charcoal grey fitting perfectly to his wide shoulders, beneath which he wore a pale-grey waistcoat over pristine white linen, with black pantaloons moulding to his long and muscular legs.

Rupert Stirling's tailor must weep with joy at how finely this gentleman wore his clothes, whereas Pandora found herself barely able to breathe at his sudden disturbing appearance in the doorway to Genevieve's parlour!

Rupert's earlier feelings of frustration with Pandora at her continued and surely deliberate elusiveness, receded slightly as he enjoyed the shocked expression on her face.

Having called at her home this morning, and then again this afternoon, and both times been informed that 'her Grace is not at home', Rupert had lost no time in ascertaining exactly where her Grace had gone to this afternoon. Noting how disconcerted Pandora was by his unexpected appearance here, he couldn't help but feel a certain sly sense of satisfaction!

'His Grace, the Duke of Stratton,' the butler announced with obvious apology to the mistress of the house for not having managed to inform her of the identity of the visitor *before* he had appeared in her parlour.

But that had been deliberately manipulated by Rupert; after chasing around after Pandora for most of the day, he hadn't wanted to give her the opportunity of escaping him yet again—for instance, by trying to leave the house by another route than the front door.

Having a woman avoid his company, in the marked way Pandora had today, was a new experience for Rupert altogether; usually he was the one who had to avoid the company of women whom he had no wish to see or speak to.

'Stratton.' Genevieve Forster had now risen to her feet in order to effect a graceful curtsy, that elegance of movement accompanied by a mischievous twinkle in her deep-blue eyes as she gave a glance in the direction of the obviously still-stunned Pandora.

Rupert handed his hat and cane to the butler before striding into the small, intimate parlour in which the two ladies had chosen to sit and converse. 'Your servant, ma'am.' He bent solicitously over the hand the Duchess of Woollerton extended to him. 'And Pandora,' he added deliberately as he turned to look down the length of his nose at her.

Pandora gave herself a mental shake as she saw the unmistakable mockery in Rupert's amused yet challenging grey eyes. If he thought to disconcert her—even though he obviously had—then she had no intention of adding to his air of triumph by continuing to be so discombobulated! 'Rupert,' she greeted him coolly. 'What brings you here on such a beautiful spring afternoon?' She was perfectly capable of issuing challenges of her own, if that was how it was to be between them.

'Why, you do, of course, my dear Pandora,' he drawled. 'My apologies if that seems…less than polite to you, your Grace.' He turned to smile charmingly at Genevieve.

'No offence taken, I assure you, Stratton,' she said drily. 'Would you care to join us for tea?'

'Not today, if you do not mind. I had thought to take Pandora for a carriage ride before the hour grows too late.'

Pandora's back stiffened. 'I have my own carriage outside—'

'I took the liberty of speaking with your groom before coming in and assured him that he could leave as you would be travelling home in my carriage with me.'

She drew in a sharp, indignant breath. 'You had absolutely no right—'

'I have every right.'

'Would it be better if I left the two of you alone so that you might settle this matter in private?' Genevieve suggested as she obviously saw the mutinous expression on Pandora's hot, flushed face.

'No!'

'Yes.'

Pandora glared across at him for his contradictory statement, becoming even more incensed by that look of hurt innocence he had affected in his expression. Hah! She didn't believe this particular gentleman possessed even an ounce of innocence! 'We really cannot ask Genevieve to leave her own parlour.'

'I'm more than happy to do so, Pandora,' that lady assured her.

Pandora sent her friend a reproving frown. 'Perhaps it would be best for all concerned if his Grace and I were to leave you to the comfort of your own parlour and finish this…discussion in his carriage back to my home, since he has chosen to dismiss my own?' A carriage which they would be sharing alone, Pandora having decided earlier not to bring Henley, as she was only visiting Genevieve.

'An excellent idea,' 'his Grace' said without apology for his actions, despite her obvious accusation. 'It has been a pleasure, your Grace,' he said to Genevieve.

'Indeed it has,' she returned lightly.

'You may be assured I shall see Pandora safely returned to her own residence.' He smiled that charming smile—a smile which she could, at that moment, quite cheerfully have slapped off his handsome face! Which, considering she had never before been a person who felt driven to violence, showed just how frustrating and annoying she found his unmitigated arrogance.

'Oh, do stop glowering, Pandora!' Rupert shot her an impatient glance minutes later as they once again sat opposite each other in the comfort of his carriage. 'But as you're already cross with me, I may as well also tell you that in your absence this afternoon I've had the locks changed at Highbury House.' He took the opportunity of Pandora's brief, incredulous silence to admire how much the colour of the gown and pretty bonnet she was wearing today both suited her so well and were an exact match in colour for those fine violet-coloured eyes—

Violet-coloured eyes, which were currently shooting sparks of flame in his direction! 'You-have-had-the-locks-changed-on-my-home?' she snapped.

He gave a haughty nod. 'Whoever entered your home last night did not break in—'

'You have no way of knowing that!'

'I know that no windows were broken, no locks smashed, which would seem to imply—'

'Whatever *you* wish it to imply!' she interrupted, clenching her fists in sheer frustration. 'You truly are arrogance personified! The single most—' The rest of her obviously intended diatribe was cut off as Rupert, already tired and irritated from the hours he'd spent chasing this woman around today, swiftly removed the distance that separated them by taking her firmly in his arms and placing his mouth against the alluring softness of hers.

Pandora was so shocked by the suddenness of having him kiss her that, for several stunned moments, she could do no more than remain acquiescent in his arms as those chiselled lips moved confidently over hers. Pleasurably. Seductively.

Sensations which she surely could not allow to continue, but at the same time *knew* she had no strength to stop!

It seemed almost as if the hours in between Rupert kissing her finger better in that frankly erotic and sensual way, and his kissing her masterfully on the lips now, had never been. As if the passion that now flared so suddenly between them was inevitable. Irresistible.

Pandora tilted her head slightly to better appreciate the feel of that mouth against her own as Rupert now sipped and tasted her lips at his leisure. Her arms moved up slowly until her gloved fingers were able to grasp the broadness of his muscled shoulders beneath his superfine, her breasts—sensitive with that now-familiar tingling—crushed against the hardness of his chest as his arms tightened about her waist and drew her even closer, the very air about them seeming charged with sexual tension.

Pandora gasped slightly as she felt one of Rupert's hands cup beneath the swell of her breast, that gasp becoming a groan as he ran the soft pad of his thumb lightly against the swollen and sensitive tip, and causing the pleasure to course hotly through her veins and the swollen folds between her thighs to dampen.

She forgot everything but that pleasure as Rupert now took advantage of her parted lips to run the smoothness of his tongue over them, before entering her mouth. His marauding tongue sought out every sensitive dip and heated hollow, claiming her, possessing her, all the while his hand continued to caress her breast. His fingers felt deliciously cool against her heated flesh as they now touched the bare swell of flesh above her gown, before he pushed that soft material aside and cupped the fullness of her bared breast in his hand, gently squeezing, kneading, before his long fingers laid claim to the pouting tip.

Pandora had never known such pleasure as that which completely engulfed her as Rupert continued that sensual assault upon the sensitive tip of her bared breast, those skilful fingers alternately pinching and then stroking the engorged nipple at the same time as his tongue plunged rhythmically into the heated cavern of her mouth. To her wicked delight, that secret place between her thighs began pulsing with the same hot demanding rhythm.

What would have happened next Pandora had no idea, but the discreet clearing of a throat outside the coach brought her back to at least some of her senses before the words spoken by Rupert's groom penetrated the fog that now seemed to have engulfed her brain. 'We are arrived at the Duchess's home, your Grace.'

Pandora pulled away and looked up at Rupert with wide, stricken eyes, quickly noting the silver glitter of his own eyes as he looked back at her, and the slight flush to his cheeks, the curve of his lips seeming fuller, more sensual than ever.

She shook her head in an effort to clear her befuddled and fogged brain, trying to remember why she had *known* that allowing this to happen would be a bad idea. A very bad idea.

Ah. Yes, she had it now. 'The answer is no, Stratton!' she snapped crisply even as she pulled completely out of his arms and turned to indicate that the groom waiting outside should open the carriage door for her. She tried not to notice that the servant's gaze carefully avoided meeting hers as he appeared to stare up at the sky instead.

Rupert reached out to grasp Pandora's arm, arresting her descent and causing her to turn back to him sharply, those violet eyes once again shooting angry sparks in his direction. An anger completely at odds with the aroused flush in her cheeks and the swell of her breasts still visible to him, the sweet curve of her lips also slightly swollen from the passion of his kisses. 'The answer to what is no?' he queried gruffly.

Her eyes widened with indignation. 'Don't attempt to play games with me, Stratton!'

The demanding throbbing of his engorged shaft clearly stated that the only game which he wished to play was one where she was naked and horizontal and he was buried to the hilt between her silken thighs!

He gave a frustrated sigh. 'I truthfully have no idea what you're talking about, Pandora.'

Her eyes burned deeply purple. 'Then let me state quite clearly, here and now, that I have no wish, either now or at any time in the future, to ever take up the dubious honour of becoming your next mistress!'

Rupert was so stunned by this heartfelt avowal that his fingers loosened momentarily on the silkiness of her bare arm, allowing her to pull free and descend from the carriage before sweeping majestically through the open front door of her house, the butler closing it swiftly behind her, as he had no doubt been instructed to do.

Rupert fell back against the upholstered seat of his carriage, too surprised still to do any more than that.

Pandora believed that his invitation to the opera yesterday, his wishing to speak with her today, their kiss just now, all to be a precursor to him wanting her to become his *mistress*?

Hell!

He might have found that assumption amusing, and her response to it even more so, if it was not also damned insulting! And what had she meant by calling it a dubious honour?

'Do you wish to return to Stratton House now, your Grace?'

Rupert looked blankly at his patiently waiting groom for several seconds, before reason finally returned and his resolve firmed. 'No, by God, I do not!' He surged out of the carriage on to the cobbled street. 'Wait here, Gregson.' He glanced up grimly at the windows of Pandora's home. 'I may be some time.'

Pandora had barely had the time to march up the staircase, enter her restored and tidy bedchamber and remove her bonnet, before the door behind her was suddenly thrown open and an obviously incensed Rupert filled the open doorway. 'What on earth—?'

'For your information, madam…' he slammed her bedchamber door shut behind him and began walking steadily, stealthily, towards her '…it is usual to wait until one is asked before one refuses.'

Pandora, having backed against her dressing table, now held her hands up protectively in front of her as she stared at him with wide, apprehensive eyes. He came to a halt just inches in front of her, his height and the powerful width of his muscled shoulders looming over intimidatingly. 'I did not— I had thought—'

'No, madam,' he bit out between gritted, even, white teeth, 'I don't believe you gave any thought *at all* to this situation before insulting me so soundly.'

Pandora didn't even pretend not to know what he meant. 'Genevieve agrees with me that it's obvious by your attentions towards me these past two days that it's your intention to ask me to be your mistress.'

'Flattered as I am that you've discussed me so intimately with your friend—' the iciness of his tone clearly indicating the opposite '—I have to inform the pair of you that the conclusions you've drawn regarding my recent so-called "attentions" are totally in error.'

'Oh…' Pandora had never felt so humiliated. So utterly and completely devastated with the emotion that she wished she might crawl away and hide somewhere. Anywhere. An option clearly not open to her when Rupert continued to loom over her so ominously. She moistened her lips with the tip of her tongue, an action that glittering silver gaze followed exclusively. 'I apologise if I have caused you insult, your Grace—er—Rupert,' she amended as those furious silver eyes narrowed in dire warning. 'It was not my intention to do so. I merely wished to—'

'Refuse the *dubious honour* of becoming my mistress before I felt compelled to voice it.'

She had said that, Pandora acknowledged with an inward wince. A remark which he'd obviously taken exception to. 'Well. That is… Of course,

I'm sure that many women would be deeply flattered to so much as be considered—'

'Oh, give it up, Pandora,' he bit out harshly. 'And accept that there's no going back from your insult to me.'

Her wince was outward this time. 'I was angry when I made that remark—'

'Because you had assumed *I* meant to insult *you* by making such an offer!' A nerve pulsed in his tightly clenched jaw.

'Well…yes. Rupert, do you think perhaps you might…move away slightly?' Her neck was starting to ache from looking up at him towering over her so threateningly. Indeed, he seemed to have swallowed up all the air in the room, making it impossible for her to breathe!

'No.'

She blinked at his uncompromising tone. 'You are in my bedchamber uninvited, sir,' she attempted to rally. 'For the second time in as many days. The least you could do is cease these attempts to intimidate me.'

Rupert gave her accusation some thought, decided that perhaps she was right and he was guilty of intimidation and took a single step back. 'Better?' he challenged.

'It is a…slight improvement, yes,' she allowed with a small sigh.

He felt some of his initial anger began to fade as he considered the amusement of their present situation instead. Pandora Maybury, with her unusual beauty, golden curls and mesmerising violet eyes, had minutes ago insulted him and his honour, more roundly, more completely, than any other living person. Perhaps because any gentleman who had ever dared to speak to him like that would have very quickly found himself at the other end of Rupert's duelling pistols.

His amusement faded somewhat as he recalled that to have indeed been the fate of Pandora's husband *and* her lover…

He moved away from her until he stood with his back to the room, looking out of the window into the street below. His carriage and four still stood on the cobbles below, waiting to take him back to Stratton House, an option he would perhaps be wise to take.

If not for the presence of the woman who awaited him there...

His shoulders stiffened with renewed resolve as he turned back to face the now cautiously watchful Pandora. 'Contrary to general belief, the offer I intend making to you is not of becoming my mistress—but my wife!'

Chapter Eight

Pandora stared across at Rupert uncomprehendingly, sure she could not have heard him correctly. He certainly could not possibly have just asked her to— No, whatever nonsense had just left those chiselled lips had been *stated*; the arrogantly Rupert Stirling did not merely *ask*!

Even so, she knew she could not have heard him correctly. That the toplofty, the elegant Rupert Stirling, Duke of Stratton, Marquis of Devlin, Earl of Charwood, etc., etc., could not possibly have just stated he wished for her, the scandalous Pandora Maybury, to become his *Duchess*!

'Whilst in some ways I find your silence a welcome relief, I also find it less flattering than even your earlier insults,' he drawled into the tense silence.

Pandora blinked before focusing her narrowed gaze upon him. 'Is this your idea of a joke?' she challenged. 'Because if it is, then it's in very poor taste.' She moved impatiently to the middle of the bedchamber. 'I believe I must ask you to leave now.' She eyed him frostily.

Not quite the response Rupert had been hoping for; and how ironic that the first—and hopefully the last—marriage proposal he made, should be seen as nothing more than an attempt at mockery on his part! Yes, this was definitely less than flattering to him…

'Would you mind explaining exactly why you think I would ever consider the idea of marriage to any woman to be in the least amusing?' he asked.

Those violet eyes flashed her displeasure. 'Because of who I am, sir. Or what the *ton* considers me to be, at least,' she added with slight bitterness.

Having learnt all that he could of this woman in the last few days, Rupert was now only too well aware of the contempt with which the *ton* had treated Pandora since the death of her husband and her lover, of how most had preferred to forget her very existence during her year of mourning, and for the main part gave her the cut direct since her return to society some weeks ago, only the Duchesses of Clayborne and Woollerton choosing to seek out and value her company.

None of which Rupert found in the least a hindrance to Pandora becoming his Duchess. In fact, he would much prefer to know the true nature of the woman who was to become his wife rather than to rudely discover it after the event.

He raised his brows. 'And exactly what is that, Pandora?'

She gave him a vexed glance. 'My husband and Sir Thomas Stanley both died in a duel.'

'Yes…?'

Her mouth tightened. 'Surely my meaning is obvious?'

'Not to me, no.'

'Oh, please!' she scoffed. 'I am disgraced, sir. Only accepted into certain homes of the *ton* because my friends insist upon it. Why should you, or any other gentleman, ever wish to ally yourself to such a woman, let alone offer her marriage?

Indeed, the fact that you have twice now entered my bedchamber uninvited shows the complete lack of regard in which you also hold me!'

Rupert watched through narrowed lids as Pandora moved restlessly about the bedchamber, her cheeks having paled to a delicate ivory and making those violet-coloured eyes appear almost purple. 'Or it could convey the eagerness I feel to share your bed?'

She eyed him sharply, suspiciously, for several long seconds before sighing wearily. 'Any member of the *ton* would happily tell you that there's no need for you to offer me marriage in order to achieve that.'

'And I believe I've already assured you—many times—that I rarely, if ever, listen to the opinions of the *ton*,' Rupert drawled. 'I certainly have no intention of seeking their approval regarding my choice of wife.'

'Then you are a fool, sir.' She paced agitatedly, the colour now back in her cheeks, blonde curls bouncing with each step she took. 'Your very name would be tainted by association.'

Rupert looked down the length of his nose.

'I am the Duke of Stratton, madam, and if you were to accept my marriage proposal you would become the Duchess of Stratton; ergo, there would be no name remaining by which I might be tainted.'

'You—'

'Yes, Pandora, it is I who must decide whom and when I shall marry.' His top lip curled back in haughty disdain. 'None of the *ton* were privy to the intimacy of your marriage, were they? Nor were they present during your liaisons with Stanley—or, at least, I presume they weren't?'

'Don't be ridiculous,' Pandora snapped her impatience with that last remark.

He nodded tersely. 'I would rather know the truth of my future bride than otherwise.'

The truth? The truth was so very different from what any of the *ton* imagined!

Could she confide the 'intimacy of her marriage' to Rupert Stirling, of all people? If he believed her, then it would clear her of every accusation that had ever been made against her a year ago. *If* he believed her…

Would anyone believe Pandora if she were to

claim that her three years of marriage to Barnaby Maybury had been nothing but a sham from start to finish? A smokescreen behind which Barnaby hid his true inclinations? Even more shocking, would anyone believe, accept, that the duel, fought by Sir Thomas Stanley and Barnaby a year ago, had not been over her at all, but another man with whom they had discovered they were both…intimately involved?

Pandora had learnt the shocking truth of her husband's inclinations on her wedding night, when he had come to her bedchamber for the sole purpose of telling her that he would not be joining her there ever again, that the mere idea of touching, let alone making love to, a woman's body totally and utterly repulsed him.

Pandora had been stunned, sickened, when Barnaby had gone on to reveal that he'd only told her these details of his private life at all because his having settled all her father's debts now meant she could never tell another living soul as to the true circumstances of their marriage if she did not also wish to bring about the ruination of her own father. The humiliation Pandora had suffered, at this shocking knowledge of her husband's desire for other men, had ensured her silence on the subject even after her father had died.

Just as Pandora had not even attempted to clear her own name of scandal a year ago, knowing that the cost of doing so would be the happiness of three other innocent people, that it was far better if everyone believed she was the guilty one than for Sir Thomas's widow and two children to suffer from being placed in a position of ridicule rather than pity.

And it was because of that latter concern she knew she still couldn't tell Rupert the truth now...

Her chin rose proudly. 'Is there not another lady who might have every reason to expect to become your wife?'

Rupert's nostrils flared at the mere thought of the woman to whom Pandora so obviously referred. Patricia Stirling. His father's widow. The same woman society believed Rupert to have been openly living with this past nine months since his father's death.

A woman that Rupert knew he wouldn't touch

intimately again if she were the only female left upon this earth.

Which she was not, thank God! 'If you're referring to my father's widow, then say so, damn it!'

'If you insist!' Those violet eyes flashed. 'Should you not, in all conscience, be making this marriage proposal to *her*?'

'I assure you, madam, that where Patricia Stirling is concerned, my conscience is completely without blemish,' Rupert said levelly.

'Indeed?' she said sceptically.

'Indeed.' A nerve pulsed in his jaw. 'Nor is it acceptable, to me or society, that I should marry my father's widow.'

Pandora eyed him scornfully. 'Then perhaps you hope to use marriage to another woman as a means of disguising your...unorthodox relationship with your own stepmother?'

'Now that you've found your tongue again it appears to have become that of a viper!' Rupert eyed her chillingly.

Those ivory cheeks bloomed with colour. 'I'm not the one responsible for creating the gossip concerning the two of you, your Grace!'

'Neither am I!' he insisted, knowing exactly who was to blame for what society thought of his present living arrangements. 'Might we forget about Patricia for the moment and continue with our previous conversation?'

She raised golden brows. 'A conversation in which you have suggested I might consider marrying you?'

Rupert's jaw tensed at the derisive incredulity in her tone. 'Yes.'

'Then, no, I don't believe we can forget the existence of the woman who, if I accepted you, would be the third person in the marriage. The French have a term for such things, I believe?'

'*Ménage à trois,*' he supplied tightly.

'Quite so,' Pandora acknowledged tautly, her cheeks still hot and flushed. 'Would that be the arrangement I might be expected to accept in a marriage between us, your Grace?'

'No it damn well would not!'

'There's no need to swear—'

'There's every reason, damn it!' Rupert glared at her coldly. 'For your information, I have not laid so much as a finger upon Patricia since the day I learnt she was my father's wife. Nor do I intend ever to do so again,' he added icily.

Pandora's brows rose sharply at his vehemence. 'I find that very hard to believe.'

'Nevertheless, I assure you it is the truth.'

Was it possible—could it possibly be that Rupert was as much an innocent victim of society's gossip as Pandora was herself? Not that she believed for one moment that he was an innocent—the talk regarding his exploits this past ten years or so could not all be false! But was it possible that he might be innocent in regard to Patricia Stirling, in the same way that Pandora was innocent about ever having been intimately involved with Sir Thomas Stanley whilst married to Barnaby?

Despite the vehemence of Rupert's denial, Pandora had difficulty believing that to be the case when he and Patricia now lived openly together and had done so since the death of his father.

No, there must be another reason he was now suggesting marriage to her, and the only reason she could think of was her original conclusion; Rupert hoped marriage to another woman would divert attention from his scandalous relationship with his young and beautiful stepmother.

Having suffered through one loveless sham of a marriage, she had no desire to repeat the experience! 'My answer to your proposal must be no—'

'Why must it?' he cut in.

'Surely it is obvious, sir?' Pandora said as he once again glowered down the length of that arrogant nose at her.

'Not to me, no,' he barked.

She sighed. 'We've only been acquainted with each other for a matter of days, and I trust you do not think me so naïve as to believe you have fallen madly in love with me during that time?' In truth, Pandora's naïvety, if not her innocence, had been completely shattered upon her wedding night. 'Any more than I can claim to have fallen madly in love with you,' she added firmly, very aware, that under different circumstances, she might well have done just that...

Rupert Stirling could, if he chose, be as charming as he was wickedly handsome. His manner towards her yesterday evening, when they'd arrived back from the theatre to find someone had broken into her home, had been both kind and protective. As for those moments of shared intimacy that had followed here in her bedchamber and those earlier today in his carriage...

She had been but twenty years of age when she'd married Barnaby Maybury, and totally naïve in the ways of men. Yesterday evening, and earlier today in Rupert's carriage, were the only two occasions upon which she had known even a taste of physical pleasure. A very enjoyable taste of physical pleasure, which caused her breasts to tighten and swell once again just at the memory of it!

But she was no longer that naïve and newly married woman. Her girlhood dreams, of having a man fall madly in love with her and for her to love him as passionately, no longer existed. As such, she could not—dare not—allow herself to be seduced by thoughts of the physical pleasure Rupert now tempted her with. 'I believe this conversation is over— Rupert?' She gave him a startled glance as his fingers curled tightly about her upper arm.

'Yes, I'm Rupert.' His teeth were bared in a

humourless smile. 'Not Barnaby Maybury. Not Sir Thomas Stanley. But Rupert. And, as such, I don't think I've ever so much as attempted to be less than honest with you during our brief... acquaintance, have I?' He deliberately used the same term Pandora had earlier, those silver eyes now glittering coldly as he looked down at her, his cheekbones as sharp as blades in the tautness of his cheeks.

'Not that I am aware, no.' Pandora conceded warily.

He gave an acknowledging inclination of his head. 'Nor will I attempt to be so now. You have asked why I wish to marry you, and so I'll tell you, and then leave it for you to decide whether or not you can accept those reasons as being sufficient for us to marry. Does that sound reasonable?'

It sounded...cold, detached, perhaps even calculated... 'Are you sure you wish to confide those reasons to me when I have already refused your offer?'

The tension lessened slightly in his aristocratically handsome face, his grasp loosening on her arm. 'Perhaps when you have listened to my reasons, you might reconsider that decision.'

Somehow Pandora doubted that very much! 'I should tell you that my plans to leave London in the next few days are well advanced. Nor do I have any intention of changing them.'

He nodded. 'I have already taken note that most, if not all, of your personal effects have been removed from this room.'

Pandora smiled wanly. 'One of the reasons for that might perhaps be because many of them were broken beyond repair.'

'You still have no idea who or why?'

'Absolutely none.' She shrugged.

Rupert might have no idea who either, but he had his own thoughts as to *why* her home might have been broken into four times in the past year. Someone, in all probability Maybury's mistress— who no doubts had a key to Highbury House, which was the very reason Rupert had arranged to have the locks changed earlier today—had left behind some sort of incriminating evidence here upon learning of Maybury's sudden death. Quite what that evidence might be, Rupert as yet had no idea, but he intended to find out the identity of this woman at the earliest opportunity.

'We digress,' he dismissed now as he released his hold upon Pandora's arm. 'Perhaps you would care to sit in that chair whilst I tell you of the reasons I must marry?'

'The reasons you *must* marry?' Pandora repeated dubiously as she moved to perch on the edge of the chair.

Trust Pandora, a woman whom Rupert had discovered these past few days to possess a sharp intelligence, to latch on to the relevant word in his statement. 'Must marry,' he confirmed bleakly, 'if I am ever to be rid of a particular and unpleasant thorn in my side.'

Those violet eyes widened. 'Patricia Stirling?'

Rupert gave a tight smile. 'Just so.'

Pandora's brows rose. 'I don't understand...'

'No one but two close friends, and my lawyer, are aware of what I'm about to tell you now.' Rupert began to pace the bedchamber. 'Let me start by telling you that you are correct in supposing that I once had an intimate relationship with my stepmother when she was still Patricia

Hampson.' His mouth twisted self-derisively. 'A mistake on my part for which I have paid most dearly, I do assure you.'

'Go on...'

Rupert breathed out heavily. 'I will start at the beginning.'

'That is invariably the best place to begin.'

He shot Pandora a chilling glance for her shot at humour. 'I'm not a man accustomed to discussing my mistakes.'

'And I'm sure they are so few in number that you won't mind making an exception in this case.'

'Pandora!'

'I'm sorry, Rupert.' She smiled ruefully. 'It's only that you looked so—so disgruntled, at admitting to having ever made even a single mistake!'

Rupert was more than disgruntled, he now had every reason to rue the day he had ever set eyes upon the beautiful but scheming Patricia Hampson, let alone shared her bed.

'Perhaps you will understand that disgruntlement when I have better explained the situation to you.' He grimaced. 'I took up a commission in the army…oh, seven years ago now. It was a hard life, but it was there that I formed my close friendships with Lucifer and Dante. We went into battle together, we drank and laughed at our victories, and all never knowing if the next battle would be our last…' His thoughts drifted off to those somehow halcyon days.

He had not been well acquainted with Lucifer and Dante until they had joined his Regiment at the same time, but fighting together, drinking together, wenching together, had formed a close bond between the three of them, until they were now closer than brothers.

'I should have seen what Patricia was about when we were introduced during one of my brief sojourns home.' He gave a self-disgusted shake of his head. 'She was the youngest daughter of an impoverished Baron from Devonshire and had already been out in society for several years. Within minutes of our introduction she made it obvious to me that she was ripe for—well, having fun, shall we say? An offer I was fool enough to accept.' He frowned as she raised mocking brows. 'I don't mind admitting, that where that woman is concerned, I was indeed the fool you called me earlier, Pandora.'

'I didn't mean to be unkind, Rupert.'

He sighed. 'For several weeks after we met Patricia and I were…together privately. And then it became time to return to my Regiment. At which time she made it obvious why she hadn't accepted any of the marriage proposals she had so far received. It seemed she had been waiting for a gentleman of suitable rank to make that proposal. And she had decided I was to be that gentleman.' His gaze hardened. 'An expectation I felt no hesitation in firmly squashing.'

Pandora's eyes were wide. 'But was she not now ruined because of her association with you?'

'This is more difficult than I had imagined…' He looked decidedly uncomfortable. 'Whatever you may think of me, Pandora, I am a gentleman, and a gentleman does not usually discuss a lady's…virtue, with a third party.'

Pandora looked at him blankly for several moments, then a deep blush warmed her cheeks as his meaning suddenly became clear to her. 'You were not her first lover.'

'Far from it,' Rupert conceded tightly. 'Nor did I have any doubt that I would not be her last, either. I'm sorry if this makes you uncomfortable, Pandora.' He winced as her gaze shifted away from meeting his. 'I'm merely trying to explain why the idea of marriage to Patricia never so much as entered my head. I— She did not take my rejection well.'

'No, I don't suppose that she did.' Pandora didn't know the Dowager Duchess of Stratton well, but she had met the other woman on several occasions in the past and, although beautiful, Patricia Stirling's nature was too different from her own, too brittle and flirtatious, too worldly, for Pandora to ever have warmed to her, let alone made a friend of her.

Rupert's eyes were now as cold as the ice they resembled. 'I'm afraid there was an argument, during which she threatened that I would pay for my refusal to marry her. I dismissed the threat as meaningless at the time and left to rejoin my regiment as I had intended, without giving her threat so much as a second thought. Which was definitely a mistake on my part.' Once again he looked bleak. 'The next letter I was to receive from my father informed me of his forthcoming marriage, to none other than Patricia Hampson!'

Pandora gasped softly. 'That was her revenge upon you, to marry your own father?'

'Oh, yes.' Rupert could still remember the shock of receiving his father's letter, of reading of that gentleman's intention of marrying the same woman whom Rupert had so recently bedded.

'Could you not have prevented the marriage?'

His eyes still glittered with remembered anger as he told Pandora bleakly, 'I was too late. The date for the wedding to take place had already passed by the time the letter reached me.'

'And did you—were you ever able to discuss the matter with your father?'

'And say what?' Rupert grimaced. 'That his wife had occupied my bed before his own?'

'Well, no, of course you could not have said that, but—he had not heard any of the gossip in society concerning the two of you?'

Rupert shook his head. 'My father had even less time for society than I and the two of us were never on close terms—I am too much like my mother, and the Duke and Duchess's marriage was an arranged and never happy one. My father and I were ever uneasy in each other's company, and as he didn't already know, I didn't feel I could tell him. I could *not* confide that his new Duchess and I had once been—intimate.'

'No, I can see how you could not tell your father that,' Pandora agreed. 'And was the Duke's second marriage a happy one?'

Rupert's mouth became a bitter twist. 'He was blindly besotted with his young and dazzlingly beautiful wife. As he was no doubt intended to be.' He frowned darkly. 'Patricia, on the other hand, took every opportunity available in which to attempt to entice me back into her bed.'

Pandora's brows rose. 'And did you ever—'

'Don't even suggest it, Pandora!' he warned harshly, jaw tightly clenched. 'I have told you, the woman repulses me. I would as soon touch a snake as I would her!'

He spoke so vehemently, and with such distaste, that Pandora could not doubt his revulsion. An entirely understandable feeling considering the circumstances under which that lady had married

Rupert's own father. 'Did your father ever know of those attempts in regard to you, do you think?'

'No, I'm sure he did not, thank God!' Rupert said. 'Indeed, the circumstances of this will dictate that he did not,' he added heavily.

Pandora eyed him warily. 'And is it—can it be that it is the circumstances of your late father's will which now prompt you into proposing marriage to me, a woman you have known only a matter of days?'

Rupert looked at her with admiration, liking her more and more as he came to know her better. He *might* indeed have only known her for 'a matter of days', but in that short time he had already come to recognise that she was not only a beautiful and desirable woman, but that she also possessed an intuition, an intelligence, which rendered it impossible for him to ever suffer the boredom in her company as he did with so many other women. With all other women, in fact...

'It is indeed,' he admitted. 'I wish you to understand that, although my father and I weren't close, he was nevertheless a man I respected for the strength of his principles and admired for his astuteness and intelligence of mind.'

Pandora nodded, remembering the late Duke of Stratton as being a handsome man in his sixties. A man who had been much liked and approved of by the *ton* and whom she had once heard Barnaby describe as being much respected by the House for the sensibility and level headedness of his political views.

'Unfortunately, with regard to his wife, those particular attributes of his nature were completely absent,' Rupert continued harshly. 'As such, the late Duke—being, in my opinion, of completely unsound mind where his young and beautiful wife was concerned—made a provision in his will which allows her to continue to live in any of the ducal homes until such time as I should marry!'

'Ah.' Pandora's breath left her in a sigh as the truth of Rupert Stirling's present—and what appeared to be scandalous—living arrangements now became clear to her. 'And since your father died she has chosen to live in whichever of the ducal homes *you* also happen to occupy?'

A low growl escaped him. 'Yes.'

'Could you not have found other lodgings?'

Rupert shrugged. 'I have tried staying at Lord Benedict Lucas's residence with him, but ultimately found that it proved far too troublesome—if not confusing—when it came to the running of the numerous Stratton estates and investments, and that mistakes were being made which would not have happened if I had been in residence at Stratton House. Tiresome as it is, unpleasant as it is, I have been forced to suffer the Dowager Duchess's constant presence in my homes for almost six months now.'

Pandora could never imagine herself throwing herself into the company of a gentleman, when that gentleman had shown her in every way possible that he did not desire her, or her company. Indeed, after their wedding night she and Barnaby, whenever possible, had chosen to live in separate residences. As such, it was inconceivable to her that Patricia Stirling should be so without pride that she now hounded Rupert by following him from house to house with only one intention in mind.

'Would marriage to me really be such purgatory, Pandora?'

She raised startled lids as she realised Rupert was now standing close enough to reach down and take her hand gently in his before pulling her up to stand only inches in front of him, at once reminding her of how pleasurably he had made love to her such a short time ago, and of her own uninhibited responses to that passion...

Chapter Nine

Nevertheless...

Pandora pulled her hand from within Rupert's grasp before stepping away from him, finding she was able to breathe more easily when not in his close proximity. 'Has it occurred to you that perhaps Patricia realised her mistake once she was married to your father? That perhaps she was, and still is, in love with you?'

'I assure you, that woman loves only one person—and that's herself.' Rupert's mouth twisted contemptuously. 'And whatever motive is behind her machinations, with regard to me, she won't lose sight of that fact.'

Pandora bit her lip. 'If that's true—'

'It is.'

She couldn't doubt him when he spoke so certainly. 'Then it is indeed a sad state of affairs and you have my every sympathy, but—'

'Don't repeat your refusal yet, Pandora!' Rupert rasped forcefully as she was about to do exactly that. 'Think about it, overnight perhaps, and let me know your decision tomorrow, in the clear light of morning.'

A frown creased her brow. 'Might I be allowed to finish?'

He straightened at the rebuke. 'Of course. I apologise.' He made her a bow.

Pandora nodded coolly. 'I was about to say that marriage to me may release you from one unacceptable situation, but it will most certainly place you immediately in another. Namely, you would find yourself married to a woman it's strongly rumoured was unfaithful to her previous husband. Indeed, it's well known that her husband was killed during a duel he fought with the man believed to be her lover, who also died.'

Rupert couldn't help but be aware that she used the terms 'strongly *rumoured*' and 'the man *believed* to be her lover'. And was that previous husband without fault or blemish himself? He already suspected Barnaby Maybury was far from innocent, and if Rupert had not spent most of the day seeking out Pandora, he might by now have had proof that he was not.

She gave him a startled glance. 'Would any fault or blemish on his part excuse such behaviour by his wife?'

Rupert studied her through narrowed lids, once again aware that those deep violet-coloured eyes appeared to be hiding many secrets—secrets which the stubborn set of her mouth told him she had no intention of confiding in him.

Secrets, which if Pandora did agree to become his wife, he was equally as determined to exact time and energy in extracting from her!

If she were to become his wife...

A circumstance which didn't look at all likely at this moment, resulting in Rupert feeling all the more determined that she *would* accept him!

'That would depend upon what those faults had been,' he finally answered her slowly.

She tapped one small foot on the floor. 'As I have said, there are dozens—probably hundreds—of women in society who would be only too happy to accept a proposal of marriage from you, so why do you persist in pressing me?'

'I believe hundreds may be an exaggeration, Pandora.' Rupert eyed her mockingly. 'As to why I have chosen you over any of them...' He took a determined step towards her, at once aware of the flush that entered her cheeks and the shallowness of her breathing, evidence—if he should need it—that she was as susceptible to the physical attraction that undoubtedly existed between them as he was. 'These past few days have shown me that we would deal very well together, Pandora. Both in bed and out of it.'

Her eyes widened as she gasped. 'You should not talk openly of such things!'

This woman was a complete enigma, Rupert decided somewhat ruefully—which was perhaps one of the reasons for his interest. On the one hand she had been a wife for three years and a widow for one, and not a faithful wife either if *rumour* were to be believed, and on the other she reacted to any of his more *risqué* remarks as a young girl might just out of the schoolroom, to the point that she blushed and could no longer meet his gaze. It was, Rupert acknowledged, as intriguing as it was frustrating—as well as succeeding in making him more determined than ever to know all of her secrets.

'All I'm asking is that you take the time to think on the advantages of becoming my wife, Pandora, before you refuse me out of hand,' he reasoned softly.

Her cheeks coloured prettily. 'Advantages?'

'I wasn't actually referring to *those* advantages,' he teased. 'As my wife, my Duchess, there would no longer be any need to remove yourself to the country, or for you to relinquish the comfort of your new friendships with the Duchesses of Clayborne and Woollerton,' he continued quickly as she would have spoken. 'Something which I am sure you have no real wish to do.'

'No...' A light of hope had entered those violet eyes at this last realisation.

Not terribly flattering to Rupert's own charms, he acknowledged self-derisively, but so determined was he now to secure this woman as his wife that he was not above using any means at his disposal. 'I will leave you now, Pandora, in order to allow you to consider my offer in peace and solitude.'

'Oh, but—'

'I will call again tomorrow for your answer. Your servant, ma'am.' He made her a formal bow—a completely incongruous politeness considering the two of them had now been conversing in her bedchamber alone for an hour or more!

'I— Yes.' Pandora was now too flustered, both by Rupert and his conversation, to do any more than instinctively make a curtsy before ringing the bell for Bentley.

Only to severely admonish herself the moment he had departed her bedchamber in the company of her butler, for not being more insistent that he accept her refusal to his marriage proposal. As things now stood, she must now expect another visit from Rupert Stirling tomorrow!

Which was perhaps what she had really wanted all along…?

Pandora dropped down weakly on to the side of her bed, her thoughts ones of confusion and contradictions. The scandal that still surrounded her past dictated that she *could not* marry Rupert Stirling. Could she...?

As he had pointed out, *if* she agreed to marry him, she would no longer be the scandalous Duchess of Wyndwood but the far more respectable Duchess of Stratton, the wife of a man whom no member of the *ton* would ever dare to challenge regarding the woman he chose to take as his wife, let alone insult that wife within his earshot or out of it.

And as Rupert had also so succinctly pointed out, *if* she became his wife, then she would no longer have to remove herself from society and retire to the country, or give up the friendships she had with Sophia and Genevieve; after years of not daring to form close friendships, for fear those friends might ask questions about her marriage, she had come to value these two new friendships all the more highly.

Looked at in that particular way, there were no disadvantages to becoming Rupert Stirling's wife.

Except Rupert Stirling himself...

He was, without doubt, the most annoyingly

arrogant man she'd ever met—as well as being the most wickedly handsome and exciting!

As such, how could she, a woman with little or no experience of such things, ever hope to engage his interest for any longer than it took him to bed her and just as quickly become bored by her? Which, she feared, would then place her in a marriage as unhappy as her previous one had been, if for totally different reasons.

No, Pandora could not, in all conscience, accept Rupert's offer of marriage, and she would tell him so when he called upon her tomorrow.

The matter now settled in her mind, Pandora felt a renewed determination to remove herself from London, and continued with her plans accordingly.

'—seem to be quite yourself this evening, Rupert?' Lord Benedict Lucas—Lucifer—prompted lazily that same evening as the two gentlemen sat sprawled in chairs at their club on either side of the small fire burning in the fireplace to dispel the chill of the evening.

Rupert had trouble bringing his attention back

to the man sitting opposite him, evidence that he was indeed distracted this evening. 'Perhaps, Benedict, that's because I am seriously contemplating the idea of marriage.'

The other man raised dark brows. 'You are?'

'Don't look so surprised, Benedict, when we are both all too aware of exactly the reason I am in need of a wife.'

His friend grimaced. 'And do you have a particular lady in mind?'

Rupert's mouth quirked. 'One with mesmerising violet-coloured eyes.'

Benedict sat up abruptly, all laziness gone from his posture. 'You surely can't mean Pandora Maybury?'

Rupert smiled at his friend's obvious surprise. 'The very same.'

'I—but—I'm aware that she attended the opera with you yesterday evening—who in the *ton* is not!—but— My dear chap, are you sure she is the right choice of bride for you?' Benedict looked slightly rattled. 'I mean to say—what of the past scandal?'

Rupert's humour faded, his eyes becoming glacial. 'I have long valued our friendship, Benedict, and sincerely hope I will continue to do so for many years to come, but I'll not allow even you to talk disparagingly of the woman I have asked to become my wife.'

His friend's brows rose at the iciness of his tone. 'You have already asked her?'

'Yes,' he clipped.

Benedict gave a slightly dazed shake of his head. 'Then why did you not just tell me that congratulations are in order?'

'Because they are not. The lady has yet to give me her reply,' he explained curtly at Benedict's questioning glance.

'I beg your pardon?' Benedict frowned. 'One would have thought she would have snatched up such an offer so fast you might have lost an arm—or some other vital part of your anatomy!'

Rupert looked pensive. 'One would have thought a lot of things about Pandora, but it's now my considered opinion that many of those thoughts would be entirely wrong.'

Benedict eyed him curiously for several long moments before stating, 'You like her.'

'I would hardly ask any woman to become my wife whom I did not desire,' he said evasively.

'No, I mean you really like *her*, and not just the beauty of her mesmerising violet eyes or her looks,' Benedict murmured speculatively.

If he did—and to date Rupert had not allowed himself to think about the subject too deeply—then it was not something he intended to discuss, even with a friend as close as Benedict Lucas. 'For obvious reasons I am in need of a wife and, because she suits my requirements, I have chosen Pandora Maybury to become that wife,' he said in a bored voice.

'And your requirements are…?'

'Beauty, brains and desirability.'

'Beauty, brains and desirability…' Benedict repeated slowly. 'And what of the ability to produce your heirs? As you know, her marriage to Maybury, although of several years' duration, was also childless.'

That was a subject Rupert had given even less thought to than his liking for Pandora! Nor did he wish to think about it now. Indeed, Rupert found the idea of Pandora being intimate with another man, even her previous husband, to be utterly distasteful. Which was a decidedly odd state of affairs, coming from a man who could not now recall even the names of some of his own past lovers.

'I believe that's a subject for Pandora and me to discuss once we are married,' he said brusquely.

'Not before?'

'My mother once told me that children are a blessing to a marriage, not a God-given right.'

'And if your new bride fails to give you your heir?'

'Then she will no doubt earn the heartfelt gratitude of my second cousin Godfrey, who will go on to inherit the title,' Rupert dismissed. 'Tell me, what do you know of Maybury himself?'

Benedict shrugged. 'Not much. He was two or three years our senior, I believe, and not a close acquaintance. I only remember him as being a slender fellow and a bit of a stick in the mud.'

None of which was any help to Rupert whatsoever in his desire to know more of the dead man. 'Never mind, I'm sure that I'll be able to persuade Pandora to speak of him herself once we are better acquainted.'

Benedict raised dark, speculative brows. 'You believe she does mean to accept you, then?'

'I have no intention of allowing her to refuse me,' Rupert announced with grim finality. 'But enough of that, Benedict—how goes it with you?'

'As always, slowly and carefully.' His friend shrugged broad shoulders. 'Now let me tell you of a piece of fine horseflesh I saw at Tattersalls yesterday.'

Rupert accepted the change of subject for the dismissal it was, knowing and accepting that Benedict was not allowed to talk of the work he carried out secretly for the Crown.

Quite why Rupert instructed his driver, much later that night, to travel back to Stratton House by a route that would take him past Pandora's home, he was unsure. But instruct him he did, only to see that, despite it being after one o'clock in the morning, her house was once again ablaze with candlelight.

Pandora really should talk to her household staff about this profligate waste of—

What the...?

The front door of the house had just been opened by the elderly butler, in order, it seemed, to allow another gentleman to step outside. A man who was dressed completely in black, from his shoes to the hat he was just placing upon his head. As if he did not wish to be seen or recognised?

'Halt the carriage.' Rupert sat forwards to give a tap on the roof of his carriage in accompaniment to the instruction. 'I said stop the damned carriage!' he repeated harshly when the groom either failed to hear or obey that first instruction.

Rupert barely waited for the carriage to stop before throwing open the door and leaping out on to the cobbled street, his evening cloak billowing about him as he strode forwards confidently to confront the man dressed in black. 'You, there! Yes, you,' he confirmed as a pale face was raised to look in his direction. 'What do you think you're doing?'

'And who is enquiring, might I ask?' came back the cool response.

'I am the Duke of Stratton and a friend of the lady whose house you have just left in the early hours of the morning,' Rupert answered haughtily, determined to know exactly what this gentleman had been doing in Pandora's house at one o'clock in the morning. He knew what it *looked* as if the fellow had been doing and it was completely unacceptable to him!

The other man eyed him calmly. 'Indeed?'

'I have said so, yes,' Rupert bit out icily.

A challenge the other man met for several seconds before turning to look enquiringly at Bentley as he stood in the doorway behind them, receiving a brief nod of confirmation for his trouble. 'In that case, I am Constable Smythe, and this is my deputy,' he added as a younger man in uniform stepped out of the house behind him. 'We were called to attend these premises earlier tonight after her Grace's home was broken into and a fire set in that lady's bedchamber,' the constable continued evenly.

'Good God!' Rupert felt the blood drain from his face. 'Is Pandora all right?'

'Her Grace has not been harmed above breathing in some of the smoke from the fire. She is badly shaken, of course—' Constable Smythe broke off his explanation as Rupert turned on his heel and hurried inside the house.

'I really am perfectly all right, Henley,' Pandora assured huskily, and not quite truthfully, as her maid fussed over her as she sat in one of the armchairs in the small parlour which adjoined her bedchamber.

Pandora had been awoken a short time ago to find that the curtains about her bed were ablaze, the heat and choking smoke making it difficult for her to breathe, let alone escape the flames. Only her terrified screams had saved her, bringing Bentley and several of the other servants running to her bedchamber, the elderly butler sweeping her up in his arms and hurrying from the room whilst Cook organised the maids in putting out those flames with bucket after bucket of water brought up from the kitchen.

Even now, over an hour after the flames had been fully doused, Pandora could not bring herself to so much as look at the scorched remains of her bed. Even more disturbing was that the constable Bentley had insisted be called to the house, upon discovering there was also a broken window in the room that had once been Barnaby's study, had proceeded to question as to whether or not the fire might have been started deliberately, rather than Pandora's original explanation that she must have somehow fallen asleep and inadvertently knocked over the candle on the table beside her bed.

Pandora had dismissed the constable's notion as being nonsense, of course. It was unthinkable, inconceivable, that someone could ever deliberately wish to harm her in that dreadful, shocking way.

'What is all that noise, Henley?' Pandora frowned her confusion as she heard the sound of raised voices outside in the hallway.

The older woman looked petrified as she turned towards the door.

'You don't suppose that he has come back?'

Pandora looked taken aback. 'Who has come back?'

'The monster who tried to burn you to death in your bed!' Henley cringed back as the voices outside grew louder.

Pandora gave a shudder at the lurid way the other woman described the events of earlier, aware that it might all too easily have come true if Pandora hadn't woken coughing from inhaling too much smoke and then seen the rapidly spreading flames that surrounded her. As it was, her bedcovers and, indeed, the bed itself had almost been consumed before the flames had been brought under control and then extinguished, leaving the bedchamber blackened, and the whole house still filled with the smell of smoke.

Not that Pandora had any ideas of sleeping in her bedchamber tonight. In fact, she wasn't sure, after the constable had put forward his theory of what might have happened, that she felt safe at the idea of sleeping in this house ever again!

'—do not remove yourself immediately I shall be forced to physically remove you!'

'Her Grace is badly shaken—'

'And *you* will be shaken until your teeth rattle if you do not step aside by my count of three—'

'Bentley, I'm sure you may safely allow his Grace the Duke of Stratton entrance,' Pandora called out wearily as she now all too easily recognised the reason for the disturbance.

Rupert, having been assailed with the smell of smoke as soon as he entered the house, now gave the overprotective butler one last deathly glare as he finally stepped aside in order to allow Rupert to throw open the door to what appeared to be a private parlour. Certainly there was no bed in it, just several small and comfortable-looking chairs and delicate tables bearing books and vases of flowers.

Pandora was seated in one of those armchairs and being fussed over by the same irritating woman from two days ago. Her golden curls were loose down the slenderness of her back and in complete disarray—golden curls that were indeed long enough to cover those generous firm breasts. Her violet-coloured eyes were so huge and dark they appeared purple in her pale, soot-blackened face and her silk-and-lace lilac-coloured robe also bore signs of the recent fire in the dark smudges upon the lace cuffs and hem, as did the matching satin slippers upon her tiny feet.

Indeed, Rupert could smell the smoke even more strongly in this room, easily guessing that her bedchamber was through one of the two doors leading off this room. Something he had every intention of viewing at a more convenient time. For the moment Pandora was his prime concern…

'Please go,' he softly instructed the woman Pandora called Henley, relieved when she instantly obeyed; he had even less patience to deal with the woman's histrionics tonight. 'Are you injured?' Rupert instantly moved down on to his haunches beside Pandora before reaching out and taking one of her delicate soot-smudged hands into his much larger ones.

'I wish that you had not shouted at Bentley,' she reproved gruffly. 'If not for him I might—' She came to a halt, her throat moving convulsively as she swallowed. 'It was he who braved the flames and carried me from my bedchamber.'

'Then before I leave he shall have my apology and my heartfelt gratitude,' Rupert assured firmly. 'But, for now—are you injured above what I can see?' he queried gently, having winced as he became aware of several patches of redness on her hands, as if she might have tried to beat out the flames with them before Bentley came to her rescue.

'I am unharmed.' Her voice sounded far more husky than usual, and in any other circumstances Rupert knew he would have found it sensually arousing. As it was, he was well aware that it was the dangerous inhalation of the smoke, which now caused Pandora to talk so throatily.

He now looked up at her searchingly, his mouth tightening as he saw the fear lurking in the depths of those purple eyes that looked directly back into his, a transparent delicacy to her ivory-coloured skin and the trembling of the softness of her bottom lip. Even her pointed and stubborn little chin seemed to have a new vulnerability about it.

Rupert made his decision quickly. 'You cannot remain here.' He stood up abruptly, his expression grim as he bent down to scoop her up effortlessly into his arms.

'Rupert!' Pandora squeaked in protest even as her arms moved up about his shoulders. 'Where are you taking me?' she gasped as Rupert walked purposefully from the parlour, only to come to an abrupt halt when they discovered Bentley standing guard outside in the hallway.

Rupert paused to address the older man with grave sincerity. 'I believe I owe you an apology for my behaviour just now, and my sincere gratitude for your bravery earlier in regard to her Grace's welfare, as well as your astuteness of mind in drawing this incident to the attention of the authorities.'

'Her Grace has become as dear to me as either of my own two granddaughters,' the butler answered stiffly. 'As she is to all of us here who have been lucky enough to find employment in her household.'

Rupert nodded as he remembered how Pandora's kindness had resulted in her hiring servants who might otherwise not have found employment—a kindness which had most certainly been to her benefit tonight. 'Her Grace will return in the next few days in order to close up this house, after which you may be assured that there will be employment for all of you here in one of the Duke of Stratton's households.'

'Rupert—'

'Yes, Pandora?' He did not so much as spare her a glance as he turned towards the staircase.

She looked up into his grim countenance, not at all sure what he had meant by that last remark. 'If, as you said, I am to return in a few days, then I must be going somewhere else.'

'Indeed.'

'Where?'

'Home, of course.'

'I—' She blinked. 'But I am already home.'

'My home,' Rupert stated. 'It is my own home to which I am taking you, Pandora.'

She stared up at him in disbelief, sure that Rupert couldn't possibly intend removing her from this house wearing only her satin and lace—and scorched—nightclothes!

Chapter Ten

'It is not that I am ungrateful, Rupert—'

'No?'

'Of course I'm not.'

'You don't sound grateful, Pandora.'

'It is only—I wish you might at least have allowed me the time to dress before carrying me from my home. Or for Henley to pack a bag so that I might dress once I arrived here.'

'It is time for bed, Pandora, a time for undressing, not dressing. Nor,' Rupert continued hardily, 'am I in any mood to deal with that ninnyhead of a maid tonight.'

'She means well.'

'I am sure that Attila the Hun believed himself to be in the right of it, too!'

'Now you are being unkind—'

'A trait for which Stratton is known far and wide, I do assure you,' a third voice cut in with scathing hauteur, bringing an abrupt end to the conversation that had been taking place between Pandora and Rupert since he had carried her out of her home and deposited her in his carriage some minutes earlier, before instructing his driver to depart for Stratton House. 'Good God, how dare you bring one of your whores into my home, Devil?' The woman's voice now rose accusingly.

'I believe you will find that it is *my* home, madam, and I advise you not to forget it,' Rupert bit out coldly as he turned with Pandora still held firmly in his arms. 'Nor will I tolerate your behaviour in calling the lady in my arms by such a foul name!'

'I will do exactly as I— Is that—can that possibly be the Maybury woman?' Patricia demanded in obvious disbelief.

Pandora had stilled in Rupert's arms the moment the other woman first spoke, relieved anew at having his evening cloak wrapped about her own scorched robes. She looked up warily at him now. She could clearly feel the leashed tension in his body as, having once again scooped her up into his arms once they left the carriage, he now held her imprisoned against his muscled chest.

A shiver run down the length of her spine as she found herself unable to look away from Rupert's furious face; his eyes had turned a hard, icy grey as he scowled at his stepmother, cheekbones sharp as blades against the tautness of his flesh, his mouth a thin uncompromising line, the squareness of his jaw rigidly clenched.

He and Pandora might have disagreed all the way here from Highbury House, concerning Pandora's reluctance to go to Stratton House with him, but never once during that time had Rupert looked at her with the intense and deliberate dislike with which he now so obviously viewed Patricia Stirling.

A woman whose existence Pandora had completely forgotten about until now, as well as the fact that she was already in residence in Rupert's home!

'It is indeed Pandora Maybury, the Duchess of Wyndwood,' he rasped. 'The lady whom I hope will very soon consent to become my own Duchess of Stratton.'

'I believe you will find that *I* am the Duchess of Stratton!'

'Not for much longer,' Rupert said with grim satisfaction.

The outraged screech that split the air following this announcement was enough to shatter the eardrums and caused Pandora to finally look up to the top of the wide, curved staircase to where the other woman stood. Tall, her ebony curls arranged artfully about the patrician beauty of her flushed and angry face, the silk robe the Dowager Duchess wore over her night rail a perfect match, Pandora noted distractedly, for the colour of Rupert's icy-grey eyes. Could that be deliberate?

'Cease that disgusting noise immediately, woman!' Rupert thundered. 'Better still would be to remove yourself and your hysterics from my sight and hearing completely!'

Patricia drew in an angry breath. 'How dare you speak to me in that tone?'

'As I am sure you are all too well aware,

madam, I will speak to you in any way I choose,' he continued icily as he walked up the staircase with Pandora, sparing only a scathing glance at the other woman before striding off down one of the hallways.

'You will not dare to sleep with that woman whilst I am in this house!'

'I assure you, if I took Pandora to my bed then it would not be with any intention of sleeping.' Rupert didn't even hesitate in his stride as he coldly answered the woman who had once been his lover. A woman he now despised more completely than he would ever have believed it possible to despise anyone or anything. 'And, as your sensibilities appear to be so outraged by Pandora's very presence, I am sure that both she and I would be thankful if you were to vacate these premises as soon as is possible,' he added.

'You are only doing this to spite me, and I refuse to be—'

'And you dare to accuse me of arrogance?' Rupert gave a scornful laugh as he bent to open a door halfway down the hallway. 'What you do or don't refuse to do is of absolutely no interest to either Pandora or myself,' he informed her.

'That is surely a little difficult to know with certainty considering your little mouse has not spoken a word since becoming aware of my presence,' Patricia jeered.

Pandora bristled, both at being called a 'little mouse' and the condescension in the other woman's tone. She had no more been born a Duchess than Patricia had, but she'd had just as many years to become one. 'My present silence has nothing to do with your own presence and everything to do with the fact that it's almost two o'clock in the morning and I'm tired and anxious for bed,' she said stiffly.

'And on that note we will both wish you a good night, madam,' Rupert spoke with satisfaction before stepping into the room and kicking the door closed behind him, a candle already alight upon the bedside table to illuminate the bedchamber.

A very masculine bedchamber, Pandora noted as she looked about them: a large mahogany four-poster bed surrounded by gold curtains, a matching tall and imposing wardrobe, and another tall

mahogany six-drawer dresser, with several beautiful paintings of horses upon the walls, the curtains at the windows matching those on the bed,
an Aubusson carpet of deep and rich gold on the
floor. It was without doubt a gentleman's bedchamber. Rupert's own room, perhaps?

Pandora's cheeks were still slightly flushed
from the deliberate way Rupert had implied to
Patricia that the two of them were about to become lovers. 'I wasn't referring to *your* bed when
I said I was tired and ready for bed!'

'"Anxious for bed" was the way you described
it, I believe?' he drawled teasingly as he placed
her gently down upon the gold cover on the bed
before straightening.

'I meant *my* own bed,' Pandora corrected
crossly as she sat up to pull his evening cloak
more securely about her. 'Which this most decidedly is not!'

'Your own bed and bedchamber are unfit for
use,' Rupert reminded her as he shrugged out of
his soot- and smoke-soiled jacket before discard-
ing it on a chair.

'And, despite what you said to the contrary only

moments ago, this is your own bedchamber.' She shook her head. 'I really feel it would have been better for all concerned if you had taken me to either Sophia's or Genevieve's home.'

'Would you really have wanted to put either of those two ladies in the same danger as you appear to be?'

Pandora's cheeks were now as white as snow. 'You are also of the opinion that this evening's fire was set deliberately?'

Rupert's jaw tightened. 'I believe Bentley was perfectly correct in bringing tonight's events to the attention of the authorities. No doubt you would have preferred he had not, just as you have instructed him in the past in regard to those other occasions upon which your home was broken into?' He raised disapproving brows.

She avoided meeting that probing silver gaze. 'I simply had no wish to…to bother the authorities with such trivial matters—'

'The fire tonight was not trivial, Pandora,' Rupert objected. 'And, as such, I have every intention of ensuring that you are under my own protection.'

'By my spending the night here?'

His jaw tightened. 'It will do for a start, yes.'

Pandora ran her tongue across the dryness of her lips. 'If you insist upon this—'

'I do.'

As she had thought... 'Then could you not find me another bedchamber in which to sleep?'

'I would prefer that you remain here.'

'But—'

'How can I protect you if you are in another part of the house completely?' Rupert cut in.

She still frowned. 'It is not proper that I sleep in your own bedchamber.'

'And who is to know where you sleep?'

Pandora gave a pained frown. 'The Dowager Duchess will know.'

His mouth thinned. 'And I very much doubt that she would wish to tell anyone of another woman's presence here, let alone that the woman spent the night in my room.'

No, Pandora accepted dully, that wouldn't suit Patricia's own intentions towards Rupert at all. Even so...

'I will sleep in the adjoining dressing room if

that will soothe your shocked sensibilities,' Rupert assured her. 'And now, perhaps you would like some hot water with which to bathe away some of the soot and grime before retiring for the night?' He purposefully changed the subject to a more immediate one.

'Rupert—'

'Pandora.'

'It's far too late to request hot water with which to bathe,' Pandora refused, still distracted by the thought of sleeping in Rupert's bed. It was far too shocking, even without his disturbing presence in the room.

'Perhaps you should leave me to be the judge of that?' He arched an arrogant brow.

Pandora's spirits had brightened slightly just now at the suggestion of bathing away some of the soot and smoke, only to dampen again as she recalled that it was two o'clock in the morning, a time when most, if not all, of the household servants would be abed. As her own household would be quiet now that all the fear and excitement had ended.

In truth, Pandora was totally bewildered still

by the fact that Constable Smythe believed that the broken window in Barnaby's study and the fire in her own bedroom were connected, and that someone had deliberately and cold-bloodedly tried, as Henley had so graphically described earlier, to murder Pandora in her bed.

Could someone really dislike her enough to actually wish to see her *dead*?

Pandora knew that many in society looked upon her with disapproval and suspicion—well, the women mainly felt that way; the gentlemen viewed her in quite a different light!—but she had not thought that anyone felt such strong emotions towards her as to want her dead.

Just the thought of her near escape was enough to make her tremble and quake.

Rupert had been waiting for the moment that the full import of this night's near brush with death finally dawned upon Pandora—indeed, he had deliberately set out to incite her temper as they drove to Stratton House in an effort to delay that reaction until he was in a place where he might more easily comfort her. Inciting her temper had seemed the safest option at the time, when just to look at Pandora, with that tumble of golden curls loose down the slender length of her spine, was enough to inflame Rupert's desire. A totally inappropriate desire on his part, he told himself, when she might have died earlier this evening.

'Pandora…? Pandora, look at me,' Rupert insisted as he moved down on to his haunches in front of her, causing her to finally raise her lashes to look up at him with eyes that were slightly unfocused, if still incredibly beautiful. He reached out to take her trembling hands into both of his. 'You will be safe here with me,' he assured gruffly.

The tip of her tongue appeared to moisten her lips before she answered him. 'Will I?'

Rupert held her gaze unwaveringly. 'Yes.'

'How can you be sure?' she whispered.

The truthful answer to that was he could not. But as far as it was within Rupert's power to do so, he meant to ensure that no harm befell this woman. Now, or in the future. Indeed, it was now his intention to ask Benedict to use his connections in the government to make suitable enquiries about the late Barnaby Maybury, and to learn the identity of the woman Rupert was sure had previously stayed clandestinely at Highbury House with her lover.

'Do you doubt my ability to protect you, Pandora?' The teasing tone of Rupert's voice was completely belied by the hard glitter in his eyes as he contemplated the fate of any person who might *dare*, in future, to harm a single golden hair upon her head.

She gave a wan smile. 'No, of course I don't. I only question whether it is possible for you, or anyone else, to ensure I will ever feel completely safe again.'

Rupert looked at her searchingly. 'Do you have any family at all?'

'None.' She shook her head sadly. 'My parents were both only children and they died of the influenza almost two years ago. Nor do I have any siblings of my own.'

Apart from his aunt and uncle and their children, Rupert had no close relatives either and, whilst he still missed the mother who had died when he was but twelve, his relationship with his father had not, as he had already confided to Pandora, been close in nature, so, whilst he mourned the death of his father, he did not particularly miss him.

He gave her hands a reassuring squeeze. 'Then, as we both appear to be virtually alone in the world, perhaps we should seriously consider marrying and making a family of our own.'

Pandora's eyes widened in the pallor of her face. 'You still wish to marry me?'

He eyed her quizzically. 'Still?'

'If Constable Smythe is to be believed, then, once married to me, *you* might also expect to one night be burnt to death in your own bed.' Pandora shuddered at the memory of the hot and leaping flames that had surrounded her earlier this evening.

'In *our* own bed,' Rupert corrected huskily.

She blinked owlishly, a warm blush colouring her cheeks as she saw the hot appraisal in those grey eyes looking so deeply into her own, and telling her—warning her!—that if she accepted Rupert's offer then the two of them would indeed share a bed once they were married. Before they were married, if the deepening of that appraisal, as his gaze now swept slowly, lingeringly, over the firm swell of her breasts, was any indication.

Pandora looked away from the heat of that appraisal. 'I— Is this— Can this be the ducal bedchamber?' It was certainly grand enough to be. Although tidy in appearance, with no clothes left about the room to distinguish it from another, there was a certain lingering smell of lemon and sandalwood in the air. The same clean smell that Pandora now associated with Rupert.

His mouth compressed. 'No.'

She looked up at him quizzically. 'No?'

'No,' he confirmed. 'Those apartments are on the other side of the house. Next to the bedchamber still occupied by my father's widow. This room is the same one which, until four years ago, was always prepared for my use whenever I was in town.'

Until four years ago… Until Rupert's father had married Patricia Stirling. Listening to the way the two of them had spoken to each other earlier, Pandora no longer had any doubts as to Rupert's antagonism towards the woman who had once been his own mistress. As there had been no mistaking Patricia's outraged reaction to Rupert's announcement of his intention to marry Pandora.

'One of the first things I will require of you, Pandora, once you have agreed to become my wife, is to choose completely new furniture and decoration for the ducal apartments,' he continued. 'Not that I am suggesting the two of us would ever wish to use them, I merely wish for all trace of that woman to be removed from this house.'

Pandora knew that the harshness of his tone and expression was not directed towards her. 'You really do dislike her...'

'I detest her utterly.' Rupert's eyes glittered with the emotion. 'Did you ever doubt it?'

She had...wondered. Until tonight, she had felt a small lingering doubt as to whether Rupert's previous vehemence towards the Dowager Duchess was completely genuine, or merely a result of chagrin because the other woman had married his father shortly after they had argued. A doubt which had been fully erased the moment she had heard Rupert in conversation—if it could be called that!—with the older woman earlier to-night.

She gave a rueful shrug. 'I have learnt that what a gentleman chooses to say is not necessarily the whole truth.'

Rupert studied the haunted beauty of Pandora's face through narrowed eyes. 'Might I enquire from which gentleman you learnt this lack of trust?'

'You are curious, perhaps, as to whether it was my husband or one of my lovers?' she came back tartly.

Rupert released her hands to sit beside her on the bed before he turned and gently placed his own hands either side of her face as he looked down into the depths of her beautiful eyes. 'Has no one ever warned you that the sort of bitter-ness you are currently expressing only succeeds in destroying the person who feels that emotion?' he chided gently.

It was a lesson which Rupert had learnt him-self this past four years as he watched his own father being played the fool by his new wife and he would not wish that disillusionment upon one so tender hearted as he now knew Pandora to be. Indeed, he hoped they would very soon start a new life together, one that would not include past disappointments for either of them.

Pandora frowned, her expression wary as she looked up at him. 'You're not really the Devil at all, are you?'

Rupert laughed softly at Pandora's use of the name which he knew society had given him during the wildness of his youth and which they still used on occasion. 'I trust you'll never try to convince anyone else of that notion, for I am sure none would believe you.'

Perhaps they would not, Pandora acknowledged, but then they hadn't seen that part of Rupert which he had chosen to reveal to her these past few days. Oh, he would never cease to be the arrogant, imposing Duke of Stratton, but she now knew with a certainty that he was so much more than that.

He was that same gentleman who had rescued her at Sophia's ball, literally, from the clutches of Lord Richard Sugdon, before escorting her safely back to her own home. Admittedly he had stolen a kiss along the way, but he had not attempted to force any further attentions upon her, merely stated it was his intention to call upon her the following day.

At which time he had bullied her into going to the opera with him that evening with two of his relatives—after which he had stolen much more than a kiss or two!—before then seeking her out at Genevieve's home earlier today and making her an offer of marriage…

Was it really possible that had happened only a few hours ago? So much seemed to have happened since then. Not least the terrible crushing fear she had suffered earlier as the heat of the flames had leapt and danced about her as she lay in her bed. If not for Bentley's timely action…!

She shuddered. 'Do you know if Lord Sugdon has left town yet?'

Rupert scowled. 'His departure is set for the day after tomorrow, I believe.'

'Do you think that he might have— He was so very angry the night of Sophia's ball…?'

'Don't think on this further tonight, Pandora,'

Rupert soothed, having already considered that Sugdon might be the perpetrator of these past two nights' mischief, in revenge for Rupert's humiliation of him, and just as quickly dismissed the idea; Pandora's home had been broken into three times before this, and as far as Rupert was aware Sugdon had no connection with Barnaby Maybury. Still, he would mention the other man's name to Benedict Lucas.

'Did you mean what you said earlier?' Pandora now looked up at him anxiously. 'In regard to finding employment in one of your own homes for all of my own household staff if I agree to marry you?'

Rupert *had* said that earlier, in an expansive fit of gratitude for Pandora's lucky escape. Nor, having said it, would he now go back on his word. 'Henley may pose something of a problem to my patience,' he acknowledged drily.

Pandora's expression lightened. 'She has a kind heart.'

'As I said earlier, I'm sure Attila the Hun also had his moments of lucidity.' Rupert gently smoothed back the hair at her temples. 'But I would no more relish having *him* as a member of my own household than I do the excitable Henley!'

'Henley is my companion as well as my personal maid.'

'If you agreed to marry me, I would then become your companion. Your personal maid, too, if you would allow it?' he added in a low tone, sure that he would enjoy nothing more than helping this woman to undress.

Her cheeks coloured prettily. 'You would have other calls upon your time and so not always be available.'

'For you I would *make* the time,' he promised.

Pandora smiled. 'I could not be so cruel as to dismiss Henley when she has no one else in the world who cares for her.'

Rupert's mouth quirked. 'If you're making the irritating Henley a part of your agreement to becoming my wife, then I accept.' He arched an enquiring brow.

Had she meant that? Pandora wondered uncertainly. Was she— Could she seriously be contemplating Rupert's proposal of marriage, after all?

There was no doubting that she felt safe in his company—at least, from dangers other than himself! And the danger Rupert posed to her was a purely physical one, a physical arousal which Pandora knew she had enjoyed, and which still held deep curiosity for her. But was either of those reasons enough for her to seriously contemplate accepting his proposal?

Rupert Stirling was not only magnificently handsome—to the point that it made her pulse quicken just to look at him and she was filled with trembling awareness as his finger slightly caressed her temples—he was also in possession of a deep-seated kindness which he chose to hide from himself as much as he did from the people he allowed close to him. As he was currently allowing Pandora close to him...

More surprisingly, he also seemed totally unconcerned about her reputation of being an adulterous wife, and as such responsible for her husband and lover dying in a duel. Something he dismissed with the claim that he would rather know the true nature of his future bride than not.

In other words, he could just be the one chance

Pandora might ever have of marrying again. If she wished to be married again, which in all honesty, she wasn't sure she did. Marriage to Barnaby had become a nightmare from which Pandora had believed she would never awaken, and marriage to Rupert might become just as much of a nightmare, if in a different way, once he became bored with her company and began to seek out other women.

That was something Pandora found she couldn't even bear to think about, let alone live through.

'Let's not talk of these things any more tonight, Pandora.' Rupert, having watched the plethora of emotions flickering across Pandora's expression and delicately pale face, now stood up briskly as an end to that particular topic of conversation. 'It has been a long and exhausting night for you, and this is not the time for making decisions. Instead I will go downstairs to acquire warm water in which you might bathe.'

'Oh, but—'

'Taking into account your disapproval of my rousing one of the maids to bring you hot water,

I have decided to see to the task myself,' Rupert continued wryly.

Her eyes widened. 'I could not possibly ask it of you.'

'You didn't ask, I offered.' His eyes reflected his amusement.

Pandora gave him a teasing look. 'Have you even been down to your kitchens before tonight?'

'Not that I recall, no,' he admitted openly. 'But there's a first time for everything, is there not? And I advise that you enjoy the experience, for it will not soon be repeated!'

Just as Rupert, once he had acquired the warm water, had every intention of thoroughly enjoying the experience of helping Pandora to bathe...

Chapter Eleven

'Would you like me to come down to the kitchens with you?' Pandora offered as she stood up uncertainly, inwardly knowing that both she, and her emotions, felt far too fragile at this moment to entertain another encounter with the shrewish and insulting Patricia Stirling.

'I'm quite capable of bumbling about on my own, thank you, Pandora.' Rupert's expression was wry as he crossed the bedchamber to open the door. 'You'll find several of my clean evening shirts hanging in the wardrobe, I suggest you use the time I am gone in which to choose one you might wish to wear after you have bathed.' He closed the door quietly behind him as he left.

Pandora's cheeks felt hot just at thinking about wearing one of Rupert's own shirts in which to sleep. There was something altogether too…too intimate about the whole notion of having that soft and silky material against her own bare flesh as she lay in *his* bed attempting to sleep. Attempting, because Pandora seriously doubted that she would be able to do so knowing that Rupert was asleep in the room adjoining this one, and as such just a door's width away…

Rupert came to a halt as he re-entered his bedchamber a short time later, his gaze sharp as he searched the deserted room for Pandora, but succeeding only in finding his evening cloak discarded across the bed. Leading him to question whether, whilst he was downstairs in the kitchen, Pandora had been foolish enough to have left the house wearing only her scorched nightgown and robe. Surely she did not fear him, and sleeping in his bedchamber, enough to have braved the dangers that possibly still watched and waited for her outside this house?

'Rupert?'

His hands tightened about the bowl of water and towels he carried as Pandora stepped out from behind the open door of the wardrobe. One of his white shirts was clutched defensively to the swell of her bosom, her hair still a tumble of blonde curls over the slenderness of her shoulders and down the length of her spine, her eyes, as she looked up at him through silky lashes, appearing as large as violet pansies in the pearly pallor of her face.

Rupert put the bowl and towels down on to the stand before crossing the room, looking down at her searchingly as he reached out to clasp her lightly by the shoulders. 'I thought you had gone.' He scowled fiercely as she gave a pained wince. 'Pandora?'

She grimaced. 'My shoulders are a little...sore. From the heat of the flames earlier.'

Rupert frowned his concern even as he released her shoulders to gently take his shirt from her grasp before moving his hands to the fastening of her robe.

'What are you doing?' Pandora looked up at him uncertainly.

He gave her a gentle reassuring squeeze. 'I wish to see the extent of— Dear God, Pandora...!' His face darkened as, having slipped the robe from her shoulders and allowed it to fall to the floor, he was able to at last see the charred remains of her white nightgown.

For remains was all there was, several patches of material burnt away at the bodice, and so revealing the redness to her shoulders and the soft curve of one of her breasts, the damage much more extensive as Rupert's gaze moved downwards; through a gaping and ragged hole near the curve of her left hip he could see more of her reddened flesh and the bottom of the gown had mostly been burnt away to reveal the same redness to the long silky length of her calves and thighs.

Rupert was filled with a murderous rage. 'When I discover who did this to you I intend to personally strangle them with my bare hands!'

Pandora's husky laugh caught on a sob. 'It's only a little uncomfortable.'

'A little?' Rupert's eyes were dark and stormy as he reached out to almost touch the redness on her shoulders. 'I should send for the doctor—'

'No,' Pandora instantly refused, although

even the air moving in the stillness of the room seemed to hurt her now hot and bared flesh. 'I—I shall be perfectly all right once I have bathed away the grime. And perhaps you have a salve I might apply to the burns to take away some of the sting?'

He reached into the pocket of his black pantaloons and produced a small jar bearing a handwritten label 'for burns'. 'Mrs Hammond keeps it on a shelf next to the cooking range and I brought it with me, just in case,' he murmured distractedly as he continued to look down at the mottled flesh revealed by Pandora's ragged nightgown. 'Thanking Bentley earlier was nowhere near enough—remind me to shake him warmly by the hand when next I see him!'

Pandora gave another husky laugh. 'He would think you had gone completely mad!'

Rupert gave a slow shake of his head. 'I may just have done that if he had not managed to rescue you.'

'But he did rescue me.' Pandora reached up to lightly clasp one of Rupert's hands within both of hers. 'Now, if you don't mind leaving? I should very much like to undress and wash whilst the water is still warm.'

'No.'

Her eyes widened. 'No?'

Glittering silver eyes looked deeply into hers. 'I am to act as your maid in Henley's absence, remember?'

'Yes…'

He nodded. 'And if Henley were here she would help you attend to both the washing and these burns.'

Pandora swallowed before speaking. 'You cannot seriously be suggesting that *you* intend to—'

'I am not merely suggesting anything, Pandora, I am stating it as a fact.' Rupert's expression was determined as his hand turned to lightly clasp hers so that he might draw her along beside him towards the bed. 'And once I have seen the extent of your burns, if I feel it necessary, I shall then demand a doctor be called.'

Pandora's heart was pounding loudly in her chest, the burning of her flesh now due to thoughts of Rupert attending to her so intimately. She could not possibly allow— He must not—

She gasped as he slipped the ribbon straps of her gown from her shoulders and allowed it to slowly fall down her body until it lay at her slippered feet, leaving Pandora completely naked to the sweep of his piercing gaze.

She knew exactly what he would see: narrow shoulders, full and uptilting breasts tipped with rosy nipples, tiny waist sweeping out to curvaceous hips and delicately slender legs. And all showing patches of redness from where the flames had licked against her flesh earlier.

It was altogether shocking for her to stand naked and exposed before a gentleman she had known but a few days. For her to stand naked in front of any man, no matter how long their acquaintance!

She breathed shallowly as she began to tingle from head to toe under the intensity of that piercing silver gaze, her skin now feeling hot and fevered, the tips of her breasts tightening as the nipples peaked, and between her thighs becoming damp and swollen.

The tip of Pandora's tongue flicked moistly across the dryness of her lips before she spoke huskily, 'I don't think this is altogether wise, Rupert...'

Any wisdom he might have possessed had left him the moment he looked upon the perfection of Pandora's naked body: full and rounded breasts that he knew would fit perfectly into the palms of his hands, a slender waist he could easily span with those same two hands, deliciously curvaceous hips, with a tiny triangle of silky golden curls at the apex of her thighs, and her legs long and creamy soft.

Perfect, that is, apart from the patches of redness left by the flames having licked against that smooth and delicate flesh.

'Let me see your back...' His breath caught in his throat as he gently turned her and saw those same blotches of red in several places down the length of her spine and another across one creamy buttock. 'Pandora!'

'I'm sure it looks much worse than it is,' she dismissed softly.

'Stay just as you are,' he instructed gruffly as he released her to turn and dampen one of the cloths in the still-warm water before gently dabbing away the sooty residue that had been left upon her skin. 'Tell me if I hurt you.'

'I'm sure you won't.' Her voice was low and husky.

Rupert frowned intently as he concentrated on sweeping the cloth lightly over her back, taking care not to touch any of the sorer-looking places, before just as carefully drying the skin with the second cloth. 'I will apply some of the salve now. It may be a little cool to your skin. The last thing I want to do is hurt you,' he groaned as Pandora flinched slightly as he spread the salve lightly across her shoulders and down her back before turning his attention to that vivid welt across her buttock.

Pandora was unsure which of her emotions was predominant at that moment, pain or pleasure. Pain, because the salve *was* initially cold against her heated skin, but pleasure, because of the gentleness with which Rupert smoothed that salve over and into her sensitive flesh and succeeded in arousing her at the same time as it soothed her...

Her breath caught in her throat as Rupert sat down on the bed to place his legs either side of hers, entrapping her, as he applied the salve to the globe of her bottom, his touch as gentle as a caress as his fingers lightly kneaded her skin. Over and around. And then again. And again. A shiver coursed down her spine as she felt the lightness of those fingers caress down the crease between her buttocks. 'Rupert...?' she murmured uncertainly.

'You have the most beautiful bottom, Pandora.' Again those fingers lightly touched against that sensitive crease.

Pandora's face was hot with embarrassment as she turned her head and looked over her shoulder at Rupert, only the top of his golden head visible as he bent in concentration on his task, his breath a warm caress against her now hot and throbbing flesh. 'I don't believe I was burnt there.'

'No.' Rupert did not look up even though he knew that Pandora was looking at him, his gaze fixed, watching, as his much darker hands smoothed the salve over both pale globes of her bottom now, cupping, caressing, before he was drawn back again and again to that tantalising crease between.

'Rupert!' He heard Pandora give a breathless gasp as he once again gave in to the temptation to touch her there.

'So perfect. So utterly perfect,' he muttered even as he withdrew his hand before lightly clasping Pandora's hips to slowly turn her to face him, her hands moving up to lightly grasp his shoulders as she swayed slightly off balance.

He breathed shallowly as he looked upon the lovely sloping breasts only inches away from his face, creamy white orbs tipped with rose-coloured nipples that caused the already thickly engorged length of his shaft to throb and ache with increasing arousal.

'What are you doing?' Pandora asked in some alarm as Rupert slowly bent forwards, his shoulders feeling hot to her touch through the thin material of his shirt.

He glanced up at her, his lips only a breath away from the pouting tips of her breasts. 'I was merely reaching for the washcloth,' he muttered. His gaze continued to hold hers captive as one of his arms moved about her waist towards the bowl of water, squeezing the excess water from that washcloth before sitting back, his gaze lowering to watch again as he gently wiped that cloth across her breasts.

Pandora continued to feel the burn of Rupert's flesh against her palms as her fingers now dug into his shoulders, the cloth cool against her own skin and causing the rosy tips of her breasts to become even more prominent.

At least, Pandora tried to tell herself that was the reason she clung to Rupert so tightly as he gently continued his ministrations, but inwardly she knew she was only deceiving herself and that it was Rupert's close proximity and the touch of his hands arousing her, both within and without.

She closed her eyes in an effort to shut out the intimacy—the temptation!—of seeing Rupert's blond head bent so close to her naked breasts, his breath now a hot caress against her skin and causing the tiny hairs upon her arms and nape to rise as she knew herself to be fully aware of him. 'Rupert, I don't think— Oh!' Pandora gave a low and keening cry, her lids opening wide in shock and then fluttering closed as she enjoyed the soft touch of his lips against the underside of her breast.

'I am merely "kissing it better", Pandora,' he whispered as he placed yet another kiss against her burning flesh, higher this time, so close to one of her pouting nipples it almost felt as if he had kissed her there.

If Pandora were to move her torso, just slightly, then she *would* touch that aching bud against Rupert's parted lips, would once again know the ecstasy he had shown her in his coach when he had kissed her there...

'Does it hurt here, too, Pandora?'

She felt the gentle brush of his fingertips against that sensitive tip, just that light caress enough to make her gasp as the pleasure coursed through her and settled between her thighs.

'Pandora?' Rupert now looked up at her with eyes of dark stormy-tossed grey as he waited for her answer.

She trembled slightly as she returned his gaze, feeling as if she was perched on the edge of a precipice, but one, if she were to indeed jump off, guaranteed to give her intense pleasure rather than pain. Was this not what Genevieve had talked of that night at Sophia's ball? The excitement of taking a lover? Of enjoying all the pleasures a man of Rupert's experience could undoubtedly show her?

Was she now going to refuse that pleasure? For she knew, without his having to say so, that if she said no to him then Rupert would accept her refusal. That he would finish helping her to wash, apply the soothing salve and then leave her.

She drew in a ragged breath. 'It hurts, Rupert,' she groaned achingly. 'So very much.' She arched her back as she tilted her breast against his waiting lips.

Rupert needed no second invitation as he parted his lips wide and drew that swollen nubbin into the waiting heat of his mouth, gently at first, then more greedily as he heard Pandora's sounds of pleasure, his hand now cupping beneath her other breast as he ran the soft pad of his thumb across the pouting nipple before squeezing it lightly between thumb and finger.

'Oh, dear heaven!' Pandora stepped even closer between his parted legs as he suckled more strongly, their thighs touching, Rupert able to scent her arousal now, both sweet and salty, and so deliciously tempting.

Rupert was breathing heavily as he pulled back slightly. 'Put both your legs over mine, Pandora.'

She blinked down at him owlishly. 'I don't...'

'Like this,' he encouraged huskily as he raised one of her legs and placed it over his thigh, and then raising the other so that she now sat across his thighs as he gently, carefully, cupped the bareness of her bottom and pulled her in even closer, the silken folds between her thighs now fully parted and cupping his iron-hard shaft through his pantaloons. 'Oh, yes...' he groaned as he began to slowly thrust against those swollen folds as he once again drew her nipple deep into the heat of his mouth, tongue laving, teeth biting as he felt and heard her rising pleasure.

Pandora arched her back, her fingers becoming entangled in the thick gold of Rupert's hair as she pressed her breast even deeper into the heat of his mouth. She had never dreamed that ecstasy such as this existed, that a man could do these things with his lips and tongue and hands—

No, that was not true, she *had* dreamed of making love many times during the barren years of her marriage, but those dreams had never been like this. So intimate. So wild. So totally, decadently pleasurable…!

It was unlike anything else she had ever known, between her thighs now drenched with moisture, the rhythmic thrust of Rupert's shaft pressing against a part of her there that gave her pleasure almost beyond bearing, until Pandora ached, longed, for something *more…*

'Please!' she gasped brokenly. 'Oh, Rupert, please…!'

She felt briefly bereft at the removal of the hand that had cupped and caressed her breast, only to gasp with renewed pleasure as that hand moved in between them and down to the inside of her parted thighs, stroking, caressing, until he centred those strokes upon the engorged nubbin he found nestled there, gently and then harder, over and over again. Pandora cried out at the pleasure rising within her and she instinctively began move into those caressing fingers, only to gasp anew as she felt Rupert plunge one of those long fingers inside her, thrusting in slowly, widening her, readying her, before it was joined by a second finger, the soft pad of his thumb continuing to stroke and press the nubbin above as he thrust time and time again into her tightness, filling her, taking her ever closer to that precipice.

He dragged his mouth from her breast, breathing hard and deeply. 'Now, Pandora!' he muttered against her hot and swollen nipple. 'I want—*need* you to come now!'

Pandora was too lost to pleasure to understand or care as to his meaning, crying out as the pleasure finally exploded between her thighs in wave after wave of endless, mindless ecstasy.

Rupert drank in the beauty of Pandora's flushed and heated face as he continued to plunge his fingers deep inside her at the same time as he stroked and rubbed that sensitive nubbin, not stopping or withdrawing from that dual assault upon her senses until Pandora's climax left her so sated she could only collapse forwards weakly against Rupert's shoulder, her hair falling about them in a wild golden tangle.

He rested his own forehead against the dampness of Pandora's shoulder, breathing raggedly as he fought for control of his still pulsing and throbbing shaft, realising as he felt the uncomfortable dampness of his underclothes that he had not been completely successful. Dear Lord, one touch of Pandora's delicate fingers and he was sure he would explode into her hand like a callow youth! A lack of control which Rupert could not remember feeling for many years, if ever.

It was all Pandora, of course. Beautiful, delicious, and enticing Pandora. Even with that welt across the delicacy of her skin she had the most tantalising bottom it had ever been Rupert's pleasure to touch, the most responsive breasts, and as for that enticing place between her thighs…!

Dear God in heaven, if he didn't leave this room in the next few minutes Rupert knew he was going to explode inside his pantaloons just thinking about her sensuous and wantonly responsive body.

The same beauty and responsive wantonness that had held Maybury and Stanley captive a year ago? Enslaving them both? Driving those two gentlemen to the madness of taking each other's lives in a greedy effort to win all of Pandora's passionate responses for themselves?

Was this now to be Rupert's own fate, too?

Pandora came back to her senses slowly, every muscle in her body seeming to ache as she felt so weak and pleasured she was totally unable to move. And yet she must move. Could not remain draped and exposed across Rupert's thighs like this for the rest of the night.

More importantly, was what had just happened to her completely natural? Her eyes had flown wide open and she had stared into Rupert's face as the hitherto unknown pleasure claimed her in wave after wave of heated and uncontrollable sensation, her abandonment complete as she could not stop herself from deepening that pleasure as she rose and then plunged down time and time again on to those pumping fingers.

And the tortured look upon Rupert's face, as he looked at her, watched her with stormy eyes, had seemed as if he were in pain rather than the ecstasy of pleasure in which Pandora was so totally lost.

The very same look which still twisted his aristocratically handsome face as Pandora finally, slowly, raised her head to look at him…

Chapter Twelve

'Steady,' Rupert was the first to break the silence that had befallen them, as he gently eased his claim on Pandora before helping her to slide from his thighs and stand up, enjoying the enticing view of her curvaceous back and that delicious bottom as she turned away to bend and pick up his shirt from where it had fallen to the floor some time ago.

She kept her back towards him as she slipped the garment over her head before lifting the wildness of her hair free until it once again cascaded down the length of her spine.

Her stiff and unyielding spine. Just as the profile she turned to him now was coolly remote as she spoke evenly. 'I— That was impulsive and unwise of us, and I—I think it best if you were to leave me now.'

Yes, that would surely be for the best, Rupert acknowledged dully. To remove himself from Pandora's vicinity. Well away from the temptation she still represented to him, when his manhood was still an aching throb of need between his thighs.

He stood up abruptly before rasping, 'Always leave the man begging for more, is that the way of it, Pandora?'

She turned to him sharply, those violet eyes dark and pained. 'I—you—that was never my intention!'

Rupert sighed, knowing that his anger was not directed at Pandora, but towards himself. It had been his intention to enjoy the delights of her body as he bathed and caressed her, but he had not expected to then find himself so mesmerised by her beauty, and her response to his caresses, that he knew he was seriously in danger of becoming totally lost to the need to possess her. Totally. Utterly. Again. And again. Until Pandora remembered no other lover but him.

Not a pleasant or comfortable realisation for a man who, in the past, had always taken any woman he desired and then just as easily—and unemotionally—discarded her.

'I apologise for that remark, Pandora, it was both crass and insulting.' He reached out to take one of her hands in his before raising it to his lips. 'I shouldn't have taken things so far as I did. You were tired and in discomfort, and surely in no condition to—' He broke off with a self-disgusted shake of his head as he released her hand before straightening swiftly. 'Is there anything else you are in need of before I leave?'

Was there anything else Pandora was in *need* of?

So many things. Words of kindness. Even affection. Anything but the strained awkwardness that now stood as a barrier between the two of them.

She took in Rupert's dishevelled appearance, the gold of his hair in disarray from where her fingers had threaded through its silky length at the height of her passion, his lips looking fuller—

from his attentions to her breasts?—his shirt hanging loose from his pantaloons.

The heat deepened in Pandora's cheeks as she turned away from the bulge of his arousal, which was still visible beneath those pantaloons. 'No, I don't believe there is anything else I require tonight.' She attempted an uncertain smile, sure she had never felt so uncomfortable, or so embarrassed, in her life.

No one had ever touched her before in the intimate way that Rupert just had. Arousing her. Claiming her. Taking her to a pinnacle of pleasure she had never dreamed existed. And all the time she had been completely naked in Rupert's arms he had remained dressed in his shirt, meticulously tied neckcloth, waistcoat, pantaloons and boots!

What must Rupert now think of her abandonment? Of the way in which she had so completely lost all control? Certainly there was none of that closeness she hungered for. The lying in each other's arms, the gentle murmurings she had always imagined would surely follow such physical closeness.

But what did she really know of 'physical close-ness'? Until tonight, her only experience in that regard had been the humiliation she had suffered on her wedding night, when Barnaby had entered her bedchamber for the sole purpose of inform-ing her he didn't find her in the least physically attractive, nor did he ever intend to touch her body in tenderness, let alone passion!

No, perhaps this distance, this coolness be-tween a man and woman who were not married to each other was how these things usually ended once the passion was spent?

All these years Pandora had wondered, and hungered, for physical intimacy, only to now re-alise that it was not as she had thought it would be at all. Oh, the pleasure was even more glorious than she could ever have imagined, but this—the distance and coolness that now existed between herself and Rupert—was surely not worth even those wondrous minutes of heady delight?

'We will talk again in the morning,' he said gently.

'I— Yes, of course we will talk again tomor-row.' Her smile became even more strained.

A smile Pandora maintained until Rupert had gone through to the adjoining dressing room and closed the door quietly behind him.

At which time she dropped down heavily on to the side of the bed, her face buried in her hands as she gave in to the tears which had been threatening to fall since the moment she regained her senses and Rupert had become a distant stranger to her.

Genevieve had been wrong—taking a lover was not fun. It was not fun at all! Oh, the lovemaking had been a revelation, more beautiful than Pandora could ever have imagined, even in her most hungry-for-affection dreams. But the aftermath—the aftermath was bewildering, emotionally painful and not something Pandora believed she would ever wish to repeat...

'What the deuce do you think you're doing?'

Pandora gave such a start, at the unexpected sound of Rupert's voice so close behind her, that for several moments she was in danger of falling from the chair she was currently standing upon in order to reach the lace glove, which seemed to have stubbornly hidden itself at the back of her wardrobe.

Instead she reached out to the shelf in front of her for balance, before turning to look over her shoulder at Rupert as he stood so elegantly and fashionably attired in the middle of her burnt-and-dishevelled bedchamber, in his superfine of cobalt blue, with a silver waistcoat beneath and pale grey pantaloons worn with black Hessians. His fallen-angel face was as wickedly handsome as ever, the gold of his hair falling rakishly over his brow as he quirked a mocking brow at her.

Pandora moistened her lips with the tip of her tongue before answering him. 'I would have thought that the open trunk beside you spoke for itself.'

Rupert's mouth firmed. 'Trunks may speak to you, Pandora, but none have as yet ever spoken to me.'

Her eyes narrowed as she released her death grip on the shelf before turning on her slippered feet to face him. 'I'm referring to the fact that the number of my personal effects already packed inside the trunk must obviously mean that I am going away.'

Yes, Rupert had already ascertained that much. Just as he had realised, when he returned to Stratton House just an hour earlier, that his own bedchamber was empty, and that Pandora was gone from the house. Something his own butler had confirmed, along with the information that her Grace, the Duchess of Wyndwood, had sent word for her coach earlier this morning, along with her maid, and had departed with said maid and coach just a short time later. It had been left up to Rupert to guess that her destination was Highbury House.

A fact that had been confirmed when he arrived here a short time ago and was greeted at the door by Bentley, the grey cast to that gentleman's face testament to his disturbed night and the shock he had suffered at having to rescue his mistress from being burnt alive in her bed. Safe in the knowledge that Pandora was indeed up the stairs in her bedchamber, Rupert had spent the next few minutes once again suitably thanking

the butler for his timely intervention and expressing his gratitude for Pandora's safety.

While the two men were talking, Rupert
couldn't help but notice that the number of boxes
in the hallway had grown in number since yesterday, informing him that Pandora was continuing with her packing.

The fact that she had looked so young and vulnerable as she perched precariously upon that
chair when he entered her bedchamber, and was
dressed in a gown of the palest lemon with a
matching ribbon threaded in her gold curls, had
momentarily robbed Rupert of breath and speech
as he tried to place this elegantly attired young
woman with the wantonly naked one he had held
in his arms last night and pleasured to an explosive release.

Looking up into her coolly smooth and beautiful face, he could still not quite believe he had
made love with this woman only a few hours
ago. 'You left without so much as a goodbye.' It
was not at all what Rupert had intended to say,
yet now that he had said it he was glad that he
had. He was…disturbed that Pandora had left

him, gone, disappeared, without so much as telling him where she was going or if she intended coming back.

Pandora turned away from that accusing silver gaze. 'I thought it was what you wished me to do.'

His eyes narrowed. 'And why should you have thought that?'

She shrugged. 'The maid brought up my breakfast tray and informed me that you had gone out.'

'And...?'

She gave an impatient shake of her head as she turned to frown down at him. 'Surely it's obvious?'

He raised those arrogant brows once again. 'Not to me, no.'

'Then you are singularly lacking in sensitivity, sir!' Pandora informed him haughtily.

'Because I chose to spend the time you were sleeping to go out and deal with several matters of business?'

She blinked. 'Business?'

'Business,' he echoed grimly. 'And would you

kindly step down from that chair, Pandora; I am getting a crick in my neck looking up at you.'

She easily guessed that it was not a crick in the neck Rupert was suffering, but that he didn't like having to look up at anyone! 'I haven't reached my glove as yet…' She turned back to the task with renewed vigour, relieved not to be the focus of that critical silver gaze, if only for the few seconds it would take to reach her missing glove.

'I'm in no mood to play games this morning, Pandora— Oh, damn it to hell!' Rupert had reached out to put his hands about her waist with the intention of lifting her from the chair, but as she turned to face him her slipper caught in the hem of her gown and she cried out as she overbalanced and tumbled from the chair, straight into his waiting arms. 'That's one way of achieving my objective,' he murmured drily as he held her tightly against him.

Her face was flushed and irritable, and she glared up at him to struggle ineffectually in his arms. 'Put me down, please.'

He arched teasing brows. 'Is that any way to thank me for rescuing you from a fall?'

Those beautiful eyes glittered. 'If you hadn't startled me, then I should not have fallen at all!'

'I'm very much afraid, Pandora, that since the first moment I met you, I seem to have done little else but rescue you from one disaster after another.' Rupert caught his top lip between his teeth in an effort to stop himself from laughing at her disgruntled expression.

'It is my wish that you put me down at once.' If Pandora had been standing on her own two feet, then she would no doubt have stamped one of them in temper.

Rupert closed his eyes and counted to ten, then counted another ten, all in an effort to prevent his mirth from breaking free and enraging her even further.

An hour ago, even ten minutes ago, he had been angry and frustrated at finding that Pandora had fled Stratton House in his absence, but now, just a few short minutes later, with Pandora held safely in his arms, all he wanted to do was laugh!

Pandora stilled as she eyed him suspiciously. 'I trust you are not about to laugh, Stratton?'

How could she, how could any woman, so

starchily address the man in whose arms she had been completely naked and aroused only hours before?

Pandora Maybury, that's who. The woman in whose company Rupert had never suffered a single moment of boredom. Dash it, how could there be time for boredom when she seemed to stumble from one mishap to the next?

It was too much, she was too much, for Rupert to be able to contain his mirth another moment longer.

Pandora looked up at Rupert as he burst into sudden, explosive laughter. Not a polite smile, or a dry chuckle, but the sort of humour which entailed him throwing back his head and letting out a loud guffaw. The sort of long and helpless laughter that made one weak and caused even Rupert to step back until he was able to sit down upon the chair from which Pandora had fallen only moments ago. And even then he did not cease his laughter completely, but continued to chuckle as he looked down at her as he shook his head in bemusement.

Pandora had been devastated, mortified with

embarrassment earlier this morning, when the maid at Stratton House had delivered her breakfast, and answered her query concerning the Duke's whereabouts with the information that he had left the house over an hour ago, nor had he left word as to when they might expect him to return.

To Pandora, the abruptness of his departure, and his knowing full well that she would not wish to spend any time alone in the house with Patricia Stirling, seemed to have but one explanation: he must be hoping, after their lovemaking in his bedchamber the night before, that she would have departed from Stratton House by the time he returned. That being the case, she had immediately sent a note to Henley requesting she bring fresh clothes and the coach to Stratton House.

To then have Rupert arrive here only minutes ago and accuse her of not saying goodbye to him was beyond anything! 'You are nothing but a cold, unfeeling, arrogant brute—'

Rupert's humour faded as quickly as it had arrived. 'Was I cold and unfeeling last night?' he prompted huskily. 'Was I arrogant then? Or a brute?'

Pandora had stilled in his arms, her cheeks flushing becomingly. 'You—'

'I am very sorry to interrupt, your Grace—er, your Graces.' An uncomfortable-looking Bentley stood framed in the open doorway. 'But Mr Jessop has arrived to see her Grace.'

Rupert's gaze remained narrowed on Pandora as he answered the other man. 'Ask him to wait in the blue salon, would you, Bentley,' he instructed distractedly.

'You—'

'Now, if you please, Bentley,' Rupert said courteously as Pandora looked set to explode at his arrogance in ordering her butler about.

'Yes, your Grace.'

Rupert didn't need to turn to know that the butler had departed. 'Mr Jessop?' he prompted as he continued to hold Pandora in his grasp.

An irritated frown creased her ivory brow. 'He's my lawyer—'

'Having previous been introduced to him, I am aware of that, Pandora,' Rupert spoke softly.

'What I wish to know is why he is visiting you again this morning?'

She breathed heavily. 'He's here because I sent for him, of course.'

'Why?'

She struggled against his hold. 'Release me, Rupert.'

'No.'

Those purple eyes darkened. 'You have already embarrassed me by continuing to hold me in your arms in front of my butler—do you now intend to embarrass me in front of my lawyer, too?'

His jaw tightened. 'Not unless that lawyer is in the habit of coming upstairs to your bedchamber, no.'

'*You* should not be in the habit of coming upstairs to my bedchamber!'

He shrugged unconcernedly. 'I will take your remark under consideration.'

'You—!' Pandora's eyes were wide, her cheeks flushed. 'Release me and remove yourself immediately from my home—and don't say no to me again, Stratton,' she warned as he was about to do exactly that, 'or I warn you I may be pushed to an act of violence!'

How she intended doing that, when Rupert still held her in his grasp, he was unsure, but caution being the better part of valour, and all that... Besides which, tempting as the notion was, Mr Jessop could not be kept kicking his heels in the blue salon all day whilst Rupert gave Pandora another leisurely demonstration of exactly why he, of all people, had a perfect right, to be not only in her home, but in her bedchamber.

A demonstration which Rupert was only willing to delay, but not to cancel altogether...

'Mr Jessop,' Pandora greeted the lawyer warmly as she entered the blue salon. Perhaps a little more warmly than she might have done if she had not been aware of Rupert's arrogant presence at her side!

Stating that there was absolutely no reason for him to accompany her had achieved absolutely nothing, as he had merely smiled that self-assured—and infuriating—smile of his and followed her down the stairs to the blue salon. As

if she were the same ninnyhead he had called
Henley and had not dealt quite capably with her
own affairs during this past year of widowhood.

'Pandora, your Grace.' Anthony Jessop made
Pandora a polite bow, but his attention was obviously distracted by the man standing beside her.

'It is kind of you to call so quickly after receiving my note.' Pandora continued to ignore Rupert's broodingly silent presence as she smiled
at the older man.

'It was my intention to call upon you this morning anyway,' the lawyer assured lightly.

Pandora arched a surprised brow. 'It was…?'

He nodded. 'But we will talk of that in a few
minutes. Your butler has just informed me that
there was a fire in the house last night? I trust
no one was harmed?'

'I—'

'Your concern is appreciated,' Rupert answered
the other man quietly. 'But, as you might well
imagine to be the case, Pandora has been over-
set by the fire, so perhaps you would just like to
state your business—'

'If you would please allow me to deal with this,

Rupert?' Pandora frowned her irritation with his interfering intervention. 'Indeed, I'm not sure how I would have managed without Mr Jessop's help this past year.'

'I've been only too pleased to be of service, Pandora,' the gentleman assured her warmly. 'And I was anxious this morning to inform you that I have received, in my opinion, a more-than-generous offer for this house.'

'Really?' Pandora brightened. 'That *is* gratifying news.'

'Indeed.' Anthony Jessop bowed. 'I have brought the necessary papers for you to sign if you find the offer acceptable?' He turned to unfasten the leather briefcase he had placed upon one of the small tables that stood either end of the sofa, before removing those papers.

Pandora took them eagerly. 'This is truly—'

'Interesting,' Rupert spoke softly. 'And surprising that you should have received an offer for this house within only days of Pandora informing you of her wish to sell it.' He easily plucked the papers from her fingers before glancing down at them.

Pandora eyed him with annoyance. 'I'm sure there's no reason for you to bother yourself with any of this, Rupert—'

'I see that the offer is being made by a gentleman by the name of Michael Jessop.' Rupert chose to ignore Pandora's indignation at his high-handedness as he quirked a brow at the other man. 'A relative of yours, perhaps?'

'My uncle.' Anthony Jessop looked slightly uncomfortable under that critical gaze. 'He owns several properties in London.'

'Indeed?' Rupert drawled. 'Then one wonders why it is that he should require another.'

'Rupert, I really don't think—'

'Perhaps you might ring and ask Bentley for some tea, Pandora?' he suggested lightly. 'We will no doubt be some time discussing this and I am sure Mr Jessop would welcome refreshment.'

At that moment Pandora's only wish was that she might strike Rupert Stirling on his infuriatingly aristocratic nose! How dare he just take over the conversation *and* the offer received for this house, as if Pandora were already his wife and of no more consequence in matters of business than—than a fly upon the wall? It was beyond arrogant. Beyond enduring after being treated in that same way during her marriage to Barnaby!

'You are perfectly correct, Rupert, in assuming that Mr Jessop and I will no doubt be some time discussing this matter. As such, we really must not detain you any longer from dealing with your own, no doubt urgent, affairs.' She gave him an insincere—and dismissive—smile.

A dismissal he totally ignored. 'As I have already informed you, Pandora, I've already seen to my own business affairs this morning, and am now more than happy to help you deal with yours.' He turned to smile at the lawyer. 'Would you care for tea, Mr Jessop?'

The other man looked more than a little flustered at the other man's invitation in what was, after all, still Pandora's home. 'I would not wish to intrude upon your time, if you and her Grace have other, more urgent matters, to attend to?'

'We do not—'

'Capital!' Rupert thanked the younger man with what was so obviously insincere heartiness. 'As it happens, Pandora and I do have other things to talk of and decide upon this morning. In fact, we were just about to discuss the arrangements for our wedding when you arrived.'

Pandora gave a shocked gasp even as she felt the colour draining from her face. 'I— But—' She broke off any attempt at making a sensible a reply, too stunned by Rupert's announcement, to think let alone speak coherently at this moment.

Rupert gave a hard smile of satisfaction as he placed his arm possessively about Pandora's waist to pull her against his side. 'There is no reason to be coy in front of Mr Jessop, Pandora, when, as you say, he has been such a good friend to you this past year.' He turned to the older man. 'The bishop has this very morning granted us a special marriage licence. I have also spoken with the vicar at St George's, Hanover Square, and he is more than happy to perform the marriage ceremony later today. Perhaps, if Mr Jessop is available later this afternoon, he might care to attend our wedding?'

Chapter Thirteen

'—Cannot believe your insufferable arrogance, your sheer high-handedness in daring to so much as *approach* the bishop regarding a special marriage licence for us when I could not have so much as received a marriage proposal from you at the time, let alone accepted it! And then to also call upon the vicar at St George's in Hanover Square with the intention of the wedding taking place this very afternoon, *and* inviting Mr Jessop to the ceremony, without discussing the matter with me first—'

Rupert had been lounging in an armchair listening for some minutes now to a similar tirade from Pandora as she paced up and down the blue salon, ever since Anthony Jessop had quite wisely made his excuses, gathered up his papers and beaten a hasty retreat, in fact.

That she had to be running out of steam some time soon called, Rupert supposed, for some sort of response on his part. 'Magnificent as you are when you're angry, Pandora, is it not perhaps time for you to stop and draw breath?'

'—is beyond what I might have expected even from you—' She broke off as his words obviously penetrated the veil of anger, those violet-coloured eyes wide as she came to a halt in front of him. 'What did you say?' She stared at him incredulously.

He gave an unconcerned shrug. 'You were starting to repeat yourself, pet.'

'Of course I was starting to repeat myself—'

'And now you are starting to repeat my own remarks—'

'Oooh, has there ever before been a gentleman as infuriating as you?' Two bright wings of colour heightened her cheeks as she really did look as if she might stamp her slippered little foot this time.

'Obviously you don't believe so,' he conceded blandly.

Pandora drew in a sharp breath. 'Did it even occur to you that I might not wish to marry again?'

'I believe the events of last night made that decision for you. Unless rumour is correct—' Rupert quirked an arrogant brow '—and you are in the habit of staying in the homes and bedchambers, and making love with gentlemen of the *ton*, whom you have no intention of marrying?'

Pandora, having been about to deliver another set-down, instead clamped her lips together in mutinous silence. How dare he? How *could* he...? Ridiculous questions both, Pandora acknowledged frustratedly, when she was already aware that Rupert Stirling dared, could and *did* do anything he pleased, and that he had done so from the moment the two of them first met.

But to be informed that the business which had taken Rupert from Stratton House this morning was to collect their special marriage licence from the bishop, a marriage licence he must have requested only the day after meeting her at Sophia's ball, before going to St George's and speaking to the vicar there, and then having the audacity to ask the obviously stunned Anthony Jessop if he would care to attend their wedding, was surely beyond that she might have expected *even* from Rupert 'Devil' Stirling!

'How are your burns this morning, Pandora?'

'Another application this morning of your cook's salve has made them almost disappear,' she admitted. 'And please don't attempt to change the subject, Rupert, when I am still so angry with you.'

His mind put to rest regarding the comfort of her burns, Rupert decided to answer her. 'I decided the first night I met you that a marriage between us would be beneficial to both of us and nothing has happened since to change my mind—'

'*You* decided? Your arrogance is—'

'Yes, yes, so you have said,' Rupert dismissed wearily. 'Obviously I would have preferred to discuss the matter with you before going out this morning, but you were sleeping so peacefully when I looked in on you earlier, and after your...

disturbed night, I believed it better to leave you that way.'

The fire in Pandora's bedchamber had been very disturbing. The time she and Rupert had spent together in his bedchamber had been even more so, but in a totally different way. Which was the reason Pandora had remained sleepless for some time after Rupert had left her the night before, resulting in her sleeping in late this morning.

She had never dreamed—not realized—

'I'm sure you must agree, Pandora, that after… our closeness last night, our marriage has now become something of a fait accompli?'

'I do *not* agree.' She frowned. 'Admittedly things became a little…emotionally charged, between us last night…' her cheeks burned at the memory '…but I don't believe it reason enough for you to have just assumed I had accepted your marriage proposal.'

'No?'

'No!'

He raised haughty brows. 'Then perhaps you would care to explain why it happened then?'

'Because you're an accomplished lover, perhaps?' Pandora acknowledged huskily.

'As you are a responsive one...'

'Which, I suppose, is only to be expected after all the years you have spent—oh, I do beg your pardon?' She turned her stricken gaze on him, apprehension in those violet-coloured eyes.

Rupert frowned slightly as he went towards her and she appeared to flinch at his approach. He came to a halt several feet away from her. 'My comment was not meant as a criticism, Pandora,' he said sincerely.

She blinked. 'It wasn't?'

He slowly shook his head. 'On the contrary, I consider myself to be the luckiest of men to have been blessed with a wife whose depth of passion so matches my own.'

Her throat moved as she swallowed. 'I'm not your wife yet.'

'A matter of a few hours only.' He gave a dismissive wave of his hand.

Pandora looked up at him quizzically. 'You are sure marriage to me is what you truly want?'

'Yes.'

Nothing else, Pandora noted dazedly, just that unequivocal confirmation. 'Have you forgotten that an unknown person, for reasons equally unknown, appears to wish me harm? And there is also my reputation to consider.'

'I have forgotten nothing, Pandora,' he assured grimly. 'In the first instance you will be safer with me at Stratton House than here, or somewhere equally as exposed in the country. In the second, your reputation, as you put it, is exactly that, hearsay and conjecture. It's my sincere hope that you will one day trust me enough to tell me the truth of that situation.'

The apprehension in her eyes deepened. 'And what makes you think that what society chooses to say of me is not the truth?'

How did Rupert know that? Perhaps because he had come to know Pandora so much better these past few days. Enough to know she was not the selfish adulteress society would have her. Her heart was good and true, in her friendships with Sophia Rowlands and Genevieve Forster, the group of misfits she had hired as her household staff, and even including her dealings with him.

No, if Pandora truly was guilty of being unfaithful to her husband, then Rupert could only conclude that she had been driven to it by that husband. How or why, he did not know as yet, but it was to be hoped that the investigation Benedict Lucas was even now putting in motion, concerning the names of the people who had visited or stayed with Barnaby Maybury at Highbury House in the years before his death, might provide Rupert with the answers to that question and others.

'It is not,' he dismissed firmly. 'And have you forgotten that I confided in you my own reasons for marrying?'

Of course Pandora hadn't forgotten that Rupert's reason for marrying was to rid himself of his father's widow once and for all, rather than any genuine feelings for Pandora herself; a truth that could not be denied when he had applied for a special marriage licence after knowing her for only a few hours and confirming that he had not offered for Pandora because he loved her or wanted *her* specifically as his wife, but because he believed her situation in life to be such that she could not refuse him.

And he was right, of course...

Pandora's flight from Stratton House earlier today, all her frantic efforts at packing since her return home, had all been in an effort to deny that which she knew to be inevitable, undeniable: she felt safe with Rupert and had absolutely no doubt that he would protect her, both from society, and whatever danger now stalked her in the night.

That he could not protect her from her own emotions, from the knowledge that she was falling in love with him, was not his fault but her own.

She had thought long and hard after Rupert had retired to his dressing room the night before, at first in complete wonder at the physical delights he had introduced her to, along with those feelings of awkwardness at her own wanton response—a response Rupert had now assured her that he thoroughly appreciated rather than abhorred. But following that, once she had been able to see past her loss of control in his arms, had come the knowledge of *why* she had behaved in that way.

She was falling in love with him.

If she had not already done so…

He was, she now appreciated, everything that a woman most desired in the man she married: handsome, strong, protective of those he considered his own, a considerate and passionate lover, and, on top of all those things, he was also wealthy beyond imagining and in possession of the title of Duke.

As such any woman would be foolish to refuse his offer of marriage, whatever his reason for making it.

Pandora, already more than halfway in love with him, would have to be mad to continue fighting her own inclination to accept him.

Besides which, once the two of them were married, there was always the hope—remote, but still there—that Rupert might one day come to feel a genuine affection for her.

She drew in a deep breath. 'Very well, Rupert, if you are still set on the idea of marrying me—'

'I am.'

'—even knowing the things about me that you do,' Pandora continued firmly, 'then I accept your proposal.'

Rupert had no idea of the process of thoughts which had led her to make her decision—nor was he sure he wished to know them—it was only the end result which was important. 'And the marriage may take place this afternoon?'

She swallowed before speaking. 'If that is what you wish, yes.'

What Rupert *wished* was that she did not look quite so much like a sacrificial lamb going to the slaughter! 'I promise—I hope—that this second marriage will be much happier one for you than your first.'

Pandora smiled uncertainly. 'At what time are we expected at St George's?'

Rupert removed his pocket watch to look at the time. 'We have over an hour before—'

'An *hour*?' Pandora echoed incredulously, her expression now one of panic. 'But I'm not dressed suitably to attend my own wedding! Nor is there time to invite any of our friends to join us—'

'I met with Lord Benedict Lucas earlier today

and he has already agreed to stand as my own witness, and I am sure that Genevieve Forster would be happy to do the same for you,' Rupert continued unruffled.

'What of Sophia?'

He grimaced. 'I believe there is a battle of wills currently taking place between your friend Sophia and my own friend Dante, and that perhaps we should leave them to…settle the matter between them in private, rather than risk that situation possibly coming to a head at our wedding.'

Pandora looked at him curiously. 'The Earl is in love with Sophia?'

'And has been so for more years than I care to think about.' Rupert nodded.

And Sophia, Pandora knew, had always protested at considering Dante Carfax as anything more than an old friend and peer of her deceased husband's nephew and heir. Perhaps Sophia might even have protested that a little too vehemently?

'Very well.' Pandora nodded briskly. 'I shall send word to Genevieve immediately.'

'Despite my invitation earlier, dare I suggest

that I would prefer it if Jessop were not present, after all?' Rupert drawled.

She gave a rueful smile. 'It would seem, as evidenced by our wedding in an hour's time, you would dare say anything!'

He shrugged. 'Is it my fault that I find Mr Jessop an ingratiating little upstart, with possible designs upon you himself?' A fact which irritated Rupert immensely, to the point he did not seem able to control that irritation whenever the other man presented himself.

Pandora snorted. 'Now you are being ridiculous.'

'Am I?' Rupert murmured softly. 'The man is far too familiar towards you for my liking.'

She gave a shake of her head. 'As I have said, he has been of great help to me since—since Barnaby died.'

'Perhaps in the hopes of ingratiating himself into your bed?'

'Rupert!'

He looked unmoved by her shocked rebuke. 'I am merely speculating.'

'Quite incorrectly, I assure you,' Pandora said

primly. 'Mr Jessop has always behaved the complete gentleman in our dealings together.'

Rupert looked thoughtful. 'Nevertheless, I must advise that you not sign any documents regarding the sale of this house until I have looked into that situation more fully.'

'I am sure there is no impropriety there.'

He shrugged. 'In that case, it doesn't signify if the matter is delayed for a few days, does it?'

Pandora didn't have the time to spend on such trivialities as Rupert's imaginings about the attentive Anthony Jessop, or anything else, when her thoughts had already turned to what she could possibly find in her wardrobe to wear for her wedding in one hour's time…

'You may now kiss the bride!' The vicar beamed at Pandora and Rupert benevolently as their marriage service was concluded without incident.

Rupert turned to his wife, fully appreciative of how lovely she looked in a cream-lace gown and matching bonnet, her mother's pearls adorning her throat, a bouquet of red roses, provided from the garden of Genevieve Forster, held tightly in her gloved hands as she gazed shyly up at him with those beautiful eyes. 'Your Grace.' Rupert sketched her a bow.

'Your Grace,' she returned softly.

'Will you allow me to steal a kiss, Pandora Stirling, Duchess of Stratton?'

She smiled. 'I don't believe it is stealing if it is freely given.'

'And is it?'

'We are now husband and wife,' she murmured softly as she raised her lips to his.

Rupert reached up to place a hand either side of her face, gazing down into the depths of those stunning violet eyes before he slowly lowered his head and gently kissed her.

At least, it had been his intention to kiss Pandora gently, before they turned to receive the best wishes of their friends. But that intention fled his mind at the first taste of her delectable lips, and his hands tightened slightly against her cheeks as he ran the tip of his tongue across her lips to part them, before he began to kiss her hungrily.

'Um-hmm.'

Rupert, lost in the pleasure of kissing Pandora, of kissing the woman who was now his wife, was only vaguely aware of someone clearing their throat noisily.

'I say, old chap, save that for when the two of you are alone, hmm?' Benedict muttered in amusement.

Pandora blinked up at Rupert slightly dazedly as he reluctantly ended the kiss, her cheeks blushing a fiery red as she turned to find both their friends watching them with indulgent affection.

Impossible as it was to believe, she was once again a married woman.

Was now the wife of Rupert Stirling, the Duke of Stratton.

A fact that was brought home to her even further as first Genevieve and then Benedict offered their congratulations, although both of them politely refused Rupert's invitation to dine with them at Stratton House later that evening, Benedict with a definite twinkle in his eye as he slapped his friend warmly on the back, Genevieve choosing to accompany him from the church.

Pandora gazed after the other couple speculatively as they appeared to chat easily together. 'You don't suppose…?'

'I try not to make suppositions about my friends, Pandora,' Rupert teased.

And Pandora had no more time for speculation as Rupert took a firm hold of her arm and escorted her to their carriage, seeing her safely seated before joining her in what was now the Duke and Duchess of Stratton's carriage.

It had all happened so quickly that it still seemed unreal to Pandora, a dream from which she might awaken, only to find she was still just Pandora Maybury, the disgraced widow of Barnaby Maybury, rather than Pandora Stirling, the wife and Duchess of the Duke of Stratton.

'Are you cold?' Rupert put his arm lightly about her shoulders to draw her into his side as he saw her shiver. 'Perhaps you're not as recovered from your ordeal of yesterday as you earlier assured me that you were?'

'I am quite well, thank you, Rupert.' She looked up at him uncertainly from beneath thick lashes.

'Perhaps I should ascertain that to my own satisfaction—and yours, I hope—once we are safely returned to Stratton House?' he suggested throatily.

Pandora felt the warmth of the blush that now coloured her cheeks. 'If you think it necessary.'

'At this moment it feels as necessary to me as breathing!' His arm tightened about her shoulders as he drew her even closer against him.

'And I'd certainly not wish to be the reason for your suffering a lack of breath.' She laughed.

'If I don't kiss you very soon, Pandora, that may sadly be the case,' he said fiercely.

She placed her hand upon his chest as she raised her face to accept his kiss, at once able to feel the way that his heart was beating rapidly in his chest. As was her own!

She was now Rupert's wife. A much-admired and coveted gentleman, whom any woman of the *ton* might consider herself truly blessed to call her husband. For all of her initial trepidation in accepting Rupert's marriage proposal, Pandora knew that she felt a certain pride in his having chosen her to be that woman.

As Rupert continued to kiss her with a passion

which held the promise of a repeat of last night's pleasure, Pandora wondered if she was about to find her very own happy-ever-after, after all, and in the arms of the most unlikeliest of men...

A hope which was dashed only a few minutes later as Rupert, having swept a bemused Pandora up into his arms as she alighted from the carriage, then proceeded to carry her over the threshold of Stratton House the moment the butler held the door open for them to enter.

'I thought I had made my feelings more than plain yesterday evening about you bringing that woman into my home.' Patricia Stirling's unmistakably chilling tones cut disdainfully into their happy laughter.

Chapter Fourteen

Rupert scowled and all humour left his visage as he continued to hold Pandora firmly in his arms. He nodded dismissal of the butler, waiting for the older man to leave before he turned his cold and icy-grey gaze upon his father's widow, as she posed to what she no doubt considered her best advantage in the open doorway of the gold salon. '"That woman", as you so rudely call her, is now my own Duchess of Stratton.'

Patricia's beautiful face twisted into an expression of disbelief before becoming one of murderous rage as she glared at Pandora, her eyes glittering with that same malevolence. 'You have actually *married* a woman who is not only a known adulteress, but was also responsible for the death of her husband?'

Rupert heard Pandora draw in a shaky breath as she stiffened in his arms, but he dared not look down at her now, knew that seeing the hurt she suffered at Patricia's deliberate and calculated viciousness would be his undoing. Instead he continued to hold her tightly to his chest as he concentrated his chilling attention on the Dowager Duchess. 'You will not address my wife in that derogatory manner or tone, madam.'

Patricia gave an unpleasant cackle of laughter. 'You have actually *married* a woman whom dozens of other gentleman of the *ton* have already bedded? The same gentlemen you might meet at your club every day and who will laugh behind your back to know they had her first? Your new bride is a woman who so publicly and repeatedly cuckolded her first husband that he was forced to fight a duel to the death over her?'

'I advise you to silence your wicked tongue, woman!' Rupert advised harshly.

'Why, you will be the laughing stock of the *ton*!' Patricia ignored the warning as she continued to jeer. 'How society will laugh when they learn that the arrogant, the oh-so-haughty Devil

Stirling has been seduced, led by his manhood to the altar, by the infamous Pandora Maybury!' She openly laughed in his face now. 'What a wonderful, delicious joke you will become, Rupert!'

If he'd had a free hand at that moment Rupert would quite cheerfully have slapped the woman's face. Not on his own behalf—the *ton* could say what they liked about him, and be damned with it—but for the vicious way in which she insulted Pandora with her every word.

That she did so deliberately he had no doubt. Patricia did everything with deliberation and purpose, from seducing him to then seducing his father when Rupert had proved elusive to the parson's mousetrap. He realised that she was now intent upon causing a rift in his marriage before it had even begun.

'Would you please put me down, Rupert?'

He looked down concernedly as Pandora made the polite request, the first words she had spoken since Patricia began her vicious assault. 'It is my intention to carry you up the stairs to the privacy of our bedchamber.'

'Perhaps later. First you will put me down, please, Rupert.' She looked up at him steadily as she firmly repeated her request.

Rupert frowned darkly as he slowly lowered Pandora to the floor of the marbled hallway until she stood on her own two satin-slippered feet, his arm moving about the slenderness of her waist as she straightened her gown and bonnet before looking up at the older woman.

Pandora smiled reassuringly at Rupert before she turned to the older woman. 'You are right in your surmise that in the past Rupert may have suffered a certain amount of…conjecture from the *ton* regarding the women he was previously known to associate with,' she spoke quietly, but with a complete sense of purpose, knowing full well what Patricia was up to—and determined not to give her the satisfaction of knowing how much her accusations had wounded her, as they were also intended to insult Rupert, at the same time planting doubts in his mind as to the wisdom of his actions.

Pandora's own confidence now relied heavily upon the fact that Rupert had assured her he knew exactly what he was doing by choosing to make her his wife, his Duchess. She had also warned him, on several occasions, of the ridicule he risked bringing down about his own head if he married her, warnings he had summarily dismissed.

With those things in mind, she had no intention of allowing Patricia Stirling's vicious tongue to drive a barrier between the two of them before they had been married for so much as a single day.

'But really, in this situation, is it not a case of "people in glass houses"?' Pandora reasoned sweetly.

The other woman looked ready to explode. 'How dare you?'

'Oh, I believe if you were ever to know me better, which I am sure neither of us wishes for...' Pandora shrugged gracefully '...then you would find that I would dare rather a lot. Indeed, I do believe that my first instruction, as the new Duchess of Stratton, must be to ask you to remove yourself from Stratton House. For all our sakes.'

The other woman's face became a mottled red,

those blue eyes bulging. 'Why, you—you bitch! How dare you presume to tell me what to do and where I must go?'

Pandora sighed at this continued unpleasantness. 'I'm trying to be reasonable about this—'

Patricia glared. 'Why, you puffed-up little upstart!'

'Obviously I'm wasting my time in trying to remain polite,' Pandora replied in a bored tone.

'In my opinion you're wasting your time altogether!' Patricia gave a scathing snort. 'How can you possibly expect or hope to hold the attention of a man as experienced and jaded as Rupert? You cannot!' she announced gleefully. 'Not if you were to dance naked in front of him for a fortnight!'

This last taunt was a little too close for comfort to Pandora's own feelings of inadequacy in the bedchamber, but she had no intention of allowing Patricia to know her poisonous dart had hit its target so precisely. 'How utterly uninspiring that would be!' Her tone had hardened at the other woman's persistence in insulting her. 'It is my opinion that a gentleman prefers a little…

elusiveness, a certain mystery, in the woman on whom he bestows his interest. Any young and virile gentleman, at least; I am sure a gentleman of *mature*, perhaps even *impotent* years, shall we say, would be far less difficult to please?'

Rupert had feared for Pandora just a few minutes ago, believing that Patricia intended, and would succeed if he did not verbally restrain her, in ripping Pandora to shreds with her viciousness. But once again Pandora had surprised him by continuing to maintain her own dignity in the face of Patricia's unpleasantness.

The slight trembling of Pandora's body against his arm told Rupert that she was nowhere near as calm as her outward demeanour so determinedly implied, her cheeks now the colour of ivory, those violet eyes having deepened to a haunted purple. And yet he also knew, by the stubborn set of her raised chin and the determination in her gaze, that Pandora would not, under any circumstances—no matter the insult—back down from this face-to-face confrontation with the viper standing in front of her.

'Are you going to just stand there and let this

woman insult your own father without a word of defence from you?' Patricia turned to demand of him.

Rupert raised mocking brows. 'You are referring to my wife, madam, the Duchess of Stratton. And whether or not Pandora's remark was an insult must surely depend upon whether or not there was any truth to it? If there is, then I cannot see how it can be called an insult.'

Patricia looked incensed. 'For your information your father was more than capable of—'

'Perhaps that is a little too much information to relate to his son, Dowager Duchess?' Pandora put in with soft reproof. 'Most especially when it is known that you shared the bed of that son before you did that of the father.'

The older woman's hands curled into claws. 'You know nothing of my relationship with Devil—'

'I believe *Rupert* has confided in me enough for me to know that it wasn't "a relationship" at all,' Pandora continued. 'It was, after all, only a matter of a few weeks' fun on Rupert's part. A soldier home on leave from the war, battle-scarred and weary, and eager to enjoy all and everything that was offered to him.'

As a set-down it was superb and Rupert knew he could not have bettered it himself if he'd tried. But he had no need to try, when Pandora was so obviously capable, and determined, to defend both herself, and him, so ably.

A sentiment Patricia might not particularly like, but so obviously recognised. 'As long as you are made aware that Rupert has only married you in a desperate effort to be rid of me?' she taunted.

'How very brave of you to openly acknowledge as much.' Pandora gave the other woman a gracious smile. 'I do so admire honesty in a person.'

'Keep your admiration for someone who may appreciate it!' The Dowager Duchess glowered at her before turning to Rupert. 'On better acquaintance, I believe the two of you may actually deserve each other!'

'It is to be hoped so.' Once again Rupert drew Pandora against his side and smiled down at her before glancing back at his father's widow. 'Do you require any help with your packing?'

Patricia drew herself up frostily. 'I believe I am

perfectly capable of making my own arrangements for moving to the Dower House, thank you.'

'Then I suggest you do so—now!' There was no mistaking the dangerous edge to Rupert's tone as he looked at her coldly. 'Now, if you will excuse us?' He bent and swept Pandora back up into his arms. 'My wife and I were about to retire to our bedchamber for several hours before dinner.' He deliberately turned his back on his father's widow as he strode across the hallway and began climbing the stairs, all the time aware of how Pandora's trembling had deepened, obviously in reaction to the viciousness of the confrontation she had just endured. 'Hold on just a few seconds more and we will have reached the privacy of our bedchamber,' he murmured softly, so that only Pandora could hear him.

Pandora's trembling increased at the mention of 'our bedchamber', their light-hearted flirtation of earlier all but forgotten with all that had followed; she certainly did not feel like that expectant bride of a few short minutes ago! Rather, she had been given another reminder, by Patricia

Stirling of all people, of exactly why Rupert had married her. The *only* reason he had married her.

Rupert frowned down at Pandora as she gave a deep and heartfelt sigh as he entered their bed-chamber and kicked the door closed behind him before placing her gently down upon the bed to sit down beside her. 'What is it?'

She gave a wan smile. 'I believe I am feeling rather…fatigued, with that unpleasant scene following so quickly on the events of last night and today.'

Rupert could have kicked himself for his lack of sensitivity; of course Pandora was feeling fatigued. She had narrowly escaped being burnt alive only hours ago, before being made love to until she attained a shattering climax. Only to then find herself married hours later and finally returning here to be insulted by the previous mistress of his bed and this house. The three former things were traumatic enough, but he believed the latter would have had most new brides screaming obscenities at him rather than expressing exhaustion!

He turned on the side of the bed before reaching out to gently untie and put aside her bonnet and smooth the hair back from Pandora's temples, allowing him to touch the tiny blue veins visible beneath the delicacy of her skin. He could also see the purple shadows of exhaustion beneath those lovely violet eyes. 'I believe you're right and it might be for the best if you were to rest here for a while before dinner.' He smiled encouragement. 'After all, we have the rest of our lives to enjoy being married to each other.'

'And will we enjoy being married to each other, do you think?'

Rupert looked down at her searchingly, the uncertainty in her expression unmistakable. 'Is it possible you already regret marrying me?'

She released a shaky sigh. 'I merely wonder if we have done the right thing in acting so hastily.'

As unflattering as Pandora's uncertainty now was, Rupert could not exactly blame her for feeling that way. How could he, when she had been so roundly insulted only minutes after their wedding had taken place? Insults which she had not only successfully fended off, but had done so in such a way as not to lose her own sense of dignity, which he admired so much. But at what inner cost to Pandora herself?

'Perhaps we should wait a little longer before making any decision in that regard,' he teased gently.

She gave another sigh. 'We seem to have rid you of Patricia Stirling's presence here, at least.'

Rupert looked down at her admiringly. 'You were magnificent just now, Pandora.'

She blinked up at him. 'I was?'

He grinned. 'I could not have dealt with the situation better myself.'

She gave a wan smile. 'High praise indeed!'

Rupert gave her a mock frown. 'I will have you know that I am known far and wide for the haughtiness of my set-downs.'

'Oh, I can believe that.' Pandora smiled slightly as some of her earlier numbness started to thaw. 'If we don't take care, we will very quickly earn the reputation of being "those high-and-mighty Strattons"!'

'I already have it on reliable authority that I am in possession of an "arrogant nose", which I apparently use in order to look down at the people who annoy or irritate me,' he drawled.

'And so you do!' Pandora could feel her sense of humour returning as they talked so easily together. After all, whatever the reason for it, this was her wedding day, Rupert was her husband, and for tonight at least, this would be their bridal chamber. 'Perhaps I am not feeling so fatigued, after all…' Her cheeks began to warm as she heard the husky invitation in her voice.

Rupert's hand stilled against her temple, golden lashes fringing narrowed grey eyes as he looked down at her intently for several long seconds. 'Perhaps…' He paused, as if seeking the right words. 'Last night was traumatic for both of us. Would it relax you to laze in a soothing bath and then for the two of us to rest here together before dinner?'

Pandora's heart began to beat loudly in her chest. 'I believe I should like that very much indeed.'

'I will ring for the hot water to be brought upstairs.' His eyes darkened to the colour of a stormy sky. 'Shall I act as your maid again?'

Pandora smiled shyly. 'Perhaps we might—attend each other…?'

Rupert was very aware, despite her denials just now, that she was in fact very weary from all that had happened to her since the fire last night. Just as he was also aware that his own lack of physical release when they had been together last night meant his self-control was not all it should or could be.

The former meant that Pandora was in all probability far too tired for lovemaking just now. Just as Rupert was unsure if he could help her bathe, or share a bed with her, *without* making love to her!

But he was certainly willing to try, believing he would enjoy watching her bathe and then climbing into bed beside her before the two of them drifted off to sleep in each other's arms.

He gave a slight inclination of his head. 'If it would please you.'

Her throat moved convulsively as she swallowed before answering him huskily, 'I believe that it would.'

Rupert stood up to pull the bell for Pendleton,

turning to watch as Pandora sat up to swing her legs to the floor before standing up.

For the first time in his life Rupert felt uncertain of how to proceed with a woman. With a wife. *His* wife.

The fact that he had a wife at all was going to take some adjusting to!

Pandora looked up uncertainly at Rupert once the butler had departed after being instructed to provide the bathwater for her Grace, not quite sure what she should do or say next. She felt a little shy still and it seemed…forward of her, to make the first move, and yet Rupert seemed equally as uncertain—reluctant?—to do so. She gave a nervous smile. 'We did not seem quite so…awkward with each other, last night.'

Rupert returned her smile. 'We were not husband and wife last night.'

She looked up at him curiously. 'Do you truly think that makes a difference?'

He shrugged broad shoulders. 'Never having been a husband before, I have no idea.'

She frowned. 'And you do not regret our hasty marriage?'

'As I was the one to arrange it, I assure you I have no regrets at all. But surely I am to be allowed the nervousness of any new husband?' he teased.

'Nervousness?'

Rupert nodded. 'I would be most displeased if I were to do or say something which caused you unhappiness.'

Pandora found his concern oddly touching, no doubt because her first husband had possessed absolutely no feelings whatsoever in regard to her happiness. 'It is decent of you to say so, Rupert—'

'Decent of me?' He reached out to place a hand beneath her chin as he raised her face so that he might look down at her searchingly. 'Were you ever happy with Maybury, even for a single day—no, pet, don't turn away from me,' he begged as she would have done just that. 'Did you care for him at all? Did he care for you?'

'No.'

Rupert frowned darkly at the flat promptness of her reply. 'It was never more than an arranged marriage?'

Her lashes lowered over those expressive eyes. 'I— We realised almost from the beginning that we did not...suit.'

'Then Maybury was a fool!' he rasped harshly.

She gasped, her lashes sweeping upwards as her eyes widened. 'My parents brought me up to believe it is wrong to speak ill of the dead.'

'Mine also.' Rupert gave a derisive smile. 'But maturity has shown me that the fact a person is dead makes no difference to them having behaved the fool before that death occurred!'

Pandora's lips twitched with totally inappropriate humour. 'You really must not say such things, Rupert.'

'For fear the devil might claim me as one of his own when it is my own time to go?' He eyed her teasingly. 'Most of the *ton* believe that to already be a foregone conclusion!'

Then, in Pandora's opinion, 'most of the *ton*' would be wrong. No doubt Rupert took wicked delight in cultivating the reputation that had earned him the name of 'Devil' Stirling, but it certainly was not all of the man, did not allow for the loyalty and affection he felt towards his friends and which they so obviously felt towards him. Or to the way in which Rupert had honoured his father's last will and testament in regard to the Dowager Duchess, despite the fact that it had caused him great personal discomfort. Nor could it deflect from the way in which Rupert had been so protective of Pandora once he became aware she was in any danger.

No, no matter his reputation, Rupert was far too honourable a man to ever suffer the fate of being 'claimed by the devil as one of his own'…

'The *ton* do not know you as I do,' Pandora declared with certainty.

He smiled slightly. 'No?'

'No,' she stated firmly. 'Nor do I believe it to be altogether proper to talk of my first husband when in my bridal bedchamber with my second.'

Rupert stared at her for several seconds before he burst into spontaneous laughter, a deep throaty chuckle that showed his even white teeth and made his eyes glow with the same humour. 'I don't believe I have ever laughed so much in the bedchamber with a lady before now.'

'With her or at her?' She arched knowing brows.

'Oh, most certainly with.' He continued to chuckle. 'You have a way of saying exactly what is on your mind that I find deeply refreshing.'

Pandora stilled. 'Would you care to know what is on my mind at this moment?'

Rupert's breath caught in his throat as he saw the warmth in her eyes. 'I believe I would, yes.'

'How big is your bath?'

Rupert's brows rose. 'I believe it is big enough and deep enough for me to stretch out my legs and luxuriate in water up to my shoulders.'

'Then it is big enough for two people to sit together?'

His smiled widened as he realised what she was about. 'Most assuredly.'

She breathed out shakily. 'Then would—would it be considered terribly…scandalous, if we were to bathe together?'

'Oh, terribly,' Rupert confirmed. 'But, as it is also a suggestion of which I wholeheartedly approve, why should either of us care whether or not it is scandalous?'

Pandora blushed at her own daring in suggesting they bathe together.

Of suggesting the two of them bathe *naked* together...

Chapter Fifteen

'You may come out from behind the screen now, Pandora,' Rupert encouraged indulgently as he glanced at the exotic Japanese screen behind which she had some minutes ago disappeared in order to disrobe. 'The last of the maids has now departed, after lighting the fire and delivering and pouring the hot water, so we are now completely alone.' One of those maids had also quietly provided the information that the Dowager Duchess had departed Stratton House in high dudgeon just minutes ago.

Rupert had disappeared into his dressing room in order to accept the help of his valet in divesting himself of his own clothing, before donning his long black silk robe, allowing Pandora those minutes of privacy to do the same. Except she now seemed reluctant to come out from behind the black lacquered screen.

Bathing with a lady would be another first for Rupert—the most recent of many where Pandora was concerned. Oh, he had seen women in their bath before now, but he could never remember being invited to join any of them. Or anticipating an unexpected pleasure quite so much...

Pandora was in a state of agitation as she stood behind the screen now wearing only her pale-cream robe, her heart fluttering frantically in her chest at her increasing feelings of nervousness. It had all sounded so daring just a few short minutes ago, the height of *risqué*. But now that it came to the two of them actually bathing together, Pandora's tummy seemed to be filled with butterflies as she felt too nervous to come out from behind the screen and face him.

What if Patricia's scornful comments of earlier should prove to be correct and Pandora failed to hold Rupert's interest for even as long as their wedding night? How would she be able to bear it if he were to eventually reject intimacy with her in the way that Barnaby had from the onset of their marriage?

No, Rupert was not Barnaby, Pandora instantly chided herself. He bore not the slightest resemblance to her first husband in looks, manner, or in his sexual preferences. The latter she knew for a fact, after the pleasures Rupert had already shown her—

'I don't bite, Pandora,' Rupert coaxed huskily from the other side of the screen. 'At least…not unless I am asked to do so.'

'Rupert!' Pandora gasped breathlessly, shocked— and at the same time filled with curiosity to know when, and in what circumstances, he might have been asked to bite someone…

A woman, no doubt. But where and why had he bitten her? And had that woman liked it when Rupert sank those beautiful white teeth into her flesh—?

'Pandora,' he now drawled teasingly, 'if you do not soon come out from behind the screen I fear our bath water will have cooled and we will have to start the process all over again!'

She knew she was being utterly silly malingering behind the screen in this way. After all, Rupert had seen her naked only the night before, when he had helped her to wash before applying the salve to her burns, and then introduced her to that delicious lovemaking; the latter was certainly an experience Pandora wished to enjoy again. And again…!

She quickly averted her gaze as she stepped out from behind the screen, having caught a brief glimpse of Rupert wearing only a long black robe which reached down to his ankles, but leaving a vast expanse of his muscled chest bare where it crossed over and was belted about his waist, the skin there lightly tanned and covered in a fine dusting of blond hair.

Her shyly averted gaze meant she missed completely the appreciative darkening of Rupert's eyes as he looked at her long golden curls loose about her shoulders and down her back. She was wearing only a pale-cream robe belted at her tiny waist, clearly revealing the outline of her pert breasts crested by those plump red berries upon which he had feasted the night before, her hips curvaceous, the bareness of her feet tiny and delicate.

But Rupert was not insensitive to the blush upon her cheeks, or the way she could not quite bring herself to look at him. A shyness on Pandora's part, which would seem to imply she had not bathed with anyone before this, either. Something which pleased Rupert immensely.

He had managed to persuade few details out of Pandora as yet about her first marriage, but he wished, for her sake, that her marriage to him be as full of new experiences as he was able to make it. Certainly he had no intention of setting up a mistress in a house in a discreet part of town, as he believed Barnaby Maybury had.

'Would you like to step into the bath first?' Rupert encouraged.

'I— Thank you.' Pandora's voice was trembling slightly as she turned away from him to unfasten her robe. 'Oh!' she gasped breathlessly as Rupert stepped behind her to slide the robe off her shoulders and down her arms.

'Climb quickly into the warmth of the water,' he said as he enjoyed the slender beauty of her naked back and her deliciously plump bottom above silky and slender legs, and caught a glimpse of that silky triangle of golden curls between her legs as she stepped lithely into the warm bathwater.

Rupert had never been in the least shy about his own nakedness and he saw no reason to become so now either as he slipped off his own robe and laid it on the chair beside Pandora's. After all, he was not the first man Pandora had seen without his clothes. Far from it, if rumour—

Oh, to hell with rumour! Who was Rupert to pay any heed to rumour? He certainly did not believe in the adage of 'Caesar's wife must be beyond reproach' whilst 'Caesar' himself could behave exactly as he pleased!

No, this must be a fresh beginning for both Pandora and himself, with no recriminations for past lovers or husbands to stand between them. Any other course of action would find their marriage floundering before it had even begun.

He looked at Pandora. Her back was towards him as she sat up stiffly in the tub, having somehow twisted and secured her golden curls loosely upon her crown, revealing the vulnerable arch of her nape and the gentle slope of her spine, the soft curve of one of her bared breasts visible as she rested one of her arms on the side of the tub.

'Move forwards a little, Pandora,' Rupert requested as he stepped up behind her, allowing him to see the flush which slowly spread up from her neck and into her cheeks as she hastily slid forwards.

Pandora kept her face averted as he stepped into the water behind her. One of his long legs slid either side of her as he slowly lowered himself into the water, trembling as he now sat snugly behind her, his bared chest against her back, his thighs cradling hers, the long length of his arousal pressing hotly against her bottom.

'Remind me to thank Mrs Hammond most profusely for her miraculous salve when next I see her,' he murmured appreciatively as his hands gently caressed the creaminess of Pandora's bared shoulders. 'There is hardly a mark or blemish left upon your delectable skin. Does it still feel sore?'

'Hardly at all,' Pandora whispered, her trembling having increased at the close proximity of his warm body to her own, and causing her to sit forwards so that her back no longer rested against the hardness of his chest.

'You'll be more comfortable if you lean back against me,' he urged as his hands moved to grasp her lightly on the hips and pull her gently back against him.

Pandora could only breathe shallowly, her fingers tightly gripping the sides of the tub as she slowly allowed herself to relax against Rupert's muscled chest, the fine dusting of blond hair there feeling ticklish against her spine as she rested the back of her head on to one of his shoulders.

'You have the most beautiful breasts I have ever been privileged to see.'

She stopped breathing altogether as Rupert's hands left her hips to move slowly, caressingly upwards, until they cupped beneath both those breasts. Seemingly disembodied hands, the fingers long, palms perfectly cupping the globes of her breasts.

It was at once the most erotic experience of her life and the most pleasurable, as Pandora looked down at those strong hands as Rupert's mouth nuzzled against the sensitive place at the side of her throat, the latter sending shivers of delight down her spine as those long fingers now captured her puckered and swollen nipples to caress and squeeze those sensitised tips to hard and aching berries.

Pandora's back arched instinctively as she felt the pleasure instantly course through her body, pushing her bottom back against him and her breasts up into Rupert's hands as his lips, tongue and teeth continued to nibble delectably at the slender column of her throat.

She groaned softly at the warmth and tingling she felt as she pressed her aching thighs together, knowing she was once again swollen there, the sensitive hidden bud throbbing with need. 'Rupert…?' she groaned achingly.

'Just relax and enjoy, pet,' he murmured against the silkiness of her throat. 'For I assure you, I don't intend to stop touching you any time soon.'

There was simply no way that Pandora could relax, her awareness concentrated totally on those hands cupping her breasts and those fingers caressing and plucking her nipples. The heated pleasure sang through her body as one of his hands now moved slowly down into the water and between her thighs, seeking out that throbbing bud before stroking her there in the same rhythm as his fingers now gently squeezed and pulled on the aching tip of her breast, making her nipples longer, firmer.

Pandora gasped softly, unable to look away from Rupert's hands, the one still cupping and pulling at her breast, the other caressing between her thighs, parting the gold curls there as she watched, revealing that ruby-red bud to her gaze as it pulsed to the tune of his caressing fingers.

It was—oh, God, this dual assault on her senses felt so *good* as her hips began to move instinctively into the stroking of those fingers against her, the pleasure growing hotter between her thighs, each plucking caress of her nipple increasing that pleasure. 'Rupert!' Pandora gasped breathlessly as that pleasure took her ever higher. 'Please, Rupert…!' she cried out, her head thrashing from side to side on his shoulder as she ached for relief from this pleasurable torment.

'Tell me what you want, pet,' he urged. 'What you *need*.'

'Harder,' she pleaded. 'Oh, please, Rupert, *harder*!'

'Like this?' He pulled and squeezed her nipple, the pulling on that turgid berry causing her channel to contract and spasm.

'Yes!' Pandora was beyond embarrassment now, beyond the awkwardness of her shyness as her hips arched up into Rupert's stroking fingers, wanting—oh, God, wanting—

'And this?' Rupert's fingers pinched that swollen, throbbing bud between her thighs.

Pandora screamed as she surged up on to the plateau of her pleasure before falling, floating on wave after wave of pleasure as Rupert now squeezed the tip of her breast to the same rhythm of two of his long fingers now plunging inside her, increasing and deepening the depth of her release until her head fell weakly back against his shoulder, her breathing laboured and gasping.

Rupert felt as if his chest was going to burst with the satisfaction he felt in watching Pandora reach her climax, revelling in the beauty of her nakedness, in the ready responses of that delicious body that had allowed him to give her that pleasure, and in doing so receive that same pleasure for himself. She was a veritable Venus come to life in his arms, a woman to be worshipped and adored, and Rupert knew he would happily spend the rest of his life making love with and to her.

For now he was happy to contemplate this one night together, their wedding night, hours and hours when Rupert intended to take Pandora in every way possible, binding her to him, claiming her, until he knew every dip and hollow of her body more intimately than he knew his own.

'Where are we going?' Pandora gasped as Rupert stood up to scoop her in his arms before stepping out of the bath, her own arms now clinging tightly about his neck as her hair slipped from its precarious hold at her crown and cascaded down over her shoulders and Rupert's encircling arm.

He smiled as he set her gently down upon her own feet on the rug. 'I thought I would ensure that you are completely dry before we go to bed.'

She stood completely naked in front of him as

he reached to take one of the thick white towels from the stand, her cheeks turning a fiery red as he moved behind her to pat her back dry of the bath water, her legs still feeling slightly shaky from the intensity of pleasure she had just enjoyed under Rupert's ministrations.

She had just enjoyed… Once again it had been she, and not Rupert, who had been given and had received pleasure.

Pandora moistened her lips before speaking. 'You are a very generous lover, Rupert, but is it not time that I—that we—'

'We have all the time in the world to give each other every pleasure imaginable, Pandora,' he assured gruffly as he dropped down on to his knees on the rug and commenced gently drying the backs of her legs. 'All of our lives, in fact.'

All of their lives…

It was wondrous, awe-inspiring to find herself married to Rupert Stirling, the Duke of Stratton, Marquis of Devlin, Earl of Charwood, his to do with as he wished for the rest of their lives.

As he was now hers to do with as she wished?

'Rupert, may I not— What are you doing?' She

gasped as she felt the touch of his lips against one of the cheeks of her bottom.

His chuckle was low and slightly wicked this time. 'I cannot help it if I find your bottom utterly delicious, Pandora. So much so that I cannot resist kissing it for a moment longer.' The warmth of his lips pressed against the other curvaceous orb.

Those chiselled lips touching her there was... altogether too intimate for Pandora's innocent sensibilities, but to turn and face him would put her in a position of even greater intimacy. Instead she stepped forwards and away from him before turning. Only for her eyes to widen and her breath to catch in her throat as she looked down at Rupert sitting back on his haunches, staring up at her with warm grey eyes, his arousal rampant and utterly beautiful between his thighs.

She had felt that arousal pressed against her several times, of course, most especially the night before when she had straddled his thighs so daringly and he had given her that first taste of pleasure, but nothing, not even that previous level of intimacy, had prepared Pandora for the male beauty of Rupert's body.

His skin was a light gold, shoulders wide and powerful, chest broad and muscled, stomach tapered and flat, and that long, thick arousal jutted out proudly from amongst the golden curls between his thighs.

'Oh, Rupert!' Pandora dropped down onto her knees between his parted thighs. 'May I...touch you...?'

'Please,' Rupert encouraged throatily. 'Dear Lord, Pandora!' He groaned at the first touch of her silky soft fingertips against the heat of his shaft.

'It doesn't hurt you?' The skin on that rampant arousal looked so taut, so full, as it leapt forwards at her slightest touch.

'Only in a pleasurable way,' Rupert moaned. 'Stroke me, pet,' he begged. 'Tighten your fingers a little and slide them up and down, and then put your other hand beneath my—yes, just like that!' These past few days of making love to Pandora had stretched Rupert's control to breaking point and it was now almost beyond bearing to have her cupping him and lightly pumping his shaft as he gazed upon her nakedness. 'Harder, love,' he urged hoarsely, back arching as he began to thrust into those encircling fingers. 'Harder! Oh, God, faster!'

'May I—?' She licked her lips as a bead of liquid appeared on the tip. 'Is it possible for me to taste you?'

'Yes!' Rupert gasped as he felt his release pumping hotly inside him as he watched Pandora slowly bend over him, her long golden curls falling silkily across his thighs as her lips parted over his hot and throbbing cock and she took him so deeply into the heat of her mouth that the sensitive tip hit the back of her throat.

If he had ever reached such a fierce and powerful release before, then Rupert had no memory of it. No memory of anything as he reached forwards to entangle his fingers in Pandora's hair as she took his fierce release, causing him to groan and writhe in ecstasy beneath the onslaught.

Minutes, hours later, Rupert finally leant forwards to rest his head against her golden curls, completely spent, drained of all strength as well as coherent thought.

'Rupert, are you all right?' Pandora was filled with alarm at his collapsed state, her cheeks paling at the fear that she might have hurt him. She had acted completely on feminine instinct minutes ago when she had asked to taste him. But had she somehow injured him? Hurt the one person she had no wish ever to hurt?

'It's all right, love.' Rupert chuckled weakly as he slowly raised his head to look at her. 'I just need a minute or two to recover, and then it will be my turn to taste you—' He broke off with a frown of irritation as a knock sounded on the outer door of their bedchamber. 'Not now!' he groaned in protest, eyes closing briefly before he shook his head. 'Ignore it, love, and maybe they will go away.' He looked down at her intently. 'Pandora, I wasn't too rough with you just now? I didn't hurt you?'

'Hurt *me*?' She knew that her cheeks were pale. 'You're the one who minutes ago seemed to be in pain.'

'That was ecstasy, not pain,' he said. 'An ecstasy I can't wait to have you repeat. As often as you wish it,' he teased.

She dared a glance at him. 'Really?'

Rupert was puzzled. 'I don't understand, Pandora. You and Maybury were married for three years. Did the two of you never share—?' He broke off as she suddenly pulled away from him.

'Don't talk of him now!' she cried, her eyes wide and accusing.

'I know you've said that the two you didn't suit, but surely—' He scowled darkly as another knock sounded on the bedchamber door. 'What is it?' he demanded impatiently.

'I really am sorry to intrude, your Grace.' Rupert's butler spoke on the other side of that closed door. 'But there is a lady downstairs wishing to see you. She refuses—she is most insistent that she must speak with you immediately, your Grace,' he added apologetically.

Pandora blinked, unsure what to make of this interruption immediately after she and Rupert had shared and indulged in such intimacies as she had never even imagined between a man and woman.

What lady was awaiting him down the stairs? And how dare she interrupt them on their wedding day?

Pandora's heart sank as she wondered if, having successfully routed Patricia Stirling, both from Rupert's life and this house, she was now to be confronted by another of the women from his reputedly wicked and licentious past?

'I will be down shortly, Pendleton,' he said tersely before turning back to look at Pandora. 'I'll get rid of this woman as quickly as possible and return to you.'

'Don't hurry back on my account, Rupert.' Pandora pulled completely out of his grasp before rising gracefully to her feet to cross the room and pick up her robe. 'As you said, we will now be spending the rest of our lives together.' She turned her back on him to pull on her robe and cover her nakedness, tying the belt securely about her waist before releasing her long hair from the collar.

'Pandora—'

'Please don't let me delay you any further.' She kept her gaze averted, but at the same time was aware of his every move as he pulled on his own robe and refastened it before approaching her.

Rupert reached out to lightly clasp one of her shoulders, his other hand moving to lift her chin so that he might look down into the paleness of her face, her eyes still avoiding meeting his. 'I'm sure, despite this woman's insistence, that it can be nothing of great import,' he finally murmured, deeply regretful that their time together had been so rudely interrupted.

'Of course not.' Her smile was brittle as she lifted her chin from his grasp. 'The sooner you are gone, Rupert, then the quicker you will be able to return,' she pointed out.

Rupert's mouth tightened and he inwardly cursed the 'insistent lady' awaiting him downstairs; a woman who had best be prepared to face the full force of his wrath! 'Will you stay exactly as you are?'

Pandora's gaze shifted to the ormolu clock on the fireplace. 'It's almost time to dress for dinner.'

And as far as he was aware, she hadn't taken the time to eat either breakfast or lunch today and consequently must now be feeling famished following the events of the day so far.

He swallowed down his annoyance that their intimacy had been so completely shattered. 'By all means dress for dinner and I will go through to my dressing room and do the same before going down to deal with our unwanted visitor.' His voice hardened over the last words, wondering who she could possibly be—certainly not Patricia, as she had departed an hour or more ago, never to return as far as he was concerned.

'I believe Pendleton said the lady is your visitor, not mine,' Pandora reminded him coolly as she once again moved out of his grasp.

Rupert's eyes narrowed as his hands dropped back to his sides. 'Pandora—'

'Please, Rupert, you really should go,' she insisted firmly.

He shot her another frustrated frown. 'I wouldn't have had this happen for the world, Pandora.'

'You can have no idea of the truth of that statement when you have no idea, as yet, precisely what "this" is,' she reasoned.

Whoever had dared to interrupt them on their wedding day was going to bear the brunt of the sharp edge of Rupert's tongue. 'I will return in but a few minutes,' he promised before walking through to his dressing room.

But one look at the identity and agitation of the 'insistent lady' who had demanded to speak with him and Rupert knew that he had spoken in error...

Chapter Sixteen

'His Grace has asked me to extend his apologies, your Grace, and advises that you start dinner without him.' An uncomfortable-looking Pendleton stood outside in the hallway when Pandora answered his knock on the bedchamber door some half an hour later. A bedchamber she had been pacing restlessly this past ten minutes or more as, having dressed, she impatiently awaited Rupert's return.

She stilled. 'And where is his Grace?'

The butler's gaze avoided meeting hers. 'I believe he had reason to step out for a while, your Grace.'

Her eyes widened. 'His Grace is no longer at home?'

'No, your Grace.'

Pandora was appalled, stunned, that Rupert could have chosen to go out on their wedding night. With the 'insistent lady' who had been waiting for him downstairs? Someone from his past, perhaps?

Was that not a big leap to have taken in her thought processes? Pandora questioned with a frown. After all, Rupert had seemed equally as surprised earlier by his visitor. Except…he had now left Stratton House without even taking the time to come back to their bedchamber to tell her himself of his departure. 'Is there anything amiss, Pendleton?' she asked the elderly man.

'Not that I am aware, your Grace.'

She sighed her frustration. 'The Duke did not state the reasons for his sudden departure?'

'No, milady.' Again Pendleton's expression and tone revealed nothing of his own thoughts on the subject. 'He merely instructed me, before he left, to inform you not to delay dinner on his behalf.'

The thoughts of eating dinner, alone, and unaware of where Rupert had gone with his female visitor, held absolutely no appeal for Pandora. In truth, she felt slightly ill, nauseous, at the abruptness of her bridegroom's desertion.

She moistened her lips with the tip of her tongue. 'And did…did my husband leave at the same time as his female visitor?'

'I believe he did, your Grace, yes.'

Pandora felt something inside of her die, as if a fist had dealt a mortal blow to her chest. Robbing her of breath. Of all thought. Except to know that Rupert had left her side on their wedding night in the company of another woman.

The humiliation, the irony, of having not one, but *two* husbands desert her on her wedding night, was not lost on her. Indeed, if that knowledge was not so painful, Pandora knew she might even have laughed at her own folly, in believing, hoping, that this second marriage to Rupert had any hopes of being any more successful than her first.

She straightened her shoulders proudly. 'I believe I will not bother with dinner either, thank you, Pendleton. If you will offer Cook my apologies…?' No doubt the poor woman, believing the Duke of Stratton to be celebrating his wedding today, had prepared a special meal for the two of them this evening. A special meal which would go as untouched as Pandora herself.

'Of course, your Grace.' The butler gave a slight bow. 'Would you care for some refreshment to be brought up to you here instead?'

'No. Thank you.' Pandora dismissed the servant, determinedly maintaining that dignity until after Pendleton had quietly left the bedchamber.

The rest of the household staff must also be aware by now that her husband had abandoned her on their wedding night and no doubt pitied her because of it. A pity which now caused hot and scalding tears to fall unchecked down the coolness of her cheeks.

She had believed that there could be no deeper humiliation than that she had suffered on her wedding night four years ago, but surely this—Rupert having left her alone and bereft on their wedding night in the company of another woman, and without so much as a word of explanation, after making love with her so passionately—was worse even than that other humiliation?

She had been so naïve and trusting when she

married Barnaby, in love with love rather than the man who had become her husband—how could she have been in love with Barnaby, when she had not really known him, and he had done absolutely nothing to encourage that emotion after their wedding?

These past four years, three of them spent as an unwanted and undesired wife, had succeeded in bringing maturity to both Pandora and her emotions.

Now she knew exactly what love was.

It was a man with the face and blond curls of a fallen angel.

It was a man called Devil…

It was two o'clock in the morning, the house eerily silent as Rupert made his way stealthily up the wide staircase two steps at a time, turning to the right when he reached the top and padding down the long hallway. He quietly opened the door of the bedchamber and slipped inside, closing it behind him and looking at the woman bathed in moonlight as she lay sleeping atop the bedcovers.

He moved silently as he stepped closer to the bed so that he might look down at her.

She wore the same cream gown she had been married in, that single string of pearls about her throat, the gold of her hair allowed to fall down about her shoulders and appearing almost silver in the moonlight, the long fan of her lashes soft against pale ivory cheeks. A frown appeared on her brow even as the fullness of her lips parted slightly and she sighed in her sleep.

Rupert felt a tightness in his chest at the underlying sadness he heard in that weary sigh. He bent to tenderly kiss the frown from her brow, allowing his lips to travel gently from that brow to her cheek, drawing back slightly as he tasted the saltiness of tears against his lips.

Tears he had caused Pandora to shed because of his abandonment of her on their wedding night?

The tightness in his chest deepened as he removed his jacket before slowly, carefully, stretching out on the bed beside her, not wishing to wake her as he smoothed the curls from her temples with gentle fingers, gladly enfolding her in his arms as she turned instinctively towards him for comfort, her head now against his shoulder, one of her hands resting trustingly upon his chest.

At peace at last, Rupert closed his eyes and fell asleep beside her.

Morning would be soon enough to tell Pandora why he had left her so suddenly the evening before...

Pandora was having the most wonderful dream as she snuggled more deeply into the arms that held her close, a dream so beautiful, so comforting, that she resisted being woken by the morning sunlight shining across the bed.

In her dream it was Rupert holding her close. Rupert's reassuring shoulder upon which her head lay. Rupert's muscled chest beneath her fingers.

Which told her more clearly than anything else might have done that she was indeed dreaming. Because Rupert wasn't here. He hadn't returned at all the evening before. He hadn't come home at all last night.

Their wedding night.

Once again she felt the hot sting of tears beneath her tightly closed lids, knowing a moment's surprise she had any tears left to cry after all the tears she had shed the evening. It was—

'I know you're awake, Pandora.'

She stilled, stiffened in disbelief, hearing Rupert's husky words at the same time as she felt the rumble of his chest against her cheek.

'Open your eyes and look at me, love.'

She could not. Dared not. Had no wish to see, to know the truth of his desertion of her the night before, as she would surely do if she once looked into his compelling grey eyes.

'Pandora?' he coaxed gently.

'Go away!' She kept her eyes tightly closed, refusing to respond to that gentleness.

'I have no wish to leave you, love.'

'You managed it with ease last night,' she reminded him dully.

Rupert's breath caught in his throat as he heard the pain in her voice. 'I no more wanted to leave you last night than I do now.'

She gave a fierce shake of her head. 'I don't believe you.'

'Why not?'

Her lids rose above accusing violets-in-spring-time eyes as she glared at him, tears shimmering on the long length of her lashes. 'Possibly because you spent our wedding night in the arms of another woman!'

'No, love.'

'Yes, *love*!' Two bright spots of angry colour entered her ivory cheeks. 'Even Barnaby was not so cruel as to—' She broke off with a pained gasp.

'Yes?' Rupert prompted as his arms tightened about her.

Her gaze avoided his as she pushed away from his chest. 'Release me, please.'

His mouth firmed. 'I've said no.'

Pandora scowled at him, at once aware of his tousled blond hair, the weariness about his eyes evidence of his lack of sleep the night before, of the fact that he was still fully dressed apart from his superfine, the shadow that covered his jaw and top lip showing that he had not shaved as yet this morning.

That he had come to her bed this morning from the arms of another woman!

Her lips trembled. 'You are despicable. A man utterly without morals of any kind. The sort of man who beds a woman who is not your wife on your wedding night.' She managed to wrench free of his hold and scoot over to the side of the bed before standing up to move in front of the window, as far away from Rupert as it was possible to be in the confines of the bedchamber. Rupert's own bedchamber, not hers. A bedchamber she had no intention of sharing with him ever again.

She gave a choked laugh as she acknowledged that her first husband had not liked women at all, and her second liked them far too much!

Rupert sat up on the side of the bed to look across the room at her beneath hooded lids. At his wife. The wife whose disgusted expression said she no longer liked him, let alone trusted him. 'I didn't spend any part of last night in the arms of another woman, Pandora,' he insisted wearily, a weariness certainly not caused by a night of debauchery.

'That is a *lie*—'

'I will never lie to you.'

She snorted. 'You are lying to me now.'

'It was two o'clock this morning when I returned to you, to our bed.'

'Don't use semantics on me, Rupert!' Her eyes flashed in warning. 'Whatever time you returned, it was from the arms of another woman!'

'No, love.' He grimaced. 'Unless you wish to count Henley as "another woman",' he added ruefully. 'And I assure you, I went nowhere near that lady's arms.'

Pandora stilled. 'Henley? My Henley?'

'Well, she's certainly not mine,' Rupert retorted.

Pandora looked confused. 'I don't understand.'

Rupert sighed deeply as he ran a weary hand through his hair, knowing that his appearance— tousled locks, shadows of sleeplessness beneath his eyes, his jaw unshaven, clothes crumpled and in disarray—must make him look every inch the adulterer Pandora believed him to be. 'Henley was the woman who came here and insisted upon speaking with me yesterday evening,' he explained heavily.

Her eyes widened. 'My Henley?'

'You really must stop repeating yourself, love,' he drawled. 'And I certainly did not spend our wedding night—or, indeed, any other night—in that particular lady's bed,' he added firmly.

Pandora swallowed before speaking, her hand trembling slightly as she pushed her golden curls over her shoulder. 'Why did Henley come here yesterday evening and ask to speak to you rather than me?'

'Ah...' Rupert sighed appreciatively. 'How reassuring it is, Pandora, to know your intelligence has at last won out over your emotions.'

She winced at his obvious sarcasm. 'What has happened? What reason did Henley have to speak with you rather than me?' she prompted insistently as he made no immediate reply.

Rupert frowned. 'Someone broke into High-bury House again yesterday evening.'

'Oh, dear Lord.' Pandora paled as she put out a hand to grasp the back of the chair in front of the dressing table. 'Someone was hurt.' Her gaze sharpened in fear.

Rupert nodded approval of the quickness of her

mind. 'Unfortunately, Bentley received a severe blow to the head—'

'I must go to Highbury House at once!'

'He isn't there, love,' Rupert told her.

'Not there?' Her eyes widened, darkened, and she seemed to sway slightly. 'Oh, God, is he—?' She swallowed hard, her cheeks as deathly pale as she obviously believed Bentley's to be.

Rupert crossed the room in two long strides and took Pandora into his arms as she looked in danger of collapsing completely. 'Forgive me, love, I'm tired and handling this badly.' He rested his head on top of her silky curls as her fingers clung on to his waistcoat.

'Bentley isn't dead,' he assured her. 'He is likely suffering a severe headache this morning, but he's alive.'

Pandora collapsed against him weakly. 'Oh, thank God! I could not have borne it if anything had happened to him.' She lifted her head to look up at Rupert. 'But if he isn't at Highbury House then where is he?'

'My estate in Cambridgeshire,' Rupert said. 'As are all your household servants. Seeing to their safe removal is the reason I did not return to you until almost two o'clock this morning. Smythe has had the good sense to discreetly place two of his men on guard near Highbury House, but I still thought it best to remove Bentley and the others from harm's way, until this situation has been settled. To have allowed you to speak with Henley yesterday evening would only have caused you more suffering, when she was, as usual, in the throes of hysteria. For which I am this time willing to forgive her, as she did have the foresight to ask to relay the bad news to me rather than you,' he added with satisfaction.

'Thank you, Rupert. I—' Pandora trembled slightly in his arms before glancing at him uncertainly. 'I have accused you unfairly.'

'Yes.' His jaw tightened. 'And, I believe, cried needless tears over it.'

'Because I thought—believed—'

'You have made it more than clear what you think of me, and my morals, Pandora,' Rupert said grimly.

'I was—it was just so reminiscent of—' She shook her head, those violet eyes once again awash with tears. 'I'm truly sorry, Rupert. I should not have— I had no reason to think...' She chewed on the fullness of her bottom lip as she stuttered to a halt.

His expression softened. 'Pandora, isn't it time that we talked of your marriage to Maybury?'

Her eyes widened. 'Barnaby? But—' She frowned. 'What does my first marriage have to do with any of this?'

In Rupert's opinion, everything! Although he was still in the dark as to exactly how or why...

After settling matters at Highbury House, Rupert had rousted Benedict from his bed in the early hours of this morning, demanding to know what, if anything, the other man's minions had learnt of the life Maybury had led at Highbury House during his years of marriage to Pandora.

He had heard that Maybury had owned Highbury House for some years before his marriage to Pandora. And questioning the owners of the neighbouring houses had revealed the names of trades people who had called at the house with deliveries, the presence of his valet, of the visits from Maybury's man of business and his lawyer, along with some of his political cronies. None of which had been of the least help in solving the mystery of whom his mistress might have been.

Hard as this might be on Pandora, difficult as she might find it to relate the details of her admittedly unhappy marriage, she now appeared to be the only person who might be able to shed some light on that particular subject.

Rupert cupped her cheeks as he looked down at her intently. 'Pandora, Maybury owned Highbury House for almost ten years before leaving it to you in his will.'

She looked puzzled. 'Yes, so?'

Rupert breathed in deeply. 'There really is no easy way to say this...' He shook his head. 'It is my considered opinion that Maybury bought the house in order that he might have secret assignations with his mistress—'

'No.'

Rupert frowned at the flat finality of her tone. 'I realise this must be painful subject for you, Pandora, but—' He broke off as she pulled free from his hands before turning away from him, her arms wrapped about her own waist, as if to ward off a blow. 'I have no wish to hurt you any more than you have been already.' He sighed, realising he was doing exactly that, whether he wished it or not. 'But Maybury—'

'Did not have a mistress,' Pandora assured him without turning.

'You cannot possibly know that with any certainty, love.'

'Oh, but I can.' She turned back to face him, her eyes haunted purple smudges in the ivory pallor of her face. 'Indeed, I can state without hesitation that Barnaby did not have a mistress, either before or after our marriage.'

Rupert studied her for several moments before slowly speaking again. 'Was he impotent?'

Pandora's smile lacked humour. 'I don't believe so, no.'

'What exactly do you mean by that? You don't *believe* so?'

'I fail to see what relevance whether or not he had a mistress has to the fact that someone has repeatedly broken into Highbury House during the past year.' Pandora abruptly changed the subject, finding that she didn't have the courage to tell Rupert all the sordid details of her disastrous first marriage.

Especially as she seemed to be making as much of a disaster of her second one!

It hadn't occurred to Pandora that Henley might have been the 'insistent lady' wishing to speak to Rupert yesterday evening. How could it, when she had no knowledge of this latest attempt to break into Highbury House?

Even so, she had severely misjudged Rupert and had accused him of being unfaithful to her on their wedding night. Something for which she believed he would find it hard to forgive her, especially now that she knew where he had actually been, of how he had been taking care of her household staff during those hours he had spent away from her the night before!

He shrugged broad shoulders. 'I believe that the circumstances of Maybury's death may have resulted in some incriminating evidence revealing the identity of his mistress to have been left at Highbury House. Personal items, perhaps. Or maybe even letters.'

'I instructed Bentley to see that all of Barnaby's personal items were packed into a trunk and placed in the attic before I moved into Highbury House.' Pandora pursed her lips at the thought of Barnaby and his lover together in what had been her own home for the past year.

Had Barnaby really been that cruel, that he could have dealt the wife he had never wanted nor liked, this final humiliation even after his death? There had been a viciousness in his manner towards her on occasion, as if he somehow held her to blame for the necessity of having to marry her at all. Enough that he had seen it as one last vicious joke to leave Pandora the house in which he and his lover had met in secret?

Yes, she acknowledged heavily, she could believe even that of the spiteful man she had come to know during her marriage to him. The sooner she accepted the offer for Highbury House, which Anthony Jessop had put forwards on behalf of his uncle, the better.

'Pandora, for pity's sake, talk to me!' Rupert looked at her pleadingly.

Could she now tell Rupert the truth of her marriage to Barnaby? At least reveal to him the secret she had kept from everyone this past four years? Would he understand, both her humiliation during her marriage, and her need for silence even after Barnaby's death, in order that she might protect Clara Stanley and her two children?

How could she not tell him all now that he had already learnt so much already of that situation?

'Pandora…?' Rupert's voice was gentle as he held his impatience firmly in check, having watched the play of emotions across her face these past few minutes. The pain. The disillusionment, followed by dignified resolve as she now raised her chin and set her shoulders before looking across at him with determination.

That resolve seemed to waver slightly as she nervously moistened her lips before speaking. 'If Barnaby had someone in his life—and I am certain that he did,' she added, 'then it was not a mistress but…a master!'

Rupert looked across at her uncomprehendingly. What did Pandora mean by that? It made no sense, except— 'Good Lord, are you saying that Maybury was involved with another *man*?'

Pandora's gaze now refused to meet Rupert's incredulous one. 'I believe it's not unheard of amongst the gentlemen of the *ton*.'

No, it wasn't unheard of, amongst gentlemen of the *ton* or otherwise. And, although Rupert did not share those preferences, he had no fault to find with them. Indeed, several of his male acquaintances in the army had been of that persuasion, and it made not the slightest difference to Rupert's feelings of friendship towards them.

But, to his knowledge, none of those gentlemen had married a woman as beautiful and desirable as Pandora, as it appeared Maybury had, in order to hide those preferences from society...

Pandora turned away to look sightlessly out at the square below, no longer able to meet his compelling silver gaze. 'Barnaby wished to further his political career,' she spoke evenly. 'Something he didn't believe would be possible if it ever came to light that he—that he—'

'Preferred the company of men to women,' Rupert put in helpfully.

'Yes.' Pandora trembled slightly. 'He explained the situation to me quite candidly after we were married. Of how he would provide for me, act as my escort during the Season, ensure that my life was a comfortable one, that I would want for nothing, but that he had no intention of ever becoming my husband in a…in a physical sense. That the mere idea of physical intimacy with me, with any woman, sickened him.'

'And he expected you to meekly accept those terms?' Rupert exclaimed with horror.

'No,' she murmured, 'he did not expect it, he *ensured* that I had no choice but to accept those terms, when he paid off all my father's debts, and warned that he would immediately demand the return of that fortune if I dared to leave or expose him.'

Rupert knew that there were plenty of marriages amongst the *ton* that were far from ideal, political and socially arranged marriages, in which both parties chose to find solace in the arms of others once the wife had provided the 'heir and the spare'. Indeed, his own parents' arranged marriage had been far from happy.

But for a man to deliberately mislead the woman he married, for him to callously and deliberately marry a woman as young and beautiful as Pandora, knowing he had no intention of ever truly becoming her husband, was beyond belief.

Or not...

If one thought about it logically, then Maybury had been extremely clever in his choice of wife. Pandora had been exceedingly young and trusting, and therefore malleable. A malleability Maybury had ensured would continue even after she knew the truth of it, by paying off her father's debts and therefore making the whole family beholden to him.

Knowing her as he did, Rupert realised that it was the latter which had maintained Pandora's silence on the subject; she was completely selfless when it came to the welfare of others, as proven by the group of unemployable misfits she had surrounded herself with at Highbury House. A selflessness she had proved included Rupert, when she had stood so steadfast at his side during that last confrontation with Patricia yesterday.

He shook his head. 'Did no one else ever guess?' Admittedly, Rupert had never heard so much as a word spoken on the subject in society, but then he did not trouble himself with gossip, and he had been away in the army for six years, only back in society for two, when the gossips had been full of the behaviour of Pandora, rather than that of the Duke.

She gave a rueful smile. 'I learnt after Barnaby's death that his valet knew the truth of it, too.'

Rupert frowned. 'Maybury's valet? How did you manage to keep him quiet?' His eyes narrowed. 'Is he the reason you have no jewellery but your mother's pearls?'

'How very astute of you, Rupert.' She looked up at him admiringly. 'I could not give him the Maybury emeralds, of course, but, yes, the despicable little man demanded my personal jewels in return for his silence on the subject.' She shrugged. 'I didn't want anything that Barnaby had given me, so it was not such a terrible hardship. Rupert, what's wrong?' Pandora looked at him in alarm as he began to swear profusely.

He controlled himself with effort. 'Do you think it possible this valet could also be the one responsible for breaking into Highbury House this last year?'

Pandora gave the idea some thought. 'I don't think so... I had no reason to like the man, but I don't believe him to have been—to have been Barnaby's lover.' She looked at Rupert anxiously. 'I— Does the...circumstance of my previous marriage disgust you?'

Disgust him? It infuriated him! And Pandora's suffering all these years enraged him. To the extent that he sincerely wished Maybury were not already dead, just so that he might have the pleasure of personally dispatching the man himself.

Was it any wonder, married to such a man, that Pandora had eventually fallen victim to the flattering attentions of other men? Men who had undoubtedly given her the warmth and comfort which her husband had so completely denied her?

'No, love.' Rupert crossed the room to take her gently into his arms. 'If I am angry with anyone it's with Maybury, not you.' He rested his head on top of her silky curls. 'How you have suffered, love...'

Rupert's understanding, his gentleness were Pandora's undoing, a choked sob catching at the back of her throat as the scalding tears once again fell hotly down her cheeks.

She buried her face against the comforting solidity of Rupert's chest, her arms moving about his waist as she clung to that strength.

'I am so sorry for the things I said to you earlier,' she sobbed brokenly. 'I've had little reason to trust anyone these past four years, but I should not have misjudged you so cruelly, when you have shown me nothing but honesty and truth. It was only that last night seemed so reminiscent of how I had been abandoned and left alone on my first wedding night. I—I couldn't believe that fate had been so cruel as to deal me the same blow twice!'

Rupert's arms tightened about her. 'I will never leave you alone again for a single night, Pandora,' he vowed fiercely. 'Indeed, I intend to keep you so busy and satisfied in our marriage bed,' he added teasingly, 'that you will never have reason to seek the comfort of other men— What is it, love?' He frowned as Pandora pulled away from him.

Her chin rose determinedly, but she could not raise her agonised gaze any further than the top button of his waistcoat as she whispered, 'There have been no other men, Rupert.'

'But what about Stanley?'

'Lies.' She at last raised her gaze to meet his. 'Sir Thomas Stanley was never my lover, Rupert.'

'But the duel?'

Her mouth firmed. 'Was not fought over me.'

Rupert looked stunned, a tightness forming in his chest as he recognised the courage in Pandora's gaze even as her lower lip trembled. For fear he would not believe her?

If he'd learnt nothing else this past few days—and some of the things he had learnt this last few minutes he could have well done without ever knowing—then it was that Pandora could be trusted to tell the truth, always. And if she said that she had never been romantically involved with Sir Thomas Stanley, or any other man, then Rupert believed her. Unequivocally.

His gaze was gently encouraging. 'Who was it fought over then?'

She shrugged. 'I believe it must be the person—the man that both Barnaby and Sir Stanley were…involved with, and who has likely kept breaking into Highbury House.'

That was Rupert's conclusion also. 'Sir Thomas is another who wed to hide his sexual preferences?'

The slenderness of Pandora's throat moved as she swallowed before answering him. 'Yes.'

It was worse than frustrating for Rupert to wish for the death of two men who were already dead! 'And you have remained silent in order to protect Stanley's family,' he guessed gruffly.

Pandora's eyes were still wet with tears as she looked up at him appealingly. 'Please understand, Rupert, I couldn't bear for Lady Clara, and her two darling children, to be placed at the centre of the ridicule they would suffer if the truth were ever known.'

Of course she could not. She was soft-hearted Pandora, a woman who would rather take all the scorn and gossip upon herself rather than see it inflicted upon another innocent woman and her two children.

Pandora was, as far as he was concerned, a

woman without equal. A soft-hearted and beautiful woman, who deserved to be spoilt, and petted, and loved for the rest of her life.

Loved…?

Dear God, what now?

Rupert turned towards the door of the bedchamber as a light knock sounded on its exterior. 'What is it?' he demanded impatiently.

'A gentleman has brought a letter which he says is in need of your urgent attention, your Grace,' Pendleton informed him apologetically. 'The gentleman is waiting downstairs for your reply,' he added before Rupert had opportunity to tell him to inform the 'gentleman downstairs' to take his damned letter and go to the devil.

'It may be news from Constable Smythe, Rupert,' Pandora said.

He drew in a deep and steadying breath, knowing that his usual control of a situation was not what it should be; in fact, he felt as if he had just been struck in the chest with a very large and heavy fist, his emotions all in disarray. Benedict had already accused him of liking Pandora, but what if—?

'Your Grace?'

'Yes, damn it!' Rupert released his wife in order to cross the bedchamber and throw open the door, hardly sparing poor Pendleton a glance even as he took the letter from the silver tray the butler presented to him.

Pandora trembled as she watched Rupert break the seal on the letter and quickly read the contents, hardly able to contain her anxiety, her need to know if this nightmare was finally over. If she, and her household staff, were to be safe at last.

'They have caught him, Pandora,' Rupert confirmed flatly.

So it was indeed over. Just as she wondered if her marriage to Rupert, the man she loved with all her heart, and who must now feel nothing but pity for her, was to be over before it had even begun...

Chapter Seventeen

Anthony Jessop was her nemesis!

Pandora felt numbed by that knowledge as she sat silently in the carriage beside an equally silent Rupert as they returned to Stratton House several hours later.

Rupert had not wished her to accompany him to Constable Smythe's offices, had assured her there was no need for her to put herself through any more suffering because of Barnaby's actions. Pandora had insisted that she must go with him, that she had to be there, that she needed to know *why* the lawyer had pretended to be her friend, whilst all the time he and Barnaby—

'Don't think of it any more, love.' Rupert's arms moved firmly about her as he pulled her tightly against his chest. 'It's over, and neither of us need ever talk of it again.'

Yes, it was over at last, Anthony Jessop having taken one look at Pandora earlier, before launching into a vitriolic attack which had confirmed that he was the person who had broken into Highbury House this past year, setting fire to Pandora's bedchamber, as well as attacking Bentley. A vicious diatribe, which had also confirmed that Rupert had been right in his earlier surmise concerning the contents of the box in the attic containing Barnaby's few belongings from Highbury House. Anthony Jessop had been looking for several incriminating letters he had written to his lover in the past. Letters he had been determined to retrieve in an effort to prevent anyone from learning of the affair.

The rest of the time they had spent at Constable Smythe's offices had been taken up with Rupert thrashing out a compromise with the constable that would best suit Pandora; having sacrificed her own reputation this past year, with the intention of saving Sir Thomas Stanley's widow and children further pain, Rupert had been determined that her efforts should not have been in vain.

It had finally been decided, with neither Pandora nor Bentley wishing to press charges, that Anthony Jessop would remove himself from England, never to return, with the promise that if he did so then he would be placing himself in a position of feeling the full measure of the law.

Pandora could not help but feel grateful to Rupert for taking this time to think of her happiness. 'Rupert—'

'We will talk once we are home and you have eaten something, love.' He glanced up to where the grooms were seated above.

She sighed as she sat back against the upholstered seat. 'I am sure I shall not be able to eat a thing.'

Rupert looked at Pandora, very aware of how pale she was, those shadows beneath her eyes seeming darker than they had earlier. And was it any wonder when let down by yet another man in whom she had believed she might place her trust?

An occurrence which did not bode at all well for Rupert being able to persuade her into trusting him…

* * *

'Better?'

'Much.' To Pandora's surprise, encouraged by Rupert, she had managed to eat a hearty late breakfast, and was now feeling much stronger, emotionally as well as physically.

'We will ring if we need anything else, Pendleton.' Rupert turned to give the butler a dismissive nod, his expression becoming grim as he stood up to pace the room in brooding silence once the two of them were alone in the breakfast parlour.

Pandora fortified herself as if for a blow as Rupert continued to pace restlessly, the food she had eaten settling like a dead weight in her stomach.

Finally he came to a halt at her side. 'Pandora, I have a question to ask you—no, I have two questions I wish to ask you,' he corrected himself. 'Neither of which you need to answer if you would rather not.'

Pandora's nervousness deepened. 'You know so much already, Rupert, that I'm sure anything else you have to ask I will answer gladly and honestly.'

'You really are the most beautiful woman, Pandora, both inside and out.' His expression softened as he fell to his knees in front of her before taking one of her hands in both of his.

She raised startled eyes, eyes that were almost on a level with Rupert's warm grey ones as he knelt in front of her. 'Rupert…?'

He raised her hand to his lips before speaking. 'My dearest, sweetest, beautiful Pandora, will you marry me?'

Her heart seemed to leap into her throat. 'But are we not already married?'

That warm gaze continued to meet hers unblinkingly. 'Yes, we are. And I have realised this past few hours that I bullied you into that marriage as surely as Maybury—' He broke off as Pandora placed her fingertips against his lips.

'We will not speak of him again,' she insisted firmly.

'No, we will not,' Rupert confirmed grimly. 'Except for me to tell you I have spent these past few hours wishing to kill a dead man.'

Pandora gave a gasp as her hand fell back to her side.

'Men are all primitive at the heart of it, love,'

Rupert apologised huskily as he reached up to cradle the smoothness of her cheek against his hand. 'And I find myself filled with murderous tendencies towards anyone who has dared to hurt you.' He gave a self-derisive shake of his head. 'It is—forgive me, Pandora, I have never felt such strong emotions before and I find myself quite at a loss to know how to tell you—how to *begin* to tell you—damn it!' He broke off with a muttered expletive. 'I love you, Pandora.' He lifted her hand to place it against the roughness of his cheek. 'This past few days have shown me that I love everything about you. Your kind heart, your loyalty, your goodness, your beauty, your passion, your— Stop me, Pandora, before I make a complete cake of myself and grovel at your feet as I beg you to marry me and make me the happiest man alive,' he groaned even as he turned his lips into her palm.

Pandora was so stunned, exhilarated, at hearing Rupert declare his love for her, that she could not have spoken if her life had depended upon it.

Actually, her life, her future life with Rupert, *did* depend upon it! But not at the cost of having such a strong man resort to grovelling at anyone's feet, least of all her own...

Pandora slipped from the chair so that she now knelt in front of him as her other hand moved up to stroke his cheek. 'I have fallen in love with you, too, Rupert. I love you so very, very much, my darling.' She gazed up at him with adoration in her eyes. 'I love your strength. Your loyalty. Your goodness. Your passion. As for your handsomeness—' She did not get any further in her declaration as Rupert's lips claimed hers in a kiss so full of his love and admiration that Pandora felt as if her own heart might burst from her chest.

Rupert loved her. Truly, deeply, loved her.

That such a thing had happened amidst such unhappiness was a miracle. A true and unshakeable miracle.

Rupert finally drew the kiss to an end to look down at her with all of that love shining in the deep grey of his eyes. 'God, love...' He drew a ragged breath into his starved lungs. 'Will you marry me, Pandora? Not privately as we did yesterday, with only two friends as our witnesses, but in full splendour, with all of the *ton* in attendance? Will you walk down the aisle to me and allow me to publicly pledge my love for you, for my Duchess?'

'Oh, Rupert!' She began to cry again, but they were tears of happiness this time.

Rupert's arms drew her close and he rested his cheek against her golden curls as he asked his second question. 'And will you wear white, Pandora, in recognition of your purity?'

She stilled in his arms before she slowly raised her head to look up at him shyly. 'I'm not sure, after our lovemaking this past few days, whether that is still possible...'

'Oh, yes, love, it's still possible,' Rupert's voice had deepened as his love for this wonderful *innocent* woman threatened to overwhelm him.

For Pandora was an innocent, Rupert had realised after he had gone over and over everything she had said to him earlier this morning. She was not just innocent of any wrongdoing, in regard to betraying her first husband, but she was also innocent in a physical sense. Amazingly, wonderfully, miraculously, she was Rupert's virgin bride.

'Then I shall wear white for you, my darling Rupert.' Those violet-coloured eyes smiled up at him as she continued. 'But I want, nay, demand that you make love with me, fully and completely, before this second wedding can be arranged.'

He shook his head. 'Never doubt how much I long for that, too, love—God, I *ache* to my teeth to make love to you,' he admitted emotionally. 'But would it not be better for us to wait? For you to have the wedding you deserve?'

'We shall still have that wedding, Rupert,' she promised huskily even as she pulled away from him to take hold of his hand so that she might draw him to his feet beside her. 'But do you not think, having been a wife for three years the first time, and for another day and night the second, that I have already waited long enough?' Her eyes gleamed up at him mischievously.

Rupert looked down at her searchingly. 'Are you sure, love?'

'I have never been more sure of anything in my

life.' She nodded. 'Well…except for how much I love you. I *ache* for you, too, Rupert,' she vowed.

'How I love you!' he groaned as he bent to lift her in his arms.

'Show me how much,' she invited as she rested her head trustingly against his shoulder as he strode from the room and up the stairs to their bedchamber with her still held securely, safely, in his arms.

Rupert's breath caught in his throat as he lay Pandora gently down upon the bedcovers to gaze down at the woman he loved with all of his heart.

His Duchess.

His Pandora…

* * * * *